ACCLAIM FOR AMY CLIPSTON

"Clipston brings this engaging series to an end with two emotional family reunions, a prodigal son parable, a sweet but hard-won romance, and a happy ending for characters readers have grown to love. Once again, she gives us all we could possibly want from a talented storyteller."

—*RT BOOK REVIEWS*, 4 1/2 STARS, TOP PICK!
ON *A SIMPLE PRAYER*

". . . will leave readers craving more."

—*RT BOOK REVIEWS*, 4 1/2 STARS, TOP PICK!
ON *A MOTHER'S SECRET*

"Clipston's series starter has a compelling drama involving faith, family, and romance."

—*RT BOOK REVIEWS*, 4 1/2-STAR REVIEW
OF *A HOPEFUL HEART*, TOP PICK!

"Authentic characters, delectable recipes, and faith abound in Clipston's second Kauffman Amish Bakery story."

—*RT BOOK REVIEWS*, 4-STAR REVIEW OF *A PROMISE OF HOPE*

"An entertaining story of Amish life, loss, love, and family."

—*RT BOOK REVIEWS*, 4-STAR REVIEW OF *A PLACE OF PEACE*

"This fifth and final installment in the 'Kauffman Amish Bakery' series is sure to please fans who have waited for Katie's story."

—*LIBRARY JOURNAL* REVIEW OF *A SEASON OF LOVE*

A Mother's Secret

ALSO BY AMY CLIPSTON

A Mother's Secret

HEARTS OF THE LANCASTER GRAND HOTEL

BOOK TWO

AMY
CLIPSTON

ZONDERVAN

A Mother's Secret
Copyright © 2014 by Amy Clipston

This title is also available as a Zondervan ebook.
Visit www.zondervan.com.

Requests for information should be addressed to:
Zondervan, *Grand Rapids, Michigan 49546*

ISBN: 978-0-7180-7998-7 (Mass Market)

Library of Congress Cataloging-in-Publication Data

Clipston, Amy.
    A mother's secret / Amy Clipston.
        pages cm—(Hearts of the Lancaster Grand Hotel; book two)
Includes bibliographical references and index.
ISBN 978-0-310-33581-8 (softcover: alk. paper)
I. Title.
PS3603.L58M68 2014
813'.6—dc23
2013049530

Cover design: Faceout
Cover photography: Brandon Hill

Printed in the United States of America

16 17 18 19 20 21 22 / OPM / 20 19 18 17 16 15 14 13 12 11 10 9 8 7 6 5 4 3 2 1

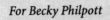

For Becky Philpott

Glossary

ach: oh
aenti: aunt
appeditlich: delicious
Ausbund: Amish hymnal
bedauerlich: sad
boppli: baby
brot: bread
bruder: brother
bruderskinner: nieces/nephews
bu: boy
buwe: boys
daadi: granddad
daed: dad
danki: thank you
dat: dad
Dietsch: Pennsylvania Dutch, the Amish language (a German dialect)
dochder: daughter
dochdern: daughters
dummle: hurry
Englisher: a non-Amish person
fraa: wife
freind: friend
freinden: friends

freindschaft: relative

froh: happy

gegisch: silly

gern gschehne: you're welcome

grandkinner: grandchildren

grank: sick

grossdaadi: grandfather

grossdochder: granddaughter

grossdochdern: granddaughters

grossmammi: grandmother

Gude mariye: Good morning

gut: good

Gut nacht: Good night

haus: house

Ich liebe dich: I love you

kapp: prayer covering or cap

kichli: cookie

kichlin: cookies

kind: child

kinner: children

kumm: come

liewe: love, a term of endearment

maed: young women, girls

maedel: young woman

mamm: mom

mammi: grandma

mei: my

mutter: mother

naerfich: nervous

narrisch: crazy

onkel: uncle

Ordnung: the oral tradition of practices required and
    forbidden in the Amish faith
schee: pretty
schtupp: family room
schweschder: sister
Was iss letz?: What's wrong?
Wie geht's: How do you do? or Good day!
willkumm: welcome
wunderbaar: wonderful
ya: yes
zwillingbopplin: twins

Hearts of the Lancaster Grand Hotel Family Trees

Glick Family

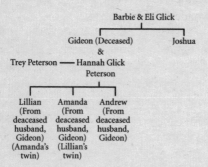

Barbie & Eli Glick

Gideon (Deceased)   Joshua

&

Trey Peterson —— Hannah Glick Peterson

Lillian (From deaceased husband, Gideon) (Amanda's twin)

Amanda (From deaceased husband, Gideon) (Lillian's twin)

Andrew (From deaceased husband, Gideon)

Lapp Family

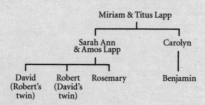

Miriam & Titus Lapp

Sarah Ann & Amos Lapp   Carolyn

David (Robert's twin)   Robert (David's twin)   Rosemary   Benjamin

Note to the Reader

While this novel is set against the real backdrop of Lancaster County, Pennsylvania, the characters are fictional. There is no intended resemblance between the characters in this book and any real members of the Amish and Mennonite communities. As with any work of fiction, I've taken license in some areas of research as a means of creating the necessary circumstances for my characters. My research was thorough; however, it would be impossible to be completely accurate in details and description, since each and every community differs. Therefore, any inaccuracies in the Amish and Mennonite lifestyles portrayed in this book are completely due to fictional license.

ONE

Joshua Glick held the reins and guided his horse through the crowd at the auction. Both Amish and *English* spectators lined the path he followed while riding behind other horseback riders. If Joshua were prideful, he would be tempted to brag that Buck, the massive draft horse he rode, was the cream of the crop—not just from his horse farm, Glick's Belgian and Dutch Harness Horses back home in Paradise, Pennsylvania, but at the auction as well.

Joshua hoped to sell at least five horses today, which would bring a nice profit.

Business had been booming ever since he bought out the other half of the farm from his former sister-in-law, Hannah, when she left the community last year. He was even beginning to suspect he needed to hire more helpers. The volume of business was becoming too much for him and his assistant, Daniel King, to handle alone.

He suppressed a smile as he thought of his farm. Joshua had promised himself he'd keep the business going as a way to provide a living for his brother's widow and their three children. Then when Hannah remarried and she and two of her children left, Joshua became the sole owner and it was no longer a source of income for Gideon's family. But now, seven years after Gideon's death, the business was becoming everything Gideon dreamed of when the brothers established it nearly a decade ago, and it was a way to keep Gideon's dreams alive. It was Joshua's connection to his only sibling, and he was going to do his best to make it the best farm it could be for Gideon. If only his brother were alive to see it now . . .

Above the noise of all the people, Joshua heard someone heckling the parade of horses. He scanned the crowd and spotted a group of three Amish boys standing with the crowd. They looked to be in their mid-teens.

"Look at that fat old mare," one of the boys said in Pennsylvania Dutch while pointing to a horse in front of Joshua's. "She couldn't pull a buggy if her life depended on it!"

One of the other two boys laughed.

Joshua turned toward the horse in front of him and returned his thoughts to his business and hopes for sales that would make the trip to the auction cost-effective.

He was deep in thought when Buck suddenly reared, kicking his massive legs and sending Joshua's stomach up to his throat as he swayed and nearly slipped off the horse. The surrounding crowd of spectators broke into a chorus of gasps and shouts. Joshua held on to the reins and climbed off the horse. He found Buck's eyes wide with fear.

"It's okay," Joshua cooed, calming the horse by

rubbing his neck. "It's fine, *bu*. Calm down. Calm down, *bu*."

Daniel ran over, appearing from behind Buck. "Is he all right?" At nineteen, Daniel was muscular from working on the farm and stood close to Joshua's height of five-foot-eleven. "Oh no! He's bleeding! Look at that cut on his rump." Daniel pulled a rag out of his pocket and placed it on the large gash. "I'll try to stop the bleeding."

Joshua examined the wound. "He's going to need stitches. We'll have to call the vet when we get home." Joshua moved to Buck's head and rubbed his neck again while studying the horse's eyes. "He's calming down." He turned toward Daniel. "Did you see what happened?"

Daniel nodded toward the crowd. "I think one of those *kinner* threw a rock. He had *gut* aim because he hit Buck right in the rear."

Irritation rose within Joshua as he looked toward where Daniel indicated he'd seen the children, probably the same boys Joshua had noticed. "Those *buwe* need to learn to respect the animals. Someone could've been hurt, and now I'm going to have a huge veterinarian bill to pay." He gestured toward the horse. "I'm going to go talk to the *buwe*. You take care of Buck. Make sure you clean and cover the wound well. Like I said, we'll have Cameron Wood treat him when we get home."

"I'll take care of it." Daniel took the reins. "I'll take him back to the barn and find the first aid kit."

Joshua headed toward the boys, who were standing by a fenced-in area surrounding a herd of ponies. The boys looked over at Joshua, and their eyes widened before they took off running.

Joshua quickened his steps. As the boys rounded the corner of the pen, the shortest one stumbled and fell, landing on his knees and grimacing.

Joshua caught up with the boy and gritted his teeth while he stood over him. "Did you throw that rock, *bu*?"

The boy shook his head and pointed in the direction the other two boys had gone. "I didn't do it. One of them did."

Joshua studied the boy while wondering if he was lying. Was he guilty and only blaming it on one of the others to escape punishment? Glancing around, Joshua found that a crowd had gathered and eyed Joshua and the boy with curiosity.

"Stand up. We're going to go have a talk." After the boy stood, Joshua took his arm and pulled him along.

"But I didn't do it!" the boy protested as Joshua steered him toward a large barn. "It was Robert! He and David ran off. Go find *them*!"

The smell of hay and animals permeated Joshua's senses as they entered the structure. He moved to the middle of the barn and stopped, facing the boy. Annoyance nipped at him. "So then why did you try to run away? That makes you look guilty."

"I didn't . . . I don't . . ." The boy looked around as if searching for something or someone. Was he searching for an excuse?

"What's your name?" Joshua crossed his arms over his chest.

"Benjamin Lapp." The boy's voice was small and unsure, matching his slight frame.

"Where's your family?"

Benjamin looked behind him, where a group of inquisitive Amish folks were gathering and watching them from the open barn door. "I don't know. They were somewhere around here."

"Do you realize how dangerous it was to throw that rock at my horse?" Joshua gestured with emphasis as agitation surged through him. "Your rock cut him when it hit him. Now he needs stitches. Do you have any idea how much that's going to cost me? Not only that, but he could have been injured much worse, especially since he reared up like that. Or he could have landed on someone. Someone could've been seriously hurt, and it would've been your fault. Do you understand?"

"I told you, I didn't—"

"*Ya ya*, you say you weren't the one who threw the rock, but you certainly took off running when you saw me." He studied the boy's young face. "How old are you?"

"Fifteen."

"Fifteen?" Joshua shook his head. "You look about twelve. If you're truly fifteen, then you should know better, *bu*. Do you live on a farm?"

Benjamin nodded. "A dairy farm." His voice seemed to lack strength, similar to his physical appearance.

"Then you definitely should know better than to scare a horse. You know how powerful those animals are. They could easily break a person's foot if they stepped on it. I knew a man whose cousin was killed when he was kicked in the head by a horse. He was knocked down, he hit his head again, and he died the next day. They can be gentle animals, but when they're startled, they can also become lethal."

Benjamin hung his head. "Yes."

"You really could've hurt someone." Joshua was on a roll and couldn't stop himself from lecturing the young man. "If I hadn't calmed down my horse, it could've been much worse. I could've been dragged if I'd fallen off and he'd started running. That wouldn't have been good for the crowd to see. I'm here to sell my horses, not entertain the crowd. This isn't the circus, you know. And now I have a vet bill to pay."

A woman made her way through the crowd at the door and came into the barn, glancing back and forth between Joshua and Benjamin. She looked to be in her early thirties and stood several inches shorter than Joshua. She had the same blonde hair and deep brown eyes as Benjamin.

"*Was iss letz?*" Her voice was all business.

Joshua pointed toward Benjamin. "This boy threw a rock at my horse and hit it on the rump and cut him badly. The horse is going to need stitches, and I'm stuck with a vet bill that I didn't need right now. He reared and kicked, but thankfully no one was hurt."

The young woman looked surprised as she turned to the boy. "Did you do that, Benjamin?"

"No." The boy threw his hands up in exasperation. "Robert did it, but he doesn't believe me. It's just like always. Robert and David make trouble, and I take the blame for it. No one ever believes me."

"I believe you." She studied him. "Ben doesn't nor-mally lie," she said without looking at Joshua.

"I'm not lying." Benjamin's eyes seemed to plead with the woman.

"He says he's not lying, but he and the other *buwe* ran away when they saw me walking toward them. They all looked awfully guilty too." Joshua pointed toward the boy as she turned her attention back to Joshua. "He needs to learn respect for horses. I could've been hurt or killed when my horse kicked. Or worse, Buck could've hurt someone in the crowd. We parade the horses through the crowd to show the people how gentle the horses are. Throwing a rock at a horse doesn't exactly convey that message. Instead of showing what a gentle horse Buck is, I scared the crowd."

The blonde looked unconvinced as a frown pinched at the corners of her lips. "Well, if Ben says he didn't throw the rock, then he didn't throw it. I believe him. I think you should give him the benefit of the doubt. You didn't see it happen, did you?"

Joshua grimaced, surprised by how outspoken the young Amish woman was. He'd never known an Amish woman to be quite so confident, especially in front of a stranger. "No, I didn't actually see him throw the rock, but I know what I saw after the incident. He looked guilty. Besides, the *bu* was standing there before the rock was thrown."

"What's all the commotion over here?" An older man with thinning gray hair, a long, gray beard, and a potbelly came in.

"This man says Benjamin threw a rock at his horse.

Now the horse needs stitches." The blonde gestured between the boy and Joshua. "Ben says Robert did it, and then Robert and David left him to take the blame."

"Joshua," Joshua said.

"What?" The woman looked at him.

"Joshua," he repeated. "My name is Joshua Glick."

"Joshua." The older man held out his hand. "I'm Titus Lapp." He gestured toward the blonde. "This is *mei dochder*, Carolyn."

Carolyn nodded at him.

"Where are you from?" Titus asked Joshua.

"Paradise." He crossed his arms over his chest again.

"We're from Gordonville." Titus fingered his beard. "Are you related to Eli and Barbie Glick?"

"*Ya*. They're my parents."

"*Ach, ya*," Titus said. "I went to school with Eli."

"Oh." Joshua nodded. "You grew up in Paradise?"

"I did." Titus hooked his thumbs on his suspenders. "I moved out to Gordonville after I met my lovely *fraa*."

"*Dat*, this isn't a social visit. This man dragged Ben in here and started yelling at him." Carolyn looked annoyed as if her father prattled off topic all the time. "We were talking about Benjamin."

"Oh, *ya*. That's right." Titus fingered his suspenders. "We were talking about Benjamin. So Ben threw a rock at Joshua's horse?"

Benjamin shook his head. "No, Robert did it. As usual, I was the one left to take the blame while they ran off. They do this to me all the time."

"Let's ask my other grandsons about this." Titus

turned toward a group of boys standing at the other end of the large barn and realized his two grandsons were among them.

"Robert! David! *Kumm!*"

Two young men, who shared similar hair and eye color to Benjamin's and looked to be about seventeen, trotted over. Their expressions were tentative.

"Joshua Glick tells me that one of you three young men threw a rock and hit his horse. Which of you did it?" Titus asked the boys.

The two older boys looked at each other and then faced Titus.

"Ben did it, *Daadi*," the slightly taller boy said.

"*Ya*." The other boy nodded. "Ben did it."

Joshua looked at Benjamin and found his mouth forming a thin line. He glanced at Carolyn, who gritted her teeth as her cheeks flushed.

"*Danki, buwe.*" Titus looked at Benjamin as the other two boys hurried off. "Did you lie, Benjamin?"

The boy, who by now Josh gathered was a brother to the other two boys, looked at the toes of his shoes.

Carolyn opened her mouth to speak, and Titus held up his hand. "Carolyn, we've been through this before. You need to drop it now, and we'll discuss it in private later. There's no need to make a scene. People don't need to hear our family issues." He turned to Joshua. "I'm sorry he threw a rock at your horse. We'll discuss this with him further when we get home tonight."

Carolyn heaved a deep sigh, and Joshua wondered why she was so disgruntled.

"The *bu* needs to learn to respect animals," Titus

continued. "Benjamin needs to pay for the vet bill, and he must apologize."

Benjamin muttered an apology while kicking a stone with his shoe.

Joshua rubbed his chin while an idea brewed in his mind. "I could use some help at my horse farm. He could work it off cleaning the stables."

Titus raised his bushy white eyebrows. "*Ya?* We might be able to work something out." He glanced at the boy. "You should go work on Joshua's horse farm for a while to repay your debt."

The boy continued to study his shoe.

"*Dat*, I don't think—" Carolyn began.

"Carolyn, I will handle this." Titus's words were kind but direct. He turned toward Joshua. "I think it would be a *gut* idea for Benjamin to work on your farm. He needs to learn responsibility for his actions, and I think your farm would be a *gut* place to start. As you said, it can be a repayment for your vet bill."

"*Wunderbaar!*" Joshua shook the older man's hand. "How about Monday?"

"*Ya,*" Titus agreed. "Since Ben is nearly sixteen, he can drive a horse and buggy now. He can get over to your place, no problem. I'll draw him a map."

While Titus and Joshua worked out the details, Carolyn put her hand on Benjamin's shoulder and directed him toward the barn exit. By now, the crowd had dispersed. Joshua watched her slender frame move outside, and he wondered why she was so against the idea of Benjamin working for him and so protective of the boy. He needed to learn a lesson in responsibility.

But there seemed to be a family dynamic he was missing. Maybe she was a big sister just looking out for her youngest brother, or maybe she was his aunt. There seemed to be something else going on, but he couldn't put his finger on what it was.

He knew it wasn't any of his business, but he was intrigued.

TWO

Carolyn climbed into the van behind Benjamin. "Go all the way to the back," she whispered to him.

They moved past David and Robert, who shot Benjamin identical smug smiles, confirming her thoughts from earlier—they both lied to get Benjamin in trouble yet again. She knew her seventeen-year-old fraternal twin nephews were menaces, but she couldn't get her father to listen to her. He was too influenced by her older brother, Amos, who was the boys' father. And since they all lived on Amos's dairy farm, Amos ruled the roost like a territorial rooster. He was very proud of his sons and refused to see their bullying ways.

Carolyn settled into a seat at the back of the van next to Benjamin. She hugged her cloak to her body and shivered. Her mother and father climbed into the van and sat up front near her nephews.

Benjamin removed his hat and pushed his blond hair back from his face. "Do I really have to work at that horse farm?" His voice was quiet, and she assumed it was to keep their conversation private. "I don't even know that man. He doesn't seem very nice. He's just going to make me do all the dirty jobs, just like *Onkel* Amos does."

Carolyn nodded. "I'm sorry, but *ya*, you do have to work for Joshua Glick. Your *daadi* said you have to, and you know you have to obey him."

Benjamin sighed and glanced toward the window.

She leaned over and touched his arm. "I know you told the truth. I was trying to get your *daadi* to listen to you. You know that, right? You know I always support you, no matter what *Onkel* Amos and your cousins say about you."

"*Ya*, I do." He looked back at her. "You always believe me, but *Daadi* always takes their side." He nodded toward Robert and David, who were speaking in low voices and laughing a few rows ahead of them.

"I know." Carolyn glanced toward the front of the van where her brother, Amos, and his wife, Sarah Ann, were settling into seats. "I think your *daadi* means well, but he's in a different position since Amos runs the farm where we live."

"They always get me in trouble," Benjamin grumbled, slumping in the seat. "Last week I was blamed for tracking mud in *Aenti* Sarah Ann's kitchen, and I didn't even do it. I had taken my boots off before I went into the *haus*, and they didn't. Yet I got blamed for it. It's not fair."

"I know, *mei liewe*." She touched his cheek. She wished she could protect her son from all the heartache in the world, but she knew that wasn't possible for any mother.

"I don't think Joshua Glick even likes me." Benjamin fingered his pants leg while he spoke. "He was very angry when he dragged me into that barn."

"That's not right." Carolyn shook her head, wondering how Joshua would treat her son while he worked on his farm. She watched her nephews whisper and laugh loudly before Amos cautioned them to keep their voices down. Suddenly, a thought occurred to her. Perhaps getting Benjamin away from his misbehaving cousins would be a good thing. She doubted Joshua could possibly be as mean as Ben's cousins were. "But maybe it will be *gut* for you."

Benjamin frowned. "I thought you said you believe me."

"I do, which is why I think maybe getting away from your cousins will be a *gut* thing. You won't have as many chores at the dairy farm since you'll be working for Joshua Glick full-time, *ya*?"

Benjamin's expression brightened slightly. "You're right. Since I'll have a full-time job, they will have to take care of all the chores on the farm while I'm gone. They won't have me around to bully."

"Exactly." Carolyn smiled. "Now you see why I'm thinking this will be a *gut* opportunity for you."

Carolyn's sixteen-year-old niece, Rosemary, flopped down on the bench seat in front of them. "What are you two talking about?"

"Nothing," Benjamin mumbled, looking out the window.

Rosemary raised her eyebrows. Carolyn shook her head as if to say "don't ask."

Her niece gestured toward her brothers, and Carolyn nodded.

Rosemary shook her head with understanding. Her

niece was the only member of the family who saw what was really going on with David and Robert.

Rosemary leaned over the seat and lowered her voice. "I saw the cutest boy today. He was working with the horses. He was tall and had dark hair and eyes."

Benjamin rolled his eyes. "Ro, can't you discuss *buwe* with *mei mamm* later when I'm not here?"

"No." Rosemary smiled. "We need something to talk about. It's going to be a long ride home."

"Tell me about it," Benjamin mumbled.

Carolyn laughed. "You just ignore us, Ben." She looked at her niece. "You can tell me about the *bu,* but keep your voice down. You know how your *dat* gets. He wants to keep you young forever."

"I know." This time it was Rosemary who rolled her eyes. She then detailed the cute boy for most of the ride home. Carolyn lost herself in her niece's story, enjoying the details of the strapping Amish boy. Carolyn prayed Rosemary's life would remain as uncomplicated as it was now and that her sweet niece wouldn't make the same mistakes she had when she was sixteen.

* * *

Carolyn stood at the sink in her brother's house and scrubbed a pot while her mother dried the dishes and Sarah Ann swept the floor.

"Benjamin got a job today," her father said as he sat at the table with Amos.

"He did?" Amos asked. "I thought he was going to keep working for me."

Carolyn turned toward them. "It wasn't planned. It just happened."

"How?" Amos looked intrigued.

Her father explained the story about the rock, and Carolyn continued to scrub the pot with such force that she thought it might break in half. She wanted to tell both her father and her brother that Benjamin was innocent, but she knew it was no use. They would never believe him.

"I see," Amos said.

Carolyn turned and found her brother rubbing his graying beard. At forty-five, he was a younger, thinner version of their father.

"It's a *gut* plan," Amos said. "He needs to work for Joshua Glick as punishment and to repay his debt for the horse's wound. That *bu* needs to learn some respect since he's always getting into trouble here. Maybe Joshua Glick can get through to him since I can't seem to get his attention."

Carolyn held on to the washrag in her hand and looked at her mother, who gave her a warning glance. Her mother could never stand for Carolyn to argue with Amos, so Carolyn vowed to try to not upset her mother. She was thankful the boys and Rosemary had gone outside after supper to finish chores and that Benjamin wasn't nearby to hear his uncle's unkind words.

"I think it will be *gut* for him too," *Dat* said.

"I bet he'll enjoy working on the horse farm." Sarah Ann smiled while sweeping near the entrance to the mudroom. "*Mei daadi* had several horses, and *mei schweschder* and I loved helping to care for them."

Amos tapped the table in emphasis. "It's *gut*, hard work, and that's what the *bu* needs."

"Work can be fun too, Amos." Sarah Ann continued to smile, and Carolyn wondered how her hard-nosed brother had won the hand of such a sweet wife.

The men discussed the weather while the women finished cleaning up.

Carolyn rinsed the last dish and handed it to her mother. She then wiped the counter and dried her hands on a dish towel as water gurgled and bubbles disappeared down the drain. "*Danki* for supper, Sarah Ann."

"*Gern gschehne*." Sarah Ann stowed the broom in the closet by the door.

"We'll see you tomorrow," Carolyn's mother said as she put on her cloak.

Sarah Ann hugged Carolyn and then her mother-in-law. "Have a *gut* night."

Carolyn hugged her cloak to her body and then followed her parents out to the porch and into the crisp night air. She marveled as they immediately began to hold hands and walk side by side toward their small house, located behind Amos's large farmhouse. Although her parents had been married for nearly fifty years, they still held hands and gazed at each other from across the room like teenage sweethearts. Carolyn longed to find a true love like her parents had always shared; however, she didn't believe she was worthy of finding a love like that because of the transgressions she committed when she was a teenager.

"Carolyn." Amos's voice sounded from behind her. "I need to talk to you."

She stayed on the porch, where her brother sidled up to her. "What do you want?" She hoped he wasn't looking for another chance to put down Benjamin. She couldn't take any more insults.

"I have someone I want you to meet. His name is Saul Beiler, and he doesn't live far from here."

Carolyn's shoulders tensed. "Why do you want me to meet him?"

"He's a widower and he has a *dochder*. He wants to meet you and see if you'll make a good *fraa*. He needs a *fraa* as much as you need a father for Benjamin." Amos gestured toward Benjamin walking toward the small house he lived in with Carolyn and her parents.

She took a deep breath to calm her soaring temper. "*Danki*, but I don't need your help. I can handle dating by myself."

"No, Carolyn, you can't." Amos shook his head. "You're thirty-one, and you're not getting any younger. You'll be blessed to find any man who will accept Benjamin."

"Amos," she began, hoping to steady her voice despite her irritation, "I'm not going to settle for a marriage of convenience. I want to marry for love, Amos, just like *Mamm* and *Dat* did."

Amos wagged a large finger at her. "You need to realize you can't live with *Mamm* and *Dat* forever. It's time for you to move on."

"Why?" Carolyn glared at him. "I work part-time in the hotel so I can contribute to the family. Benjamin isn't a burden on anyone. I've always cared for him, even though I had him when I was sixteen. I took responsibility for my actions."

"But the shame still follows you wherever you and Benjamin go. The sooner you're married, the sooner that shame is forgotten. Besides, Benjamin needs a full-time *dat* who can guide him and discipline him the way he needs to be disciplined. Today is a prime example of how Benjamin gets in trouble. If he had a father permanently in his life, he would learn how to behave."

"I think Benjamin is doing just fine." Carolyn gritted her teeth and tried in vain to keep the tears from stinging her eyes. "I'm sorry you think I'm still bringing shame to the family."

"Carolyn, just listen to me." He held up his hands as if to calm her. "I'm only trying to help you and Benjamin. I'm not doing this to hurt you. Saul is a *gut* Christian man. He is well respected in the district—he might even be a deacon one day. He'll be a *gut* father and a *gut* husband. He makes a decent living and can support you and Benjamin. He'll also make you and Benjamin respectable in the community."

Carolyn reluctantly nodded, knowing she had to accept her brother's guidance since he owned the land on which she and her son lived and that it was no use to argue with him. "Fine. I'll consider it. *Danki* for thinking of me. *Gut nacht*," she mumbled as she went down the porch steps and started across the field.

As she walked, she glanced up at the glorious sunset, taking in the orange, red, and yellow hues bursting across the sky. She looked toward the three-bedroom house where she lived with her parents and Benjamin. It was the same home where she'd given birth to her son. It was the same home where she had to tell her parents the news that she had given in to her boy-friend's constant pressure and wound up pregnant at the tender age of sixteen.

Her shoes crunched the frozen ground as she remembered the warm June day when she brought her baby boy into the world. Her life changed forever when she held that beautiful baby in her arms. She could no longer attend youth group events or enjoy buddy days spending time with her best girlfriends. Her childhood evaporated, and she felt alienated, lost somewhere between true adulthood and young adulthood.

She was also heartbroken since her boyfriend had disappeared before she had a chance to tell him that he was going to be a father.

Yet the most painful part of being a teen mother wasn't the social events she missed or facing mother-hood without Ben's father; it was the way the members of the community regarded her. People began to treat her differently from the moment the news spread of her pregnancy, even before the baby was born. Both male and female members of her church district would shake their heads and frown with sadness in their eyes whenever she walked past them. Women friends and family members would whisper their words of sympa-thy to Carolyn's mother well within earshot of Carolyn, causing her eyes to overflow with tears.

The most heartbreaking of all was when her father found out she was going to have a child. He cried, and then he stopped speaking to her for nearly two months. She sobbed and begged him to forgive her, but he remained silent. He eventually forgave her, but their relationship remained strained for years. Carolyn prayed to God, begging him to repair the distance between her father and her, but the distance remained.

She hadn't been baptized into the church before she had Benjamin, so she didn't have to confess her sin before the church. However, she decided to join the church after Benjamin was born. She wanted Benjamin to be raised within the stability of the Amish community, and she committed herself to becoming a church member.

Carolyn climbed the steps leading to the front porch of the house as she contemplated her precious son. Although Benjamin inherited Carolyn's blonde hair and brown eyes, at times she caught glimpses of her former boyfriend's expressions in his face. It seemed as if the heartache of his abandonment were haunting her through Benjamin's smiles, but that hurt soon transformed into love, a deeper, more meaningful love than her former boyfriend could ever provide.

Although Benjamin was created in haste and out of wedlock, he was Carolyn's angel. Raising him without the benefit of a stable marriage was difficult, even grueling at times, but she loved him with all her heart. And she was determined to shield him from all the hurt and shame she'd endured when he was born. Benjamin was innocent despite the mistake that brought him into the world. She constantly reminded him how much she loved him, so that he would never doubt her feelings for him. She never wanted him to carry the blame for or the shame of her mistake.

Carolyn moved across the small porch and sank into

the swing. She pushed it back and forth and breathed in the brisk February air while thinking about her brief conversation with her brother. Amos was the only member of the community who never forgave her mistake. She was thankful that he provided a home for her and her son on his farm, but she'd prayed thousands of times that he would soften his heart toward them. She knew that employment away from Amos and his mischievous sons was a good option for Benjamin.

Carolyn smoothed her hands over her cloak as she contemplated Joshua Glick. She'd noticed him at the auction early in the day when he was repairing a buggy in one of the barns. He looked to be in his mid to late thirties and was tall and lean. His dark hair was a stark complement to his deep blue eyes. His clean-shaven face was tan from the hours he must have spent with his horses. She noticed that he was confident and kind with his horses, as if he could relate to them on a deeper level than the average Amish man. She immediately recognized his expertise with the animals when he was working in the barn, too, and she admired his talent.

Yet she was then taken aback when he scolded her son with authority, as if Benjamin were one of his own children. She hoped Joshua would hold on to his temper and be a fair and good employer. She wanted her son's first experience working away from home to be positive.

"*Mamm?*" Benjamin's voice broke through her thoughts. "Are you coming inside?"

"*Ya.*" Carolyn stood and faced him in the doorway. "I'm coming in." She walked over toward the door and smiled, silently thanking God for her precious son.

THREE

During the Sunday service, Joshua sat with the other unmarried men while he sang along with the familiar German hymns in the *Ausbund*. It was the Esh family's turn to host the three-hour service, which was held in the barn of one of the church district families every other Sunday.

He held back a yawn as he stared down at the hymnal. The long day at the auction had worn him out, but it was worth it to showcase and sell a few of his horses. He'd also gotten to bed much later than he expected after having the vet stitch up Buck, but he managed to travel to church on time in his horse and buggy. Glancing across the barn, he spotted his father sitting with the other older, married men, and his father greeted him with a nod.

The service began with a hymn as Joshua redirected his thoughts to the present. He joined in as the congregation sang the hymn slowly. A young man sitting behind Joshua served as the song leader as the service began. He began the first syllable of each line and then the rest of the congregation joined in to finish the verse.

While the ministers met in another room for thirty minutes to choose who would preach that day, the congregation continued to sing. Joshua saw the ministers return during the last verse of the second hymn. They hung their hats on the pegs on the wall, indicating that the service was about to begin.

The minister began the first sermon, and his message droned on like background noise to the thoughts echoing in Joshua's head. Although he tried to concentrate on the preacher's holy words, he couldn't stop looking across the barn to where the married women were seated.

Just a little over a year ago, Joshua would gaze toward the same area of the congregation and find Hannah, his former sister-in-law, sitting there. He thought about Gideon suffering a massive heart attack in the back pasture at the horse farm. Although the emergency medical technicians had tried to revive him in the ambulance on the way to the hospital, it was too late.

Joshua always wondered if he could've saved him if he'd found him earlier in the day. Although Joshua knew it was a sin to doubt God's plan, he sometimes remembered the details of that day and wondered what he could've done to save his brother. What if he had done CPR longer? What if Hannah had called the paramedics sooner? What if the ambulance had driven faster? Joshua knew nothing could bring his brother back, but that reality did little to take the pain away. He missed him so much sometimes that his heart ached with regret and guilt over his death.

While the minister continued to talk in German,

Joshua lost himself in memories of his brother and their horse business.

The first sermon ended, and Joshua knelt in silent prayer along with the rest of the congregation. After the prayers, the deacon read from the Scriptures, and then the hour-long main sermon began. Joshua willed himself to concentrate on the sermon and then the prayers.

Relief flooded Joshua when the fifteen-minute kneeling prayer was over. The congregation then stood for the benediction and to sing the closing hymn. While Joshua sang, his eyes moved to where the young women sat and settled on his niece, Lillian. Although it had been a year since Lillian's mother, sister, and brother left the community, he still sometimes expected to see Lillian's fraternal twin, Amanda, sitting beside her during the service.

Lillian sat up straight and pushed her glasses farther up her nose while singing the hymn. She was the picture of Hannah in younger days with her bright red hair and green eyes. Joshua still had a difficult time accepting that Hannah had left Lily living with Joshua's parents while she moved Amanda and Andrew into the bed-and-breakfast with her new husband. Joshua had heard recently that Amanda had gotten her GED and was taking classes at the local community college and Andrew was attending fourth grade at the local public elementary school.

Lillian continued to smile and act as if everything was okay, but Joshua knew the truth. He could see the sadness in her green eyes, no matter how happy she said she was.

When the service was over, Joshua helped a few
of the other men convert the benches into tables and
then sat and talked with them while they awaited their
lunch. He looked up as his mother moved past him and
nodded a greeting.

*   *   *

Barbie Glick smiled at her son, Joshua, on her way to
the kitchen where she helped the other women prepare
to serve the food to the men.

"*Mammi*," her granddaughter Lillian said as she
sidled up beside her. "Have you met Lena Esh?"

Barbie shook her head. "I don't think I have."

"She was sitting with Anna Mary and me." Lillian
motioned toward the other side of the kitchen where
her best friend, Anna Mary Esh, stood with a girl who
had the same brown hair and eyes. "That's Lena. She's
Anna Mary's older sister who just moved back here
from Ohio. She's almost thirty."

"She just moved back here?" Barbie filled a tray with
dishes of peanut butter spread as she spoke. "Where
was she living?"

"She lived with her cousins for a few years, helping
to take care of her sick *mammi* in Sugar Creek, Ohio,
and then decided to join the church and come back to
be with her family. She's working in the Esh family's
bakery now." Lillian picked up a pitcher of coffee and
grinned. "She'd be perfect for *Onkel* Josh. You said
you'd like him to finally get married. Maybe she could
be the one to steal his heart."

"Oh, *ya*?" Barbie studied the girl, taking in the slight frame and pretty smile of the church's new member. "You think so?"

"Oh *ya*." Lillian pushed the ribbons back from her prayer covering. "Lena is really sweet, and she already thinks *Onkel* Josh is handsome. I pointed him out to her earlier. Anna Mary told me Lena is eager to get married and start a family. I think Lena and *Onkel* Josh would get along just fine." She motioned toward the door. "I'm going to go fill coffee cups."

"I'll be right there with the peanut butter spread." Barbie carried the tray over to where Lena was talking with Anna Mary while they filled bowls with cheese spread. "*Gude mariye.*"

Lena and Anna Mary returned the greeting.

"I hear you're working at the bakery," Barbie said to Lena while balancing the tray in her hands.

"*Ya.*" Lena nodded while glancing down at the bowls of cheese spread. "I love to cook and bake."

"That's *wunderbaar.*" Barbie smiled. "I also hear you lived with your cousins for a while."

"I did." Lena's shoulders hunched a little. "I cared for my grandmother for a number of years. After she passed, I realized I was supposed to come back to my family, find a husband, and be his helpmate. That's what God intended for us to do." She smiled at Anna Mary and then looked at Barbie again. "I want to fall in love and get married soon. I'm almost thirty, so I feel like it's time to start a family."

Anna Mary nodded, causing the ribbons to bounce from her prayer covering. "We're glad you came back."

"I'm so *froh* to be back. I missed my family so much. And the bakery is so fun. *Mei mamm* says I'm a really *gut* baker. She says I'll make a husband *froh* because I'll make *gut* food and keep him well fed." Lena's cheeks blazed a bright pink. "I don't mean to be prideful."

"You're not prideful," Anna Mary told her sister. "Lily says I'm a *gut* teacher's assistant too. I love teaching with Lily. Maybe you can help me make some *kichlin* to bring in for the scholars next week. They would love to have some of your chocolate chip *kichlin*."

"That's a *gut* idea." Lena's smile was wide with excitement. "I want to see your schoolhouse too. You have to invite me to come in and visit the class one day. Do you think the scholars would like chocolate chip *kichlin* or another kind? I can always make oatmeal raisin and peanut butter. What about peanut butter with chocolate chips?"

Barbie nodded slowly while she listened to Lena discuss her favorite cookie recipes. The young lady's demeanor and voice were humble, and she seemed respectful when she talked to Barbie.

Barbie's smile widened as a thought filled her— Lena was the complete opposite of Hannah, her former daughter-in-law, who never heeded Barbie's suggestions or took her advice on child-rearing or housekeeping. No matter how much Barbie tried to train Hannah to keep a house and raise her children the way she had raised her boys, Hannah did the opposite.

Lena would be the perfect, dutiful, respectful daughter-in-law who would be certain to listen to Barbie and obey her. And Barbie was certain that if

Lena did marry Joshua, Lena would never consider leaving the community and taking away Barbie's grandchildren as Hannah had done last year. It was obvious that the young lady took her church vows seriously and was determined to be a dutiful helpmate to her future husband.

Barbie was intent on getting Joshua married. He was nearly forty, and she longed for more grandchildren—especially since Hannah had left the community and taken two of Barbie's precious grandchildren with her. She saw Amanda and Andrew periodically, but she missed them desperately at church.

Lena would be the perfect wife for Joshua. She was young and pretty, and she could bake and cook. Barbie was certain Lena could keep a house too. If not, then Barbie would teach her how. She just had to point Lena out to Joshua and motivate him to leave the farm and start dating. Her son worked constantly and never attended the gatherings for the older singles in the community. She had to get him to step away from the farm and start living a full life.

"I think the scholars would love your peanut butter *kichlin*," Anna Mary said after Lena stopped talking about recipes. "That's a *gut* idea."

"Lena," Barbie said, "have you gone to any of the socials for the older singles since you've come back?"

Lena shook her head. "No, I haven't gone yet."

"You should go," Barbie said. "You'll meet the bachelors in the community. I know there are some older bachelors who could use a *gut fraa* like you."

Anna Mary jabbed her sister's ribs. "I told you that

you should go. It's the only way you're going to meet someone. You said you want to get married."

Lena shrugged. "Okay. I'll go."

"*Gut*." Barbie smiled as she started toward the door. She had successfully convinced Lena to go to a social gathering for the older singles in the community. Now if she could just get Joshua to go and meet Lena.

. . .

After lunch, Joshua had said good-bye to his friends and was hitching his horse to his buggy when his father walked up behind him.

"How was the auction?" his father asked as he began to help him.

"It went really well." Joshua nodded. "I sold five horses."

"*Gut, gut!*" *Dat* clapped his hands. "You've gotten busy. You should consider hiring more help."

"There was one issue at the auction. A *bu* threw a rock at Buck and now Buck has a gash in his rump. Cameron Wood came over last night and stitched him up."

"That's awful," *Dat* said. "Is Buck all right?"

"He's fine. I found the *bu* who did it. He's going to start working for me tomorrow to repay the vet bill debt. The *bu's* name is Benjamin Lapp. He's fifteen." Joshua gestured toward his father. "You know his *daadi*."

"I do?" *Dat* looked confused.

"You went to school with him. Titus Lapp. He lives over in Gordonville."

"Oh *ya*! Titus Lapp." *Dat* fingered his beard as he spoke. "He married a *maedel* named Miriam, and they have two *kinner*."

Joshua shrugged. "*Ya*, that sounds right."

Dat leaned against the buggy. "How is old Titus?"

"*Gut*, I guess." Joshua shrugged. "Maybe he'll come to the farm with Benjamin sometime and you can stop by and see. Benjamin is going to help out until the summer."

"Sounds like the *bu* needs to do some work. And you need the help, so it will work out perfectly," *Dat* said.

"*Ya*, I hope so. The *bu* is small. He actually looks a lot younger than he is, but maybe working on my farm will help him develop some strength and muscles. I know it's helped Danny fill out some."

"What are you two talking about?" His mother walked around from behind the buggy.

Joshua shared the story of the boy coming to work for him, and she crossed her chubby arms over her wide dress and nodded in agreement.

"Sounds like a *gut* plan." *Mamm* suddenly smiled. "Did you see the new *maedel* at service today?"

Joshua shook his head while he finished hitching the horse. "No, I didn't."

"Her name is Lena, and she's Anna Mary Esh's older *schweschder*. You know Anna Mary. She's Lily's teacher's assistant at the schoolhouse. She started helping Lily out at the school a couple of months ago."

Joshua tried not to frown as his mother talked on about things that didn't really interest him. "I know Anna Mary."

"Oh, *gut*. Anyway, her older *schweschder* Lena just came back to Paradise after living with her cousins. She wound up joining the church out in Sugar Creek, but she wanted to come back here to be with her *mamm* and *dat*. She's almost thirty. She's working at the Esh family's bakery, and she likes to bake and cook. You should meet her."

"*Mamm*," Joshua began, doing his best to keep his voice even despite his growing agitation, "please don't start trying to fix me up with someone. I told you already I'm too busy to date. I have a business to run."

"Listen to me, Joshua." His mother gripped his sleeve. "It's not natural for you to be alone. You need a *fraa* to run your household for you. You can't do all the cooking and cleaning yourself. I won't be here to take care of you forever. You need to stay strong and healthy so you can run your farm. You need a *fraa* to cook *gut* food for you."

Joshua gritted his teeth to bite back disrespectful words. "*Mamm*, I take *gut* care of myself, and I don't expect you to cook or clean for me. I can handle it all on my own. I've done pretty well since I moved into the *haus* on the farm. I haven't starved yet, have I?"

"No, no, you haven't. You look healthy so far." She waved off his rebuttal. "Just give me a chance to tell you about Lena. She's perfect for you. She's young and *schee*. She's just what you need. You'll get to know her, marry her, and you'll have a houseful of *kinner*. Don't you want what Gideon had?" She sniffed, and her blue eyes misted over with tears when she mentioned his late brother. "Gideon was such a *gut dat*. I know you can be one too. Hannah has taken two of *mei grandkinner*

away from our community. You can bring us more
grandkinner. You can help repair my broken heart."

Joshua looked at his father, hoping he would change
the subject and stop his mother from ranting about
the painful subject of Gideon, Hannah, and the children they all missed. Instead of chiming in, his father
looked resigned to his mother's determination.

"Just go to a social and meet Lena," his mother continued. "You'll like her, Josh. I'm certain you'll want to
get to know her better."

"Fine," Joshua said with a sigh. "I'll go to a social
and meet her, but don't start planning my wedding just
yet. I never said I was desperate to get married. You're
just desperate to get me married."

"*Wunderbaar!* You'll finally go to a social!" His
mother clapped her hands. "I know you'll be *froh* to
meet Lena." She looked past him and gasped. "There
she is with Anna Mary. Look toward that group of
maed. They're standing with Lily."

Joshua looked toward a group of young women talking by the pasture fence and spotted a young woman
standing with his niece and her friend. The young
lady was average height and had light brown hair. She
laughed while Anna Mary and Lily seemed to be talking nonstop beside her. She angled her face toward
Joshua, and he noticed her delicate features. Lena
then smiled at Lillian, and her face seemed to light up.
Joshua had to admit she was attractive, but what did he
know about dating? He'd pined for Hannah for nearly
half of his life, and she'd walked away from him and
the community without looking back.

"You should go talk to her now, Joshua." *Mamm* nudged him with her hand. "Just go say hello."

Joshua eyed his mother. "I can't go talk to her now. I need to get home and feed the horses." His mother opened her mouth to speak, and he raised his finger. "I told you I will go to a social. Please don't push this. You know I don't like to be pressured into things."

"Okay, okay." She nodded. "That will be just fine."

"I'll see you both later. I'm going to head home." Joshua shook his father's hand and gave his mother a quick hug before climbing into the buggy.

He guided the horse out to the main road while thinking about his mother. He loved her, but sometimes he wished she would concentrate on something else. She'd always pressured him to find someone and get married, but lately it seemed to be her one focus, her one goal in life.

He was certain her heart was broken after Hannah chose to leave and take Amanda and Andrew away from the Amish church. And in some ways, it made sense that she hoped Joshua could provide more grandchildren to help heal the hole in her heart. Yet, at the same time, he wasn't focused on finding a wife and starting a family. He wanted to run the best horse farm he could in honor of Gideon's memory. Finding a wife didn't fit in with his plans right now. He was too busy to date, but his mother wasn't known for taking no for an answer.

Joshua considered Lena while he merged onto another road, heading toward his farm. She looked to be a nice enough young lady. He was certain his mother wouldn't stop nagging him until he attended a social and met her, but he'd only told her he would to get her to drop the subject. Joshua had no intention of attending a social with the rest of the older single folks in his church district. If he were meant to meet Lena Esh, then God would place her in his path. If his mother asked about the social, he'd simply tell her he was too busy and he'd try again the following week. She would have to accept that answer for now. He prayed she would find something else to occupy her time and take her focus off Joshua's life.

He turned onto his street and made his way toward his horse farm. Soon the sign advertising Glick's Belgian and Dutch Harness Horses came into view and Joshua thought again about Gideon. He missed his older brother and thought of him nearly every day as he walked out to the stables, thinking of how Gideon would be pleased if he could witness how busy and successful the farm had become during the past few years.

Joshua guided the horse up the rock driveway and past the two-story, white clapboard house where he now lived. It was the house where Gideon had brought Hannah after they were married and then welcomed his three children. The house seemed too big and too empty for only Joshua, but it made sense for him to move onto the farm after Hannah left.

He climbed down from the buggy, unhitched the horse, and led it toward the stable while thinking about his life. He knew God intended him to stay on the farm after Gideon died, and for a long time he believed God intended for him and Hannah to be together.

As he stepped into the stable, he pondered what life would be like if he had a wife and a family. He pushed the thoughts away, knowing he didn't have time to find a wife. Dreaming about it was crazy. He was where he needed to be. After all, he was nearly forty and still single. Maybe God didn't intend for everyone to be married.

Yet deep in his heart, he wondered if there was more for him than his lonely life on the horse farm.

* * *

Later that evening, Barbie checked to make sure the back door was locked before heading to bed.

"*Mammi.*" Lillian walked through the kitchen clad in her long nightgown. "I thought you had already gone to bed."

"I was heading that way." She watched her granddaughter place a book in her tote bag. "Are you getting ready for school tomorrow?"

"*Ya.*" Lillian yawned and stretched her arms. "I had fun at youth group today. We played volleyball until our arms hurt over at Nancy's *haus.*"

"That's *gut.*" Barbie sat on a kitchen chair. "Have a seat. Let's talk for a minute. How's Leroy?"

"He's *gut.*" Lillian's smile was wide as she sat across from her. "I really like him. I can't wait until we're both baptized so we can really date." She suddenly frowned. "Sometimes I really miss Amanda while I'm at youth group. I know she chose to go with *mei mamm* and go to college, but sometimes I feel so lonely. It was hard enough losing *mei mamm*, but I also lost *mei zwilling-boppli* and *mei bruder*."

"I know, *mei liewe*." Barbie touched her hand while wondering how Hannah could've walked away from her daughter and started a new life without her. "But you still have me. You'll always have your *daadi* and me."

"*Danki*." Lillian's expression brightened again. "So, do you think *Onkel* Josh and Lena will get together?"

"I hope so." Barbie rested her chin on her palm. "He promised me that he'd go to one of the social gatherings for the older singles. I hope they meet and start dating. Maybe we'll have a wedding to plan in the fall."

"*Ach!*" Lillian clapped her hands. "That would be *wunderbaar*." She suddenly frowned again. "But he's awfully stubborn. What if he doesn't go to the social? What can we do to get them together?"

"Hmm." Barbie rubbed her chin. "We'll have to come up with a *gut* plan."

"Okay." Lillian cupped her hand to her mouth to block a yawn. "We'll have to think about that. I'll let you know what I come up with. I better get to bed. *Gut nacht, Mammi*."

"*Gut nacht*." Barbie considered the issue of Joshua's bachelorhood while her granddaughter disappeared up the stairs. Barbie never took no for an answer. She would find the right wife for Joshua no matter how long it took.

FOUR

Joshua glanced toward the driveway just as a horse and buggy steered in. He'd been expecting Benjamin Lapp to arrive anytime. The young man stopped the horse by the barn and Joshua crossed the pasture to meet him.

"*Willkumm!*" Joshua shook Benjamin's hand.

"*Danki.*" Benjamin scanned the property. "This is a *schee* farm."

"*Danki, danki.*" Joshua gestured toward the horse. "Why don't you unhitch your horse and you can bring him to the stables. I'll show you around."

"Okay." Joshua gave him a little history of the farm as Ben guided his horse toward the stables. Daniel King stepped out as they approached.

"Benjamin." Daniel shook Benjamin's hand. "It's *gut* to see you. Are you ready for some hard work?"

Benjamin shrugged. "*Ya.*"

"*Gut.*" Daniel motioned for Benjamin to follow him. "Let's get started shoveling out the stalls."

Joshua walked toward the barn where his telephone and answering machine were kept. He found the red button flashing and listened to the messages. The first two were from potential customers wishing to make an appointment to come and see the horses. He wrote down their names and numbers so he could call them back.

When the machine began the third message, his mother's voice rang through the speaker. "Joshua, this is your *mamm*. I need you to bring me that casserole dish I left at your *haus* Friday. I'm planning on making you another casserole, and I have to have that dish. Please bring it this evening around five. See you then. *Danki*."

Joshua sighed while wondering what casserole dish his mother needed. He called the customers back, made appointments with them for the following day, and then strolled into the house. He crossed from the mudroom into the kitchen and grimaced at the mountain of dirty dishes clogging the sink. He had planned to take care of the dishes this morning, but he was sidetracked outside by the constant work required to keep a successful farm running.

Joshua scanned the kitchen, finding piles of newspapers, unopened bills, catalogs, and notepads peppering the long table. When Hannah and her family lived in this house, it was spotless. Now it was nothing but a messy bachelor residence. Actually, it was a *lonely* and messy bachelor house. Hannah would be so ashamed if she saw it.

Hannah.

Joshua wondered if that ache he felt in his heart when he thought of her would ever go away. He wanted to move past the hurt and betrayal she had left behind, but he didn't know how to let go. He knew he needed to pray and ask God for help healing his heart, but he didn't even know how to ask for help. How silly was that? He couldn't even open up his heart to pray for healing.

He moved to the sink and sifted through the heap of pots, dishes, and bowls until he found the casserole dish his mother had requested. Then he washed all the dishes and picked up some of the mess on the kitchen table before returning outside to continue his chores.

* * *

Carolyn stepped into the break room at the Lancaster Grand Hotel that afternoon after she finished cleaning the rooms on the second floor. She found her friends and fellow housekeepers, Ruth Ebersol and Linda Zook, already sitting at the table, eating their lunches.

"Hello," Carolyn said, pulling her lunch bag from the refrigerator. "How is your day going?" She poured water into a plastic cup and then sat across from them.

"It's been *gut*," Linda, a petite brunette in her early thirties, said. She shrugged as she unwrapped a cheese sandwich. "The usual. Dirty rooms and unmade beds."

Ruth laughed. Her graying hair peeked out from under her prayer covering. "You sound as if this is the worst job in the world, Linda. It's not so bad, really. And the sun is shining and February is almost over. March will be here soon. It's been a fine day. I've been training the newest member of our housekeeping team."

"We have a new coworker?" Carolyn raised her eyebrows with surprise as she pulled her sandwich out of the bag. "I didn't know Gregg was hiring someone new."

"*Ya*, her name is Madeleine Miller. She's going to come and join us for lunch in a few minutes. She had to go talk to Gregg." Ruth gestured toward the door. "You'll like her. She's very sweet, and she's *English*."

"Really?" Carolyn lifted her turkey sandwich.

"She's going to replace Hannah." Ruth sipped her cup of water. "It will be nice to finally have the extra help again. Gregg wasn't sure we needed it for a while, but business has picked up considerably. I'm glad he decided to hire someone."

The door opened, and a woman who appeared to be in her late twenties stepped into the room wearing a gray dress and a black bib apron. Her dark brown hair was pulled back in a long ponytail, and her gold name tag said "Madeleine."

"You must be Carolyn." Madeleine approached Carolyn and shook her hand. "It's nice to meet you. Ruth has told me all about you."

"It's nice to meet you too." Carolyn tapped the seat next to her. "Join us for lunch."

"Thank you." Madeleine placed her lunch bag on the table and then sat next to Carolyn. "Gregg seems really nice."

Ruth nodded while chewing. "He's a *gut* supervisor. He's fair, and he also expects us to do our best."

"Do you live close to the hotel?" Carolyn asked as she wiped her mouth with a paper napkin.

Madeleine nodded. "I live a couple of miles away in Paradise. I moved here a few months ago. I'm sort of starting over."

Carolyn and Ruth exchanged intrigued expressions.

Linda folded up the wrapper for her sandwich. "What made you move here?"

"Well," Madeleine said as she glanced around at her newest friends, "my grandparents were Amish, and I used to visit them here frequently when I was a child. I spent nearly every summer with them when I was little. After they passed away, I found out I inherited their house, and I decided to move here instead of selling it."

"Oh." Carolyn nodded. "You think you might stay in the area for a while?"

"It's more than that." Madeleine studied her apple. "I actually have always been fascinated with the culture. I've always moved around a lot, and I would like to find a real home. The summers I spent with my grandparents were always my favorite. I feel like I belong here."

Carolyn met Ruth's curious gaze and raised her eyebrows.

"Are you saying you want to be Amish?" Ruth asked.

"No," Madeleine said slowly. "But I've always wanted to move here and learn more about the community where my grandparents lived." Madeleine turned toward Carolyn. "Did you grow up Amish?"

"*Ya*." Carolyn gestured toward the other women at the table. "We all did."

"What was it like to grow up Amish?" Madeleine asked with curiosity shining in her eyes.

Carolyn remained quiet while Ruth shared stories of growing up on a farm not far from where she lived now. Linda chimed in and talked about her parents' farm and how wonderful life was before her parents passed away.

Carolyn smiled and nodded but remained silent while they spoke. She had never shared the story of her teen pregnancy with her coworkers, and she didn't want to open up today, especially since she didn't know Madeleine very well. Although she was no longer ashamed, she knew how some people judged her.

"Well, it's about that time." Ruth stood and tossed her plastic cup into the trash can behind her. "Back to work."

Linda turned toward Madeleine. "Ruth said I can take you with me this afternoon while I clean. Would you like to join me?"

"That would be wonderful." Madeleine packed up her lunch bag. "I'd love to work with you."

Carolyn placed her empty lunch bag in her tote and then placed it in her locker. She waved good-bye as Madeleine and Linda headed out of the break room.

"Are you okay, Carolyn?" Ruth sidled up to her. "You were awfully quiet during lunch."

Carolyn shrugged. "I didn't have much to add to the conversation. My childhood isn't worth sharing. You and Linda had wonderful stories to share about your childhood."

"What are you saying? I'm sure you do too." Ruth crossed her arms over her big apron.

Carolyn paused and touched her temple while mentally debating if she should tell Ruth her biggest secret, the secret that could change their friendship forever. *Will Ruth still look at me the same way once she knows the truth about Benjamin?*

Ruth frowned. "I'm sorry. I never meant to make

you feel uncomfortable. It's not my place to pressure you into telling me something that's not any of my business." She moved past Carolyn. "I need to get back out there to clean the meeting rooms."

"Wait." Carolyn tugged at Ruth's sleeve. "I'll tell you."

Ruth gave her a sad smile. "You don't have to. I was wrong to pressure you."

"No, it's okay. I've wanted to tell you for a long time." Carolyn paused and drew in a breath, while praying the news she was about to share didn't change her close friendship with Ruth. "I have a son."

Ruth's eyes rounded with surprise. "Did I hear you correctly? Did you say you have a son?"

Carolyn nodded. "Benjamin isn't my younger *bruder*. He's my son."

Ruth gasped. "I had no idea."

"I know." Carolyn ran her fingers over the counter while she spoke. "I was young, and I thought I was in love. My boyfriend pressured me, saying he loved me and if I loved him too, well . . ." Her voice trailed off. "I was only sixteen when I had Benjamin."

"Oh, Carolyn. I had no idea." Ruth touched Carolyn's shoulder. "It must've been so difficult for you and your family."

"It was. I never got used to the stares and whispers." Carolyn shook her head as she thought about her former boyfriend. "My boyfriend wasn't there when Benjamin was born. He doesn't know he has a son. He left the community."

"Where did he go?"

"He had talked about going to a former Amish

community in Missouri. He wanted me to go with him, but I couldn't bring myself to leave my community." Carolyn shrugged. "He didn't even have the courage to tell me to my face that he was leaving. He left a note for me with one of the other boys who worked with us. All it said was, 'I can't stay here. I wanted you to go with me. I hope you understand that I need to go now.' How was I supposed to understand why he left? But I'm just thankful that God gave me the courage to face the consequences. I've always tried to be the best *mamm* I could without a husband to support me."

Ruth's expression was filled with sympathy. "I can't imagine how difficult it was to become a *mutter* at such a young age."

"It was terrible. Some days I would just hide in my room and cry until *mei mamm* forced me to come out. I missed out on so much of the fun of being young. I couldn't go to singings, and I never dated after that."

"You've never dated?"

"Not since I was sixteen." Carolyn smoothed her hands over her apron while she thought about her youth. "*Mei mamm* told me I could go to singings, but *mei dat* made me feel guilty about it. He constantly reminded me how hard *mei mamm* worked at home and how unfair it was for me to go out with *mei freinden* while *mei mamm* looked after the *kind* that was born after my terrible sin."

Ruth sighed. "I'm so sorry."

Carolyn smiled. "You don't have to be sorry. I love my son. He wasn't planned, and being his *mamm* hasn't been easy. But I love him with all my heart. I want to shield him from the shame I've had to bear all my life."

"Is that why you never told me?" Ruth leaned back against the table in the middle of the room. "Were you afraid I would judge you?"

"No." Carolyn frowned. "I don't know. How can you not judge me? I don't want our friendship to change."

"Our friendship won't change, Carolyn. You'll always be *mei freind*. We all make mistakes. We're all human. None of us are perfect in God's sight."

"I know, but people still treat me differently. *Mei dat* treats Benjamin like he's his own *kind*, and people who don't really know us think Ben is my nephew. But *mei dat* treats me differently. It's as if he'll never go back to seeing me as his *dochder*. I know he's forgiven me, but I wonder if he'll ever act like he's truly forgiven me."

She shook her head as her thoughts turned to her brother. "And then there's Amos. He reminds me constantly of the mistake I made and the sacrifices my parents have made to raise Ben like their own. He's pressuring me to get married so that my son is legitimized and has a full-time *dat*. I guess Amos thinks I need to move out so that my parents can enjoy their golden years together, alone. I pray constantly that Amos will forgive me."

"But you are forgiven in God's eyes." Ruth squeezed Carolyn's hands. "He has forgiven you already. He forgave you as soon as you asked him to."

"*Danki*, Ruth. *Mei mamm* has said the same thing and tells me to keep praying for *mei dat* and Amos. I do pray for them, but I'm also aggravated. I know I made a mistake, but I want a normal life for my son. I dream at night that someday I'll find the right man who will love both me and my son." Carolyn sighed. "Amos wants to find me someone who will marry me as soon as possible. In fact, he's found a widower who will accept me despite my past sin. He doesn't understand that I don't want a marriage of convenience. I want to marry for love. I want a man who will accept Ben and me and then build a family with us. I want a man to fall in love with me, not just see me as a decent wife and housekeeper."

Ruth nodded. "You keep praying for that. You'll find it."

"*Danki*, but I don't think I ever will. I'm certain God is punishing me for my past sin. I'm supposed to be alone."

"No, that's not true. Our God isn't a vengeful God. He forgives you."

"I'm not so sure about that. I also pray that Amos will see all the *gut* that came out of my sin. Ben is a *gut bu*, but *mei bruder* doesn't see that side of him. He only sees what he wants to see. He believes his *buwe* are perfect, but they like to make trouble." Carolyn shared the story of what happened at the auction.

When she finished the story, she reflected on Benjamin's new job. "I think it will be *gut* for Ben to get away from his cousins. They like to get him in trouble at the farm. They play pranks and then tell their *dat* Ben did it. Amos always believes his sons before Ben."

Ruth clicked her tongue and shook her head. "That's

a shame Amos and his sons treat Benjamin so badly. I'm sorry to hear that. But I think it's a *gut* thing Ben is going to work for Joshua Glick. Joshua is a *gut* man."

"You know him?"

"Oh, *ya*. He's in my church district. You did know he's Hannah's former brother-in-law, *ya*?"

"Oh, that's right." Carolyn snapped her fingers. "I do remember that now that you mention it."

"Joshua started the horse farm with his brother, Gideon, many years ago when Gideon and Hannah were first married. Gideon died of a heart attack seven years ago, and Joshua has kept the farm going. He seems abrasive at times, but he's a very *gut* man. I think he'll treat Benjamin well."

"I hope so."

"*Danki* for telling me the truth about Benjamin. I will guard your secret within my heart." Ruth paused and touched Carolyn's arm again. "Carolyn, I want to give you a little advice with Benjamin. I have a son who left the community many years ago. He also went to a former Amish settlement in Missouri."

"*Ach*, Ruth." Carolyn frowned as sympathetic tears drenched her eyes. "I had no idea."

Ruth's smile was once again sad. "Now we both have shared a secret. I just wanted to warn you not to alienate Benjamin. If you do, he may leave, just like my Aaron did."

"I would never alienate him. I've always been the best *mamm* I could to him. I've tried to make a *gut* life for him. That's why I work here and save some of my money for him and for his future."

"I know you want to be a *gut mamm*, but with the way your *dat*, your *bruder*, and your nephews treat him, he may feel different and alienated. Just promise me that you'll be careful." Ruth sniffed and wiped her eyes as tears trickled down her cheeks. "I don't want you to lose your son like I lost mine. It's been more than fifteen years, and I haven't heard from him. I miss him every day. I don't want that to happen to you."

Carolyn considered her friend's words. "*Danki*, Ruth." Carolyn glanced at the clock above the door. "We'd better go. Gregg may come looking for us if we stay in here too long." She started for the door and silently thanked God for Ruth's wonderful friendship.

FIVE

Carolyn stood at the kitchen sink at home and washed out a mixing bowl after putting a meat loaf in the oven. She spotted a horse and buggy moving up the rock driveway and dropped the bowl into the hot, sudsy water.

Carolyn turned toward her mother, who was setting the table. "Ben is home!" She wiped her hands on a dish towel and then grabbed her cloak from the peg by the back door. "I'm going to go see how his day was." She rushed out of the house and met Benjamin at the barn.

She approached the buggy just as Benjamin climbed down. He was covered in mud from his neck to his boots, and he smelled like the inside of a barn in the middle of a sweltering summer day. His hands were nearly black with dirt and mud. He lifted his straw hat, and his sweaty blond hair was plastered to his head.

She gasped as she took in the sight of him. "You're a mess!"

Benjamin grimaced. "I'm exhausted. I've never worked so hard in my life."

Anger swelled inside Carolyn. "What did he have you doing?"

"Mucking out stalls." Benjamin glanced down at his trousers. "Every muscle in my body hurts. He worked me like an indentured servant. I think I could lie down and sleep for a week."

"Why would he do that on your first day?" Carolyn demanded. "That's cruel!"

"Ben!" Her father grinned as he approached them. "You look like you've been dragged by your horse."

"I feel like I have been, *Daadi*."

Carolyn's frustration surged as she studied her son. "Who does Joshua Glick think he is?"

"What do you mean?" her father asked.

"Why does he think he can work Ben so hard on his very first day?" She pointed at Benjamin. "He's just a *bu*."

"That was the deal, Carolyn. Ben's repaying Joshua for hurting his horse."

"No, this wasn't part of the deal." She pointed toward the buggy. "I'm going to go have a talk with him."

"Don't do that." Benjamin's eyes widened. "I can handle it. You don't need to get involved."

"*Ya*, I do need to get involved." Carolyn nodded with emphasis. "I'm your *mamm*."

"Let me handle it, *Mamm*." His brown eyes pleaded with her. "I'm fifteen. I'm a man now."

"He's right, Carolyn," *Dat* chimed in. "You don't need to get involved."

"*Ya*, I do need to defend my son."

"Carolyn, this isn't your place," *Dat* pressed on. "You need to let me handle this."

"I'm going, *Dat*. Please tell *Mamm* that I'll be

back soon." She climbed into the buggy and guided it toward the road. This time she was going to do what *she* thought was right.

* * *

After Daniel and Benjamin had gone home for the evening, Joshua headed over to his parents' house with his mother's casserole dish sitting next to him in the buggy. He guided the horse into his parents' driveway and found another horse and buggy parked near the barn. Joshua stopped his horse and buggy near the other one and then climbed out.

As he approached the porch, he found his mother and Lillian standing by the back door, talking to two young women. When he reached them, he realized they were Anna Mary and Lena Esh, and he inwardly groaned as it became apparent that he'd been set up. His mother didn't want the casserole dish; she wanted him to meet Lena.

"Josh!" his mother's voice sang as he looked up at her wide grin. "You're here!"

"Hello." He nodded at the women, and Lena smiled. He held up the casserole dish and felt like a heel. What was he doing holding up a casserole dish while surrounded by a group of eager young women?

"*Wie geht's, Onkel* Josh." Lily gestured toward the Esh sisters. "Lena and Anna Mary came by to deliver *kichlin* Lena made."

"*Mei schweschder* made these *appeditlich kichlin* for our scholars. Lily is going to bring them to class tomorrow." Anna Mary held up two boxes. "Lena works at *mei mamm's* bakery. She's the best baker."

"That's *wunderbaar*." Josh forced a smile.

"I hope the scholars enjoy them," Lena said. "I enjoyed making them. I tried a new chocolate chip cookie recipe, and I think it came out well. If they like them, I'll make more."

He had never felt so uncomfortable and out of place in his life. It was as if he were a contestant on one of those *Englisher* dating game shows his elderly neighbor had once detailed in a conversation. It was also obvious his niece was now plotting with his mother to get him to date Lena. Annoyance stole over him. He appreciated their good intentions, but he just wanted to be left alone to run his farm.

"Here's your dish." He handed it to his mother. "*Gut nacht.*"

"Wait!" his mother said. "Don't go just yet. I have supper ready inside. Come in and join us. I've already invited Anna Mary and Lena to stay too."

His mother's smile was eager and expectant. He felt trapped, like a wild horse locked in a stall.

He tried to think of an excuse, any excuse. "Well, I was going to finish cleaning up the house. It's a mess."

"Don't be *gegisch*. I'll clean it for you tomorrow." *Mamm* motioned for him to enter the house. "*Kumm.* Stay for a bit."

Joshua sighed and held the door as the four women filed into the mudroom. He hung his coat and hat on a peg and then followed them into the kitchen, where platters of food cluttered the long table. The aroma of peanut butter spread, fresh-baked bread, pickles, and macaroni and cheese penetrated his nostrils, and his stomach growled in response. Although Joshua wanted to flee the uncomfortable scene, he was hungry, and he desperately wanted to make himself a sandwich. He'd been so busy working that he never had lunch. Daniel and Benjamin had stopped working around noon to eat. Joshua, however, had continued training a horse, and he eventually lost track of time.

His mother made a sweeping gesture toward the table. "Please help yourselves. My husband told me he will return home late today."

Lena sat at the table. "*Danki*." She bowed her head to pray.

Mamm pointed at the seat across from her and motioned for Joshua to sit.

He dutifully complied and then lowered his head to give a silent blessing. When he looked up again, *Mamm* was standing by the doorway leading to the family room with Anna Mary and Lily. Anna Mary placed the two boxes of cookies on the counter near the sink.

"Anna Mary," Lily began with her voice a little too loud. "Let me show you the quilt I'm working on before we eat. It's going to be a gift for Naomi's birthday."

The three women disappeared into the family room, and Joshua was left alone with Lena. *This was most definitely a plan, and I was naïve enough to fall right into their trap*, he thought.

Lena filled her plate with pretzels, macaroni and cheese, and bread.

Joshua cleared his throat and tried to think of something to say while loading his own plate. "It all smells *appeditlich*, *ya*?"

Lena nodded. "*Ya*, it does. I hadn't realized how hungry I was until I smelled the food."

"I thought the exact same thing. I skipped lunch." Joshua smeared peanut butter spread over a thick piece of bread. "So, you work at the bakery?"

"I do." Lena's brown eyes met his. "I really enjoy working there."

"What are your favorite desserts?" he asked.

Between bites of macaroni and cheese, Lena listed her favorite things to bake. She finished describing her favorite recipe for chocolate cake, and then the room fell silent. The only noise was the drone of low voices coming from a nearby room.

Joshua finished his peanut butter sandwich while struggling to think of something to say. "I run a horse farm," he finally said.

"Oh." Lena nodded. "That must be very hard work."

"It is," Joshua said while spooning more macaroni and cheese.

"Do you have a lot of horses on your farm?" Lena asked.

"*Ya*, I do." He shared information about his farm while she nodded and listened intently, her eyes fixed on him.

He was still talking about his horses when *Mamm*, Lily, and Anna Mary returned to the kitchen, all smiling like expectant children on Christmas morning. He was certain their excitement was directly related to his interaction with Lena.

Mamm sat across from Joshua and aimed her smile at him. "I see you two are getting along well."

Joshua frowned at his mother, but the gesture didn't dampen her mood. Although Lena seemed like a fine young woman, he didn't appreciate being set up with her.

Anna Mary and Lily joined them at the table, and after a silent prayer, all three women began to fill their plates with food and talk nonstop about everything from housework to news about people in the community.

Joshua was thankful when his father joined them in the kitchen and he had someone to talk to who didn't want to discuss baking or talk about the people in their church district. He made small talk with his father about the farm until their plates were clean. After another silent prayer, the women began cleaning up the kitchen while Joshua and *Dat* headed for the mudroom.

"*Danki* for the meal," Joshua called to his mother while putting on his hat and coat.

"*Gern gschehne.*" *Mamm* approached him as she reached for her cloak. "Let me walk you out."

Joshua fought the urge to groan, knowing she would want to discuss Lena again.

"Good-bye, *Onkel* Josh," Lily called with her hands submerged in the soapy sink.

"Good-bye." Joshua waved to Anna Mary and Lena, who smiled and waved.

Joshua followed his parents outside and stood on the porch with them.

His mother clamped her hands together and smiled. "So, you liked Lena?"

"She was nice." Joshua sighed as he decided the direct approach was best with her. "*Mamm*, I appreciate your effort, but I don't think there will ever be anything between Lena and me."

"What are you saying?" His mother looked confused.

"I'm not interested in her." Joshua shrugged. "She's a nice *maedel,* but I don't have time to date. I'm too busy running the farm. I have customers calling daily, and I have horses to train and feed. My life doesn't leave any room for a relationship right now."

Mamm gave *Dat* a pleading expression. "Eli, tell him he's talking *narrisch*. Tell him he needs to date. Explain to him that the Lord wants us to bear fruit, and it's not natural to be alone."

Joshua hoped his father would back up his feelings.

Dat shook his head. "He's old enough to make his own decisions, Barbie. I think you need to just let God take control."

Joshua swallowed a sigh of relief. *Danki, Dat!*

"You're both *narrisch*." *Mamm* waved off *Dat's* words. "Lena is perfect for you, Josh. That's why you need to go to those socials, to get to know her. But I was afraid you'd break your promise to me, so I brought you over here to meet Lena."

"*Mamm*, I told you I'm not interested. Please back off." Joshua tried his best to keep his words respectful despite the exasperation building inside him. "I need to go. See you soon."

Before his parents could respond, Joshua headed to his waiting horse and buggy. During the ride home, he silently prayed for patience with his mother and also asked God to redirect her efforts from his love life to something else.

He considered Lena as he drove the rest of the way. Although she was attractive, he felt no spark for her, and therefore he couldn't imagine trying to forge a relationship with her. How could he possibly get to know her better if they had nothing to talk about?

If he did want to date, he would want to find someone who was more interesting to him. He also would want to feel an attraction to the woman.

But he wasn't interested in dating. He only wanted to work on his farm. Why couldn't his mother understand that?

He arrived home and then went into one of the barns to check on the animals. He noticed a stall that needed to be repaired and went to work on it.

* * *

Carolyn's temper flared as she guided the horse past a sign that read Glick's Belgian and Dutch Harness Horses. She was determined to give Joshua Glick a piece of her mind. She led the horse up the rock driveway toward a row of barns. After halting the horse, she hopped down from the buggy and marched toward a large barn where the doors were open wide. The loud bang of a hammer sounded from within.

"Joshua Glick!" she called over the racket as she stepped into the barn. "Joshua Glick?"

The hammering stopped, and Joshua stepped into her line of sight. "Carolyn? May I help you?"

"I'd like to talk to you about Benjamin." She started toward him. "He came home covered in mud and muck."

Joshua shrugged. "So? That's how I look every day after I work out here." He turned his back to her and resumed hammering a nail into a stall door.

Resentment boiled within her as she watched him work. "Excuse me, I'm speaking to you." He looked over his shoulder at her. "Don't you think you worked him a little hard on his first day?"

"No, not really." He swiped the back of his hand over his sweaty brow. "Work is *gut* for the *bu*. All *buwe* need to learn what real work is." He started hammering again.

"I don't think it's your place to decide how hard Benjamin needs to work." She raised her voice over the hammer. "You're taking advantage of him, and it's not right. He's just a *bu*."

Joshua stopped hammering and faced her. "Well, my deal is with his *daadi* Titus, and I intend to follow through. I need the help, and the *bu* owes me for the vet bill he caused. Hard work is a *gut* way to teach *kinner* respect." He frowned. "Maybe the *bu* will think twice before he throws a rock at a horse again." He started toward the tack room at the back of the large barn.

"Wait just a minute!" Carolyn rushed to catch up with his long strides. "I also don't think it's your place to decide what's best for Benjamin." As she took another step, her shoe slid on slick mud, and her hands flew up in an attempt to right herself. But much to her dismay, her feet flew out from under her, and she landed on her bottom in a pool of muck with a loud splat. Her cloak, stockings, and shoes were covered in the dark, smelly brown muck. Anger and embarrassment rained down on her. Why hadn't she watched where she'd been walking? Now she was as dirty as Benjamin! She was certain she smelled just as bad as he did too. To make matters worse, she'd taken a spill in front of this man whom she barely knew.

Joshua spun and faced her. "Are you all right?"

"I'm fine," she muttered as humiliation heated the tips of her ears. A lock of hair fell from beneath her prayer covering.

"Let me help you." He held out his hands.

"No," she grumbled. "I'm fine." She grabbed a post, pulled herself up from the smelly puddle, and stared down at her soiled clothes.

"Can I give you a rag?" He held out a stained towel.

"*Danki.*" Her words were hardly audible. She wiped the towel down her cloak and skirt, but the mud remained in place. She handed the towel back to him. "I think you need to go easier on Benjamin." She hoped she sounded more confident than she felt, standing in front of this man while covered in muck.

"No, that wasn't the agreement I had with Titus. Benjamin is going to work for me, not stand around while I do all the chores." He gestured around the barn. "There's plenty that needs to be done here, and I need the help."

She was at a loss as to what to say. The fall had taken both her dignity and her words. "Fine. *Gut nacht.*"

He studied her as if she were crazy. "*Gut nacht.*"

* * *

Carolyn drove back home and found her mother washing the dinner dishes. She quickly changed her clothes and then returned to the kitchen.

"I kept some food warm for you." Her mother retrieved a plate from the oven.

"*Danki*." Carolyn took the plate and then sat at the table. After a silent prayer, she began to eat the meat loaf and mashed potatoes.

Benjamin and her father entered the kitchen from the outside.

Benjamin gave her a worried expression. "What did you say to Josh?"

"I told him that he was being too hard on you." Carolyn turned to her father. "I said that it wasn't his place to discipline Benjamin."

"You shouldn't meddle. You were wrong to go over to Joshua's after I told you not to." *Dat's* tone was stern as he removed his coat and hat. "It's not your place to interfere."

"*Ya*, it is." Carolyn placed her fork on the table beside the plate. "Benjamin shouldn't come home looking as if he'd walked to Philadelphia and back in the middle of a hurricane."

"I can handle it myself." Benjamin's expression was serious. "You have to let me grow up and be a man."

"He's right," *Dat* said. "Let him finish out his end of the deal. It's *gut* for him."

Carolyn turned to her mother, hoping to find her support. Instead, her mother nodded in agreement with her father. Carolyn heaved a heavy sigh, knowing she'd been overruled yet again. She had to put her faith in the Lord. He certainly would watch over Benjamin.

* * *

Barbie and Lillian sat in the family room later that evening. Barbie read the Bible while Lillian read her latest Christian novel.

Barbie gazed over at her granddaughter and caught her pushing up her glasses while she studied the page in front of her. "Is that a *gut* book?"

"Oh, *ya*." Lillian nodded without looking up. "I can't put it down."

Barbie smiled as she turned back to the book of Matthew. She heard footsteps in the kitchen announcing that Eli had come in from working out in his wood shop. "It must be time for bed. *Daadi* is in the kitchen."

Lillian nodded and closed her book. "I'd love to keep reading, but I don't want to yawn while trying to teach the scholars tomorrow." She stood. "I better get ready for bed."

Eli appeared in the doorway. "You two are up late."

"My book is so *gut*." Lillian hugged the novel to her chest. "*Gut nacht*. See you in the morning."

"*Gut nacht*." Eli crossed the family room and sat beside Barbie on the sofa. She immediately smelled sawdust and noticed the dust on his trousers and shirt.

"*Gut nacht*, Lily." Barbie watched her granddaughter run up the stairs. "She's such a *gut maedel*. I don't understand how her *mamm* could leave her behind."

"Hannah did what she thought was right. It's not

our place to judge her." Eli pointed toward the Bible. "What are you reading?"

"The book of Matthew." She looked down at the page. "I love this verse. 'Let your light shine before men, that they may see your good deeds and praise your Father in heaven.'" She met Eli's gaze. "That's why I'm trying to find Joshua a *fraa*. That's my *gut* deed. I think the Lord led Lena here so she can marry Joshua and give us more *grandkinner*."

Eli shook his head and frowned. "Barbie, I know you think you're doing something *gut*, but you need to let God lead Josh and Lena. It's not your place to interfere. Our parents didn't interfere when we were dating. Let Joshua make his own decision. He's a grown man."

"Now you sound like Josh." She shook her head while wondering why her husband could never see things her way. "I'm only trying to help."

Eli sighed. "I know you think you're helping, but you're only going to upset him. He's always been the stubborn one. Gideon would let you take control at times, but Josh has never been like that. He's set in his ways. Right now he's only focused on the farm, and you need to respect that." He touched her shoulder. "I know you mean well. You have a *gut* heart. That's why I married you. But you have to let Joshua find his own way."

"If I do that, then I'll never have any more *grandkinner*." She sniffed as tears soaked her eyes. "My heart breaks every time I think of Andrew and Amanda. They belong in this community with us. They should be Amish like their *dat* was. Hannah stole them from us."

"I know." Eli patted her shoulder. "I know you miss

them, but you have to let God guide Joshua. If he's meant to be a *dat*, then he will become one in God's time. Trust God, Barbie. If you try to make something happen that's not supposed to happen, then you'll just lose your son altogether. We've lost one son. Don't drive the other one away."

Barbie gasped and stood up, placing her hands on her hips. "How dare you accuse me of pushing Joshua away! I'm only doing what I think is *gut* for him."

"Now, now, Barbie. Don't put words in my mouth." Eli held up his hands as if to calm her. "I didn't mean it that way. I know you have all *gut* intentions. I'm only trying to warn you to back off a little before you upset Josh. You know how he gets when he's upset. He might stop coming to visit us. We don't want to lose him. That's all I'm saying."

Her irritation subsided as she studied Eli's face. "Fine. I'll back off a little, but I still want to see him get married."

"I do too." Eli stood and touched her hand. "Let's head to bed. It's getting late."

Barbie followed Eli upstairs toward their bedroom. As they got ready for bed, she sent a prayer up to God, asking him to warm Joshua's heart toward Lena. She asked God to help Joshua find more to life than work. She also prayed that Joshua would find the right woman for him soon. And she asked God to help Hannah realize that she needed to mend her relationship with Lillian.

SIX

By Thursday morning, Carolyn couldn't stand her curiosity about Benjamin's new job any longer. He seemed less exhausted when he came home at night, but when she'd asked him about his work, he didn't have much to say. Her irritation with Joshua Glick had subsided some, and she wanted to see more of the farm for herself; her anger and subsequent fall into the muck hadn't afforded her much opportunity to take it all in. So Carolyn decided to ride to work with Ben and then take his horse and buggy to do some errands while her parents were also out. Her primary goal, however, was to satisfy her curiosity.

As Benjamin guided the horse into the driveway leading to the horse farm, Carolyn gazed at the scenery she'd missed Monday when she was blinded by her outrage. She took in the large, beautiful white clapboard house with the sweeping wraparound porch and the row of newly painted red and white barns and stables near a white split-rail fence.

"This is so *schee*," she said, despite her lingering frustration. She had to admit that the property was lovely.

"I knew you would like it." Benjamin guided the horse toward the row of stables. "Josh keeps the place immaculate, but his *haus* is a wreck."

He chuckled, and Carolyn studied him. Although she enjoyed the sound of her son's laughter, she was surprised at how quickly he'd changed his opinion about working at Joshua's farm.

"So you don't mind that Joshua has you working so hard?" she asked.

He shrugged. "I'm starting to think that maybe *Daadi* is right. Maybe this job will make a man out of me. I'm tired of being called a *bu* all the time. Maybe I'll earn some respect by working hard."

Instead of protesting, she nodded. Benjamin had always been small for his age. Although he was nearly sixteen, he seemed to be stuck in the body of a thirteen-year-old with thin arms and short legs. Yet Carolyn had always thought her son was handsome. She prayed he would soon grow taller and have the confidence to attend singings with the other young people in the community. She longed to see him make more friends and maybe someday fall in love and have a family. She wanted him to have all the things she dreamed of—a family and a happy home.

Her thoughts turned back to Joshua Glick's farm and Benjamin's temporary job.

"I know Joshua is working you hard, but has he been nice to you?" Carolyn asked as Benjamin brought the buggy to a stop.

Benjamin shrugged. "*Ya*, he's been fine. He wants

things done his way, but he's not mean like *Onkel* Amos is sometimes."

Carolyn frowned. She was glad her son was away from his uncle and cousins, but she also wished she could take away the hurt he'd suffered when they treated him badly because of her own mistake.

Carolyn climbed out of the buggy and looked across the pasture to where Joshua worked with a horse. She watched as he moved the horse back and forth, guiding it with the bridle, and she found herself drawn to his stewardship toward the animal. He turned toward the stables, and when he spotted the buggy, he waved. He started toward them, and Carolyn couldn't look away. She studied how he carried his muscular, lanky body with grace. He walked over to Benjamin and Carolyn and smiled as he reached them.

"*Gude mariye*," Joshua said, lifting his hat to wipe the back of his hand across his brow. "I'm surprised to see you here, Carolyn. What brought you over for a visit today?"

Carolyn smoothed her hands over her apron, hoping it wasn't covered in dust after sweeping her mother's kitchen earlier. "I thought I would drop Ben off so I could run a few errands with this horse and buggy while I'm off work today. My parents needed our other horse and buggy."

"Oh, *gut*." Joshua gestured toward the row of barns. "You left quickly Monday after our brief conversation, and I wasn't able to show you around. Would you like a tour?"

"*Ya.*" She was surprised at the offer. "That would be nice."

"Okay." Joshua turned to Benjamin. "Ready to start shoveling?"

"*Ya.*" Benjamin touched Carolyn's arm. "I'll see you later."

"Leave a message if you need a ride home." Carolyn watched Benjamin trot toward a large stable. She turned toward Joshua, who was watching her, and she suddenly felt self-conscious. "This is a *schee* farm."

"*Danki.*" Joshua crossed his arms over his wide chest. She couldn't help but notice that his blue shirt accentuated his deep azure eyes. "Where do you work?"

"The Lancaster Grand Hotel," she said. "I work part-time as a housekeeper on Mondays, Wednesdays, and Fridays. I know that's a little unusual for our community, but I like getting out and meeting people." She was almost certain she caught the hint of a frown.

"Hannah used to work there." His tone changed as he said the words, as if they tasted bad.

"*Ya*, Hannah Glick. I worked with her. She's your sister-in-law."

"She used to be my sister-in-law." He started toward the barn. "Let's get that tour started. I have a lot of work to do."

Carolyn watched him for a moment, stunned by the sudden change in demeanor. Had she said something to offend him? She trotted to catch up with his long strides. "I didn't mean to keep you from your work."

"Oh, no. It's fine." His smile was back, and her heart thumped in her chest.

She fought against her body's reaction to his face and looked toward the stables. It was silly to be attracted to this man. She didn't even know him. "How long have you had this farm?" she asked.

"This land has been in my family for years. My parents inherited it after *mei mamm's* parents passed away. They had tenants living here and caring for the land until *mei bruder*, Gideon, married Hannah and moved in. Right after he moved here, Gideon told me he wanted to go into business with me." He stopped in front of the stables and swept his eyes over the property. "The horse farm was all his idea. Our parents loaned us the start-up money, and we started the farm. In the beginning, we only had a few horses."

Carolyn peered into the stable, and the aroma of animals and hay wafted over her. Her eyes moved to where she'd fallen on Monday, and embarrassment crept up on her. She hoped he hadn't told anyone about her unladylike behavior. "How many horses do you have?" she asked in an effort to keep the conversation moving.

He pointed toward the stalls. "We have twenty-nine box stalls. We normally have anywhere from forty to fifty horses here at one time."

"This is spectacular." Carolyn studied the horses. "They are such magnificent animals."

"They are. They're really smart too. I don't think everyone gives them credit for their intellect. I love training them and working with them." He laughed a little. "You know, when we first started the business, I thought *mei bruder* was *narrisch*. It was so much work that I was overwhelmed."

Josh pointed toward the house. "But I soon fell in love with the work. It's a labor of love, but it's a blessing in so many ways. I actually slept in the spare bedroom for a while since Gideon and Hannah didn't have any *kinner* at first." He paused for a few moments as if contemplating his words. "I'm *froh* God led Gideon to the horses. It's been *gut* comfort for me since Gideon died and Hannah moved away."

He cleared his throat and looked down at the ground. "I'm a little surprised I told you that. I haven't actually said that out loud to anyone before."

"Oh." Carolyn studied him as he kicked a rock with his shoe. It was obvious he was embarrassed that he had opened up to her, and once again she found herself surprised by Joshua Glick. He was turning out to be more than just the outspoken man she'd seen at the auction and then argued with on Monday.

An awkward silence passed between them, and Carolyn internally groped for something to say.

"So, you live here now?" She pointed toward the house.

"*Ya.* I moved in when Hannah and her *kinner* moved out last year." He met her gaze, but his expression seemed guarded. Was he afraid of revealing too much again? "The *haus* is too big for me, but it's convenient living here. I can just walk out the door and I'm at work. I get more done in the daylight since I don't have to travel from here back to the little *haus* where I lived on my parents' farm." He pointed toward a second stable. "Ben is working in here with Danny King."

Carolyn followed him to the other stable, where

they found Benjamin and Daniel. Daniel glanced up and waved, and she returned the greeting. She then followed Joshua toward the row of barns.

"All our equipment is kept in those three barns, and there's a small pond at the back of the pasture." Joshua pointed toward the back of the property. "Hannah used to like to go sit back by the water." He shook his head, as if to shake away the memory.

"It's beautiful," Carolyn said while scanning the area. "I would love to live in a place like this."

Joshua studied her. "Don't you live on a farm?"

Carolyn nodded. "I do, but it's not the same. I live with my parents in the *daadi haus* on *mei bruder's* property. I've always dreamed of having a family and a farm of my own. I appreciate my family, and I love them, of course, but I would love to have something of my own."

"It always sounds like a *gut* idea when you talk about it and dream about it." Joshua rubbed his clean-shaven chin. "But it's a lot of work."

"But you just said the horses are like a comfort for you," Carolyn reminded him with her hands on her hips for emphasis. "You admitted just a few moments ago that you fell in love with the farm after a while."

Joshua smiled. "*Ya*, you're right. I did say that, but it's a lot when you're alone. I'm thankful that I have Danny to help me."

"And Ben," she added.

"Very true." Joshua looked toward the stable where Ben was working. "He's a hard worker and a quick learner."

Carolyn couldn't stop her smile. It was a relief to hear someone compliment her son for once. She looked toward the pasture and silently admired the beautiful horses grazing. A comfortable silence fell between them.

"Are you still angry with me for working him too hard?" Joshua asked.

Carolyn studied him. His direct question startled her. "No, I don't think so. He seems happy here."

"Good." He smiled. "I'm glad he's here. I'll work him hard, but I promise you that he'll learn a lot from me."

"That's *gut*."

"Well, I better get back to work," Joshua said.

"*Ya*, I better get to my errands." She looked up at him. "It was *gut* getting to talk to you."

"*Ya*." He nodded. "It was *gut*. See you soon."

Carolyn made her way to the waiting horse and buggy. Before climbing in, she turned back toward the pasture and watched Joshua return to the horses. She lingered for a few moments, taking in Joshua interacting with the horses, and she wondered why she felt such a growing respect for the man.

She had not dated since Benjamin was born, and she'd gotten used to being alone. Benjamin was all she needed for years, and she also couldn't relate to the young people who were her age in the community since her life experiences had been so different from theirs. Yet now she found herself staring at this near stranger and wondering what it would be like to get to know him better.

She shook her head, attempting to erase the crazy

notion of dating a man like Joshua Glick. Yet the thoughts haunted her as she guided the horse toward the main roads and the market. No matter how hard she tried to suppress it, Joshua's smile floated in the back of her mind like a gentle whisper from a dear friend.

* * *

Joshua watched Carolyn climb into the buggy and then guide the horse toward the road. Soon the buggy disappeared down the rock driveway, but her image lingered in his mind. Carolyn was the most complicated woman he'd ever met. She'd argued with him on Monday after Benjamin's first day at work, but today she'd visited him as if the argument had never happened. She seemed stubborn but also elegant as she complimented his farm. She was as intricate and mysterious as the morning sunrise.

Although Carolyn and Lena were close in age, he was struck by the stark differences between the two women. Lena was attractive, but Carolyn had something mysterious in her deep brown eyes, which were an intriguing complement to her blonde hair peeking out from beneath her prayer covering. Both women were unmarried, but Carolyn seemed more mature and wise beyond her years. He easily fell into a conversation with Carolyn and didn't have to strain to come up with topics of conversation, like he had with Lena.

He contemplated their conversation and wondered why he had begun to open up to Carolyn about his deep attachment to the farm and all he'd lost when Gideon died and Hannah left. He'd never wanted to tell anyone how he felt about his life before. What was it about Carolyn Lapp that brought his deep emotions to the surface? He shook the question off and glanced toward the stable while wondering how Daniel and Benjamin were doing.

But as Joshua walked to the stables, questions pinged through his mind. He pondered why a beautiful, intelligent, mature young woman like Carolyn wasn't married. She'd confessed to him that she wanted a family and a farm, so why hadn't she found someone and made that dream come true?

He stepped into the stable and heard Daniel and Benjamin talking and laughing near the back. Benjamin seemed to fit in at his farm, and Joshua needed the help with all the work. He wondered if Benjamin would consider staying on as a helper when the summer season began. He decided to keep that idea in the back of his mind and see how the next couple of months went.

Joshua grabbed a shovel and stepped into a stall, where he began to dig. His mind wandered back to questions about Carolyn. She intrigued him, but he knew he couldn't consider dating her. He was too busy. He didn't have time to get involved with a woman, no matter how attractive and interesting she was.

And besides, when he had fallen in love before, he got hurt. It was safer if he stayed alone, and at this point as his fortieth birthday loomed in the next couple of years, he believed that he was supposed to be alone.

* * *

Hannah stared out the window from the passenger seat of Trey's BMW on Saturday morning as the car moved through the familiar streets she'd known when she was married to Gideon. She felt like a different person as she glanced down at her denim jumper and her clogs. Although she wore her long red hair in a bun, her prayer covering was gone, and a plain gold band decorated her once-naked ring finger. She looked over at her husband, and he smiled at her.

"Are you okay?" His voice was warm and smooth.

"*Ya*, I'll be okay." She looked back out the window as the street leading to her former in-laws' farm came into view.

"I can't wait to see Lily," Andrew announced from the backseat.

Amanda leaned between the front seats. "What time are you picking us up, Trey?"

"You name the time," Trey said while steering into the long rock driveway.

"How about two o'clock?" Amanda asked. "I have to study for that biology exam this weekend."

Hannah could hear the worry in her daughter's voice. "You'll do fine, *mei liewe*. You've gotten straight A's so far in biology, so why are you worried?"

Amanda sighed. "Thanks, *Mamm*. I'm just worried I'm not cut out for college."

Hannah faced her daughter and took her hands. "You will do fantastic. Stop doubting yourself."

"Thanks." Amanda gave Hannah a quick hug by leaning between the front seats. "I'll see you later." She pushed the car door open and headed toward her waiting twin sister.

"Bye, *Mamm*! Bye, Trey!" Andrew yelled before leaping from the car and running up the driveway behind Amanda.

Hannah looked through the windshield toward where Lily was hugging Amanda by the bottom step of the porch leading into Barbie's mudroom. Then as Andrew hugged Lily, a knot formed in Hannah's chest.

Hannah stared at Lily and tears filled her eyes while the twins talked. Although Hannah was happy in her new marriage and in her new life running the Heart of Paradise Bed-and-Breakfast with Trey, she missed having all three of her children together. Being separated from Lillian left a gaping hole in her heart.

Trey touched Hannah's arm. "Go talk to her."

"The last time I tried to talk to her, she slammed the door in my face." Hannah's voice was thick with her heartache. "I don't think I can stand more of that rejection. It's difficult enough not seeing her every day. Facing the hate she has for me is even more painful than missing her."

"She doesn't hate you, Hannah." Trey cupped his hand over hers. "You'll always be her mother, and she'll always love you. You can't give up on her. She wants you to reach out to her. Eventually, she'll forgive you."

"I don't think I can do it." Hannah cleared her throat. "I just can't."

"Yes, you can. Just go, Hannah. Try to talk to her." He nodded toward the windshield. "Take as long as you need. I'll wait here for you."

Hannah took a deep breath and pushed the door open. Lily met her gaze and then looked quickly back at her siblings. Hannah's heart thumped in her chest as she made her way toward her children.

Lily looked over at Hannah again and then pointed toward the back door. "You can go inside. *Mammi* made *kichlin* for you."

"Which kind?" Andrew asked.

"Oatmeal raisin." Lily grinned. "Your favorite."

"Awesome!" Andrew pumped his arm before racing up the porch steps and disappearing into the house.

Hannah studied her twins as they stood together with their stark differences never more pronounced. Although they were fraternal with different hair and eye color, they looked even less alike now as Lily wore her prayer covering, plain dress, and bib apron. Amanda had quickly adapted to college life, choosing jeans, blouses, and sweaters more often than skirts and dresses. Her blonde hair hung in a braid that nearly reached her behind since she still refused to cut it. She wore a tiny bit of makeup that Hannah could only see if she examined her face, which made Hannah happy. Although Hannah wanted her daughter to make her own choices, she took comfort seeing Amanda ease into this new life with grace. She no longer dressed Amish, but she still looked like a respectful young lady.

Amanda's expression was hesitant, and Hannah assumed her daughter wanted to be sure Hannah and Lillian were going to be civil toward each other before she went inside. Amanda had assumed the role of peacekeeper since they left the community. She was the one who asked Lily to calm down when she got upset with Hannah.

"Lily," Hannah began, her voice still thick. "It's *gut* to see you. I've missed you."

Lily lifted her chin in defiance. "That didn't stop you from leaving me behind."

"Lily," Amanda said. "Just give *Mamm* a chance. She's really missed you. You haven't seen what I have. She cries about you nearly every night. She still loves you even though she isn't Amish anymore."

"I think you should stay out of this." Lily's words were more determined than unkind. "This is between *Mamm* and me."

Amanda turned to Hannah, who nodded as if to tell her it was okay to leave. "I'll leave you two alone to talk. See you later, *Mamm*." She hurried up the porch steps and disappeared into Barbie's house.

"Lily, I have missed you. I will always miss you." Hannah reached for Lily's hand, but Lily quickly took a step back. "How are you?"

Lily shrugged. "I'm fine. I've adjusted to living here. *Mammi* and *Daadi* are *gut* to me."

"I'm so glad to hear it." She was so thankful that Lily finally talked to her. This was the first almost-civil conversation they'd shared since last year. Relief consumed Hannah, and she found the confidence to push on and try to keep her talking. "How's teaching?"

"It's *gut*. I love it." Lily crossed her arms over her chest as her eyes scanned Hannah. "I can't believe you're wearing a ring. The Amish never wear jewelry. And you've taken off your *kapp*. You've completely forgotten where you came from. You've thrown away all the traditions that mean so much to us."

Tears stung Hannah's eyes. "That's not true. I still dress plainly. I could never forget all our beliefs."

"It seems as if your choice to throw away our traditions has rubbed off on Amanda and Andrew." Lily gestured toward the house. "They're both dressing *English*. Andrew is in jeans and his hair is cut short. And Amanda's hair isn't covered, and she wears jeans and makeup. I can't imagine what *Mammi* is going to say. How would *Dat* feel about this? I guess they're influenced by you."

"I'm not influencing them." Hannah tried to keep her tone even, despite feeling offended by Lily's comments. "I'm letting them make their own choices. I want them to be comfortable in our new life. This is a new start for all of us. Amanda is *froh* going to college. She wants to fit in. She doesn't want people staring at her or treating her differently. I have to allow her to do what she feels is right, and she's still dressing modestly. Andrew loves school. He wants to look like his new friends."

"He should be going to my school." Lily spat out the words as she glared at Hannah. "He shouldn't be in an *English* school. He should be in this Amish community." She pointed toward the ground. "That's what *Dat* wanted for us. Have you forgotten about *Dat* completely since you have a new husband?"

"No, I haven't forgotten your *dat*. How could I forget the first man I ever loved and the father of my *kinner*?" Hannah took a deep breath and tried to hold back her tears. "I'm the one who decides what's best for Andrew. Right now, he belongs with me, Lillian." She pointed to her chest. "He's my son, not yours. I know what's best for him."

"Bad things happen in the *English* schools, and he'll be influenced by *kinner* who don't behave and don't believe in God."

"Lily, if Andrew told me he wanted to come back to this community, I would let him. If he told me he wanted to go to your school, then I would send him there. Right now he's happy living with me." Hannah pointed toward the house. "When you get inside, ask him how he feels, and he'll tell you that he loves his new school. Go ahead and ask him, and see what he tells you."

"I *will* ask him." Lillian lifted her chin in defiance. "If he were in my school, I could protect him and remind him about God. He's going to forget everything he learned from our church. He should be at the Amish church services too. He's going to stop believing in Jesus."

"That's not true." Hannah shook her head as tears clouded her vision. "Trey and I take Andrew and Amanda to our church. They both believe in God. Their faith is just as strong as it was when we were living in this community. They're happy, Lily. Can't you tell they're happy? They are the same siblings they were when we were all living on the farm together. They love you and miss you, just like I do."

"No." Lily sniffed and wiped her eyes. "They aren't the same. Nothing is the same. You broke our family apart. You changed everything, and nothing will ever be the same. I know I'm supposed to forgive you, but I will never find a way to heal my broken heart."

"Lily." Hannah took a step toward her. "I still love you. You have to believe me."

"No." Lily shook her head as tears streaked her pink cheeks. "I don't believe anything you say to me, and I never will. You need to leave now." She climbed the steps toward the back door.

"Lily!" Hannah called after her daughter. "Lillian, please talk to me! Give me a chance to make things right between us. I love you, Lillian!"

Lily entered the house, shutting the door behind her. Hannah stood as if her feet were cemented in place and stared at the door for several minutes, praying that Lillian would come back and talk to her. She needed to finish the conversation with her daughter.

When the door remained closed, Hannah finally walked back to the car while tears trickled down her cheeks. She choked back a sob as she climbed into the passenger seat and closed the door.

"Hannah." Trey pulled her into his arms. "I'm so sorry."

Hannah rested her cheek on Trey's shoulder as the tears flowed.

"Just give her time." He whispered the words into her ear while stroking her back. "She'll come around. Have faith, Hannah."

"I don't know." Hannah sniffed and willed herself to calm down. "I don't see how she'll ever forgive me." She moved out of his embrace and wiped her eyes with the back of her hands. "She's still so angry. I can't stand the hate in her eyes."

"I told you before that she doesn't hate you. You'll always be her mother. She could never hate you." Trey wiped a stray tear away from her cheek with the tip of his finger. "She talked to you today for the first time. That means she's making progress."

"It doesn't feel like progress. It feels like a horrible nightmare that won't end."

"No, it's not a nightmare. It's getting better. I watched Lily close the door in your face the last time we came over here." He pointed toward the back door. "Today she was waiting outside for her siblings, and she stayed and talked to you. That's progress."

Hannah finally nodded in agreement. "You're right. This was the first time she talked to me."

"Just have faith, Hannah. I promise you that Lily will forgive you someday."

"I pray you're right." She sighed and touched his cheek.

He suddenly frowned. "Do you regret marrying me? Was this more heartache and trouble than you ever anticipated?"

"No." Hannah shook her head. "I'm thankful we found each other. I'm thankful God led you to me. I could never regret marrying you. I love you, Trey."

"I love you too." Trey leaned over and kissed her.

Hannah closed her eyes and prayed that someday her daughter would forgive her and repair the hole in her heart.

SEVEN

"A mos invited us all to go over and play games tonight," Carolyn's mother said as she dried the last pot from supper.

"He did?" Carolyn glanced over at *Mamm* while sweeping the floor. "Why would he do that? It's been a long time since he's invited us over for games on a Sunday night." The words slipped from her lips before she could stop them.

"Now, Carolyn." *Mamm* placed her hand on her slight hip and faced her. "You know Amos means well. He's just a little cranky sometimes."

"Cranky? I would say he's more than cranky. Sometimes he's downright mean to Ben."

Mamm sighed. "I know. I've seen it. I've asked your *dat* several times to speak to Amos. I was praying it would help."

"You have?" Carolyn was surprised since her mother rarely spoke out against her father or her brother.

"I have. I just haven't told you." She smiled. "Just because I haven't said anything to you about it doesn't mean I haven't noticed it and tried to fix it behind closed doors."

"*Danki.*" Carolyn smiled. "I'm thankful you did that for Ben."

"I promised you I would help raise him like he was my own, and I've done my best to do that." *Mamm* turned back to the sink. "So, about game night. We're all invited. We need to head over there soon."

Carolyn continued sweeping the floor. "I wonder what the special occasion is."

"Maybe the special occasion is that it's been too long." *Mamm* put the last pot away.

"Maybe." Carolyn swept up the pile of dirt into a dustpan and tossed it into the trash can. She appreciated her mother's positive attitude toward her brother, but she had an overwhelming suspicion there was more to game night than playing games. Her brother hadn't hosted a game night or attended one at their parents' house in more than a year.

After finishing up the kitchen, Carolyn and *Mamm* retrieved Benjamin and *Dat* from the barn and headed toward Amos's large farmhouse at the front of the property.

Carolyn spotted a buggy parked near the pasture and turned to her mother. "Is someone visiting?"

Dat gestured toward the buggy. "Amos said his *freind* Saul was going to join us."

"Saul?" Carolyn swallowed a groan when she realized Saul was the widower Amos wanted her to meet. She stopped in her tracks and faced her mother. "I'm not going."

"You're not going?" *Mamm* looked confused. "Why?"

"Can't you see?" Carolyn's voice rose as anger surged through her. "Amos planned this so I can meet Saul."

Mamm continued to study Carolyn with confusion. "I don't understand."

Carolyn turned to her father and Benjamin, who also looked confused. "You two go on. I'm going to talk to *Mamm* for a moment."

The men shrugged and then continued to the house.

"Carolyn, why are you so upset?" *Mamm* asked while they stood by the pasture fence. "What's wrong with playing games with Amos's family and his *freind*?"

"Amos hasn't told you about Saul?"

Mamm shook her head.

"He's a widower who has a *dochder*. Amos says I need to get married because Ben needs a stable *dat*, and I need to stop being a burden to you and *Dat*. He also said that I bring shame on the family and I need to be married off so the community forgets about my mistake and my teenage pregnancy."

"What?" Her mother's eyes widened. "That's *gegisch*. You're not a burden, and you don't bring shame on our family. Everyone has forgiven you for what happened, and Ben is growing into a nice young man. You can live here as long as you want. Besides, Ben has more fathers than he needs. Your *dat* and Amos are like father figures to him."

Carolyn shook her head. "You may think I don't bring shame on the family, but Amos is ashamed of having me here. He wants to marry me off as soon as possible."

"You can get married when you feel the time is right. You don't need Amos trying to help you find a husband."

"That's exactly how I feel. I'm not going to marry someone just to get married. If I ever get married, it will be for love. I want a marriage like you and *Dat* have. I want a relationship with mutual respect." Her voice rose as anger bubbled up inside her. "But even more than that I want love. I don't need someone to support Ben and me. I work at the hotel, and I contribute to the family. I want a man who—"

"Carolyn, stop." *Mamm* put her hand up to silence her. "I know what you're saying, and you're right. You won't be forced into a marriage you don't want." Her expression warmed. "We shouldn't stand out here and debate this. It's rude, and we're going to make everyone suspicious. Let's go in and play games with our family and Saul. It doesn't hurt to meet him. You might actually like him. You never know if God put Saul in Amos's life so that you could meet."

Carolyn raised an eyebrow with disbelief, and *Mamm* laughed.

"You're just as stubborn as your *dat*." *Mamm* took Carolyn's hand. "Let's go play games and have fun. You work hard at the hotel. You need to have some fun too. Besides, you love playing games. Let's go before we miss our chance to join in. You might actually enjoy yourself."

I doubt it. Carolyn frowned as they climbed the porch steps and entered Amos's kitchen, where Rosemary sat at the table while talking with a girl who looked to be about ten. A few decks of Dutch Blitz cards sat in the middle of the table. Rosemary's brothers sat at the other end of the table and frowned as if they were bored.

Carolyn's father and Amos stood on the other side

of the kitchen and talked to a tall man with dark hair and a beard. Carolyn's body tensed with uncertainty as she studied the man, who seemed to be in his midthirties. He stood close to six feet tall, and his expression was unreadable as he spoke.

"Saul," Amos said as he made a sweeping gesture toward Carolyn. "This is *mei schweschder*, Carolyn."

Saul nodded at her, and she immediately noticed that he had sad brown eyes.

"Nice to meet you." Carolyn hoped her smile seemed genuine despite her feeling awkward. He seemed to examine her as if she were a horse at auction.

"Hello." Sarah Ann brought a platter of homemade granola bars to the table. "Would you like a snack?" She pointed toward the counter. "Rosemary made some pretzels too."

Carolyn inhaled the aroma of the pretzels. "Rosemary, they smell *appeditlich*. Did you use your special recipe?"

"*Ya*, I did. *Danki*." Rosemary sat up a little taller. "I was just telling Emma about my recipe. She said she wants to try it."

"Hi, Emma. I'm Carolyn." Carolyn nodded at Emma and then helped her mother bring cups of water to the table.

Sarah Ann brought the platter of pretzels, along with plates and napkins, to the table and then clapped her hands. "I think we're ready to start the game."

Carolyn and her mother sat across from Rosemary and Emma. Sarah Ann sank onto a bench beside Rosemary and began opening the decks of cards.

The men, however, moved toward the back door. "Where are you going?" Sarah Ann eyed Amos with annoyance. "I thought you were going to play."

"We're going to sit on the porch and talk." Amos gestured toward the back door. "Saul doesn't like to play games."

Carolyn glanced at *Mamm*, who responded with a warning expression. Carolyn enjoyed playing games with her family, and she wondered why Saul didn't enjoy them. He seemed rather standoffish, which seemed odd to Carolyn since he was supposedly looking for a wife.

Amos's sons stood up and followed the men, who were all pulling on their winter coats.

"We'll join you," David said.

"*Ya*. Dutch Blitz is boring," Robert chimed in.

They filed out to the porch and then their muffled voices sounded beyond the kitchen walls.

"*Mei dat* doesn't like games." Emma shrugged. "He told me that *mei mamm* did, but she died six years ago when I was only four."

"Ben and I like games, right, Ben?" Carolyn smiled at her son as he moved over next to her.

"*Ya*, we do. We play them all the time with *Mammi*, *Daadi*, and Ro. I don't feel like going outside with the men." Ben grabbed a deck of cards.

"Why don't you young people and Carolyn play?" Sarah Ann suggested. "*Mamm* and I don't need to." Carolyn wondered if Sarah Ann thought she should get to know Emma better. Amos must have told her he hoped she would marry Saul.

Ben shrugged. "We can all play."

"No, don't be *gegisch*," Sarah Ann said, waving off the comment. "Your *mammi* and I can go into the *schtupp* and look at some material we have for a new quilt we're making."

"*Ya*." *Mamm* stood. "We do need to get started on that quilt tomorrow if we're going to have it ready for the store in time. More orders are coming in every day."

"I'd like to see your material too." Carolyn stood. She wasn't sure she wanted Sarah Ann and her *mamm* supporting Amos's plans like this.

"You're not going to play?" Emma's smile transformed into a frown as she looked at Carolyn. "If you leave, then we won't have enough players."

Carolyn couldn't stand to break the little girl's heart. "Oh."

"You can play," Sarah Ann said. "We can show you the material another day."

"Great!" Emma's expression brightened. "We'll have fun now."

Carolyn sank back into the seat. "*Ya*, we will."

Sarah Ann and *Mamm* headed toward the family room while Ben and Rosemary set up the game.

Carolyn enjoyed two rounds of Dutch Blitz. She laughed and enjoyed the company of her niece, son, and new friend, Emma. She was bright and sweet, and Carolyn felt sorry that the young girl had lost her mother.

Soon they were all yawning, and Carolyn cleaned up the snacks while the young people continued talking.

The back door opened and Amos stuck his head into the kitchen. "Emma, your *dat* is ready to leave."

"I'm coming." Emma stood and faced Carolyn. "I hope to see you soon."

"*Ya*, I hope so too." Carolyn gave her a little wave.

Emma said good-bye to Ben and Rosemary and then called good-bye into the family room where Sarah Ann and Carolyn's mother were still talking about their plans for the week's quilt making. Then, pulling on her cloak, Emma hurried out the back door.

"She seems like a sweet girl," Rosemary said while sweeping the kitchen.

"*Ya*, she is nice. I'm certain she's had a difficult time since she lost her *mamm*." Carolyn tried to imagine being Emma's stepmother. Although she liked the girl, the idea didn't feel right. The idea of marrying Saul felt like wearing a shoe that was the wrong size.

Mamm stepped into the kitchen. "Did you all have fun?"

"*Ya*, we did," Rosemary said while sweeping the pile of crumbs and dirt into the dustpan. "Emma is a *gut* player."

"That's nice." *Mamm* pushed the bench under the kitchen table and gathered up the pile of napkins. "I guess it's time to head home."

Benjamin and Carolyn said good night to Sarah Ann and Rosemary and then pulled on their coats before they followed Carolyn's mother out the door to where her father and nephews stood on the porch.

Carolyn glanced down toward the driveway and found Amos standing by Saul's buggy. Soon the buggy began to rattle down the rock driveway, and everyone waved as it disappeared from view.

"*Gut nacht*," her parents said in unison as they started down the steps to go home. *Dat* immediately took *Mamm's* hand in his, and they walked close to each other as they made their way to the house. Carolyn smiled while silently admiring her parents' close relationship.

Carolyn's nephews rushed into the house with the door slamming behind them. Carolyn wondered if they were the reason Benjamin decided to stay inside and play the game with the women. She shook her head while thinking how ironic it was that Amos insisted Benjamin needed discipline when it was his sons who could use some lessons on how to behave and treat others with kindness.

"Are you coming, *Mamm*?" Benjamin stood at the edge of the porch steps.

"*Ya*." She smiled at her son. "I was lost in thought."

"I can see that." He tilted his head and his brown eyes glistened in the light shining out the kitchen windows. "*Was iss letz?*"

"Nothing, *danki*." Despite the cold evening, her heart warmed at the sight of his concern. She was so blessed to have such a wonderful son. Why couldn't her brother see his kind heart? "Let's go home. It's getting late, and we both have work in the morning."

Carolyn fell into step with Benjamin as they started toward their house with their shoes crunching on the rock driveway.

"Carolyn!" Amos called her name as he approached them walking toward the house. "I'd like to have a word with you."

Carolyn's jaw clenched. She turned to Benjamin. "I'll see you at the *haus*."

Benjamin nodded. "*Gut nacht, Onkel* Amos."

Amos nodded in return and then looked at Carolyn. "Saul said he wants to see you. He's going to come visit you."

"Why would he want to come and see me?" she asked. "He didn't even talk to me tonight."

"He said he was too self-conscious to talk to you in front of everyone. He's a little shy in groups. He wants to come by and talk to you alone. Is that all right with you?"

"I suppose it's fine. I don't have much of a choice." She bit back an irritated sigh and considered the best approach for dealing with her overbearing brother. "Amos, I appreciate your concern about Ben and me, but this doesn't feel right. I don't need you to try to find someone to marry me. I can handle my own life and my son's life without your help."

"Can you?" Amos shook his head. "I don't think you realize how perfect Saul is for you. He's a solid member of the community and he runs a successful business. He can take care of you and Benjamin. He needs a *fraa* for himself and a *mutter* for Emma. He also will accept Benjamin and your past without any questions."

Carolyn crossed her arms over her apron and lifted her chin in defiance. "I don't think he's right for me, and it's my decision whom I marry. *Mamm* and *Dat* didn't pick Sarah Ann for you."

"I didn't have a *kind* before I was married either." He rubbed his long beard. "You're blessed to have found a man who will accept you and Benjamin, and you have me to thank for that. You never had the opportunity to date when you were younger because your hands were full. I don't think you have the time to try to date the traditional ways. I think this is the best way for you to find a *gut* man."

Carolyn shook her head. "I told you I want to marry for love. I don't love Saul. I don't even know him."

"You need to get to know him. Give him a chance. He's a *gut* man. He doesn't live far from here at all. His farm is over in Paradise."

Carolyn's mind immediately turned to Joshua when her brother said "Paradise." She pushed any thoughts of him away. She really didn't know him any better than she knew Saul.

"Carolyn, just give him a chance." Amos's eyes pleaded with her, and she was surprised to see her brother almost humble while discussing this subject.

"Fine." She considered Benjamin and wondered if maybe this was a sign from God that she needed to find him a father. She then threw her hands up in surrender. "I'll give him a chance."

"I'm *froh* to hear you say that." Amos gestured toward the house. "I best get inside. *Gut nacht.*"

She repeated the farewell and started toward her parents' house while wondering what had possessed her to agree to see Saul. Why had she given in and let her brother push her around yet again? She was convinced deep in her heart that she could never love Saul, but she was conflicted about dating him. What if dating him was the right choice for Benjamin? What if Benjamin felt slighted because he never had a father in his life?

And what if she was supposed to marry someone like Saul because God didn't feel she deserved a marriage based on love? Maybe settling for a marriage of convenience was punishment for her past transgressions. The thought caused her chest to constrict.

"*Mamm?*" Benjamin's voice called through the darkness as she stepped onto the porch of their white clapboard house. "Is everything okay?"

"Ben?" Her eyes adjusted to the dark, and she spotted his silhouette seated on the swing. "What are you doing out here?"

"Waiting for you." He tapped the seat beside him. "Sit with me for a minute."

Carolyn sank onto the swing and it gently moved back and forth. Her mind flittered through her favorite memories of Benjamin's childhood. "Do you remember when we used to sit out here and watch thunderstorms when you were little?"

"*Ya.* Of course I do." He laughed a little. "*Daadi* would get so worried and tell us to come in before we got hit by lightning."

Carolyn chuckled as she hugged her cloak to her body. "I remember sitting on the porch and watching storms with *mei daadi* before he passed away. You would've loved him. He was so funny." She stared toward the main house. "He would've loved you too."

"What did *Onkel* Amos say to you?" Benjamin's tone was cautious as if he were afraid of getting into trouble for asking about adult things.

Carolyn turned toward her son and internally debated telling him the truth.

"It was about me, right?" His voice became unsure.

"No." Carolyn shook her head. "Well, in a way."

"What did I do now?" He sounded exhausted, as if this subject wore him out.

"No, no, Ben. You haven't done anything wrong." Carolyn fingered the seam on her cloak while choosing her words. "*Onkel* Amos wants me to get married. He thinks it would be *gut* for you to have a *dat.*"

"But I have *Daadi.*" He shrugged. "In my mind, he is my father. He's the only father I've ever known, and that's fine with me."

"I know that, and I'm thankful my parents have been here to help me. They've always been *gut* to you and me." She paused, hoping to choose words that wouldn't hurt Benjamin's feelings. She didn't want him to feel as if he were a burden to her or her family.

"Wait a minute. Saul is a widower. Emma said her *mamm* died six years ago." Benjamin sat up straight as if an idea flashed through his mind like lightning. "Is that why *Onkel* Amos invited Saul over tonight? Is he trying to find someone to marry you and be my stepfather?"

Carolyn couldn't lie to her son. "*Ya.*" She whispered the word.

"And he thinks Saul would be a *gut* husband for you and father for me?" he asked.

"*Ya*, that's right."

"Do you like Saul?"

"I don't even know him." Carolyn shook her head. "I don't know how I can make that decision without getting to know him."

"Are you going to date him?"

Carolyn nodded. "I told Amos I would give Saul a chance and try to get to know him."

"Is that what you want to do?"

Carolyn sighed and stared back toward her brother's house. "I don't know what I want to do." She turned toward Benjamin. "Do you want me to get married?"

Benjamin shrugged. "I want you to do whatever makes you *froh*."

"Does that mean you're satisfied with your life?"

"Why wouldn't I be? I have everything I could ever need, and I know you love me. That's all anyone ever needs, right?"

"*Ya*, that's true, but you never had a regular family like everyone else."

"That doesn't matter to me, *Mamm*." Benjamin rested his ankle on his knee.

"You don't think living here is hard? You've never had an easy time with the way your uncle and cousins treat you."

"I'm used to it." He was silent for a minute. "Do you ever feel like you missed out on having a normal life because of me?"

"What do you mean?" Carolyn studied her son and wondered where his thoughts were going.

"You could never go to singings."

"It's okay. I wanted to be with you."

"Did you ever date after I was born?"

Carolyn shook her head.

"So I ruined your life." His voice was small and unsure again.

"No, no! Don't you ever say that. You're the biggest blessing in my life, Benjamin. God gave you to me for a reason. You're my angel." She touched his arm. "I never considered you a mistake, so don't you ever think you are one. Do you understand?" She emphasized the words.

"*Ya*." He nodded. "Does that mean you never wished you were married?"

Carolyn contemplated the question. "*Ya*, I would like to be married, but if it's not in God's plan for me, then I will be satisfied. I have something some women never have, and that's a son like you. Some women never get the opportunity to have *kinner*."

"That's true." He was silent for a moment, as if he were contemplating something. "I don't think you should rush into marriage with anyone. It's for life, so you can't change your mind after the wedding."

Carolyn smiled at her son. "You're a smart *bu*."

He yawned. "It's late. We better get to bed."

"You're right." Carolyn yawned in return.

As they headed into the house for the night, Carolyn sent up a silent prayer asking God to guide her friendship with Saul. She then smiled as she sent up another prayer thanking God for her wonderful son.

EIGHT

Joshua wiped his brow before lifting the hammer and bringing it down on the new post he was adding to the back pasture fence on Wednesday afternoon.

"Josh," Benjamin began as he held the post in place, "I want to ask you something."

"Go ahead." Joshua let the hammer fall to the ground.

"I've been working here for over a week now." The boy's voice was hesitant.

"*Ya*." Joshua took a drink of water from the thermos he'd brought from the house. "What are you getting at?"

"I'd like to do more than just shovel out stalls and fix fence posts." Benjamin pointed toward the barns and stables. "I want to learn what you do."

Joshua studied the boy, impressed and surprised by his enthusiasm. "Really?"

"*Ya*, really." Benjamin's emphatic nod nearly knocked his hat off his head.

"What do you want to learn?" Joshua prodded.

"I want to learn how to train horses, how to shoe them, and everything else you do every day."

"Why do you want to learn everything I do?" Now

Joshua was intrigued by the boy's yearning for knowledge.

Benjamin pushed his hat back and wiped his sweaty brow. "I like working here. It's better than working on my family's dairy farm. I think I want a farm like this when I'm older."

"Really?" Joshua placed the thermos on the ground and then picked up the hammer.

"Yes, really." Benjamin's expression was determined, and Joshua was overwhelmed by the boy's interest. Joshua had always dreamed of teaching his nephew everything he knew about horses, but that dream evaporated when Hannah took the boy out of the community and into the *English* world. Maybe this young man could become a surrogate nephew to him.

"You do realize mucking the stalls is part of learning about the farm," Joshua said. "By working in the stalls, you're learning how to be around the horses."

"I know, but I want to learn more than just how to shovel manure."

"All right. Here's the plan. After we finish this fence, I'll show you how to brush and water the horses. Once you show me that you've mastered those two tasks, we'll move on to more. Does that sound good?"

Benjamin clapped his hands. "Great! I can't wait."

While they finished working on the fence, Joshua contemplated his conversation with Benjamin. He had an overwhelming feeling that the boy wasn't the one who had thrown the rock at his horse. He now wondered if Benjamin had been telling the truth and his older brothers had lied, which also could have been the reason Carolyn was so irritated during their first conversation. Maybe Carolyn knew the other boys were lying, and she was trying to convince her father to believe Benjamin. And that was also why she was so upset after Benjamin came home exhausted and filthy his first day at work.

He pondered Carolyn Lapp. She was obviously very protective of Benjamin, which he found intriguing. Although Joshua and Gideon were close, his older brother never protected him like Carolyn protected Benjamin. Joshua clearly remembered being teased by the one mean boy in school, and Gideon rarely defended him against the bully. Joshua had to tell his father what was going on before the boy was corrected.

Joshua wondered why Carolyn would take such a keen interest in her nephew. Carolyn Lapp was a true mystery.

* * *

Benjamin burst into the kitchen at his grandparents' house later that evening, causing Carolyn to nearly knock her pot of noodles off the stove.

"Ben!" she yelled. "You startled me!"

"Mamm!" He rushed over to her. "I had the best day!"

She smiled. "Really? What happened?"

"Josh and Danny taught me how to brush the horses." Benjamin grabbed a cookie from the jar on the counter as he continued. "It was so *wunderbaar*! I'm actually learning how to take care of horses now. This is the best job. I think I want to run my own horse farm when I'm older. Maybe I'll find some land and own a place just like Josh's." He kissed Carolyn's cheek and then hurried off to his room.

Carolyn beamed as she watched him disappear. Her heart warmed at the sight of her son's enthusiasm. She silently thanked God for giving him the opportunity to find happiness.

"What was all the ruckus?" *Mamm* appeared in the doorway leading from the family room into the kitchen.

"Ben is home from work. He's *froh* because he learned how to brush down the horses today. He loves the job, and he says he might want to run his own horse farm someday."

Mamm grinned. "That job is the best thing that ever happened to that *bu*."

"I know. I was just thinking the same thing." Carolyn smiled as she stirred the noodles in the pot. She had to find a way to thank Joshua for bringing joy into her son's life.

* * *

Carolyn guided the horse up the rock driveway toward Joshua's farm. She'd spent all of that Thursday morning baking and wanted to drop off two pies for him as a thank-you for having Benjamin work on his farm before she picked up some groceries. She brought the horse to a stop at the top of the driveway, picked up a basket containing the shoofly and apple pies from the seat beside her, and climbed from the buggy.

As she walked toward the house, Carolyn glanced toward the pasture and saw Benjamin and Daniel helping Joshua train a horse. She stood mesmerized and studied her son as he worked with the other two men as if they'd been a team for years. Tears burned her eyes when she realized Benjamin had finally found a place where he fit in after years of struggling to feel as if he belonged with his cousins. She felt as if her most urgent prayer had finally been answered.

"Thank you, God," she whispered while gripping the basket handle.

A few moments passed before the men realized Carolyn was standing there. They waved to her, and she returned the gesture. Joshua started trotting toward Carolyn. Her stomach flip-flopped as he approached, and she tried to keep her sudden and overwhelming attraction to him in check as he climbed through the split-rail fence and smiled.

"Hi." Joshua adjusted the straw hat on his head. "Ben said you might stop by today."

"*Ya*." She held up the basket. "I was baking this morning, and I wanted to bring you a couple of pies. I had planned to send them over with Ben, but I didn't get to bake last night. Since I have to work tomorrow, I had to bring them over today." She realized she was babbling because she was nervous. She quickly stopped speaking. Why did this man make her so self-conscious? She'd never been self-conscious before.

"Oh. *Danki*." He examined the pies. "They smell *appeditlich*, but you didn't have to bake for me."

"I wanted to thank you."

"Thank me?" He looked confused. "Why would you have to thank me?"

Carolyn gestured toward the field where Benjamin and Daniel were still working. "Ben has talked nonstop about this farm in the last few days. He told me the other day that he wanted to ask you to let him do more than just shovel out the stalls and repair fences. I told him to be honest with you and let you know that he wanted to learn." She couldn't stop her smile. "Then he came home last night excited because he learned how to brush a horse. I've never seen him so *froh*, and I'm really thankful you gave him a chance to learn a trade and find joy."

"I'm glad he likes working here, and I'm glad to have him. Ben is a great kid, and he's doing a great job. He's a hard worker, and he's not afraid to try new things."

Carolyn couldn't stop her grin. "*Danki.*"

"*Gern gschehne.*" He glanced down at his dirty coat and hands and then laughed. "I would take those pies from you, but I don't know if I should touch them right now. I need to be hosed off before I can think about eating."

Carolyn nodded toward the house. "Do you want me to put these in your refrigerator?"

"That would be great." He jammed his thumb toward the pasture behind him. "I better get back to work."

"Okay. Let me know how you like the pies."

"I will. *Danki.*" Joshua climbed through the fence and headed back toward Daniel and Benjamin.

Carolyn crossed the driveway and found her way up

the porch, through the mudroom, and into the kitchen. Her mouth gaped when she found the kitchen in disarray, just as Benjamin had described. A large stack of dishes clogged the sink and piles of journals, papers, and catalogs peppered the kitchen table.

She opened the refrigerator and found it nearly bare. Carolyn wondered what the man ate and when he had last been to the market or grocery store. She placed the pies on the top shelf and then examined the sink, taking in the disheveled mound of dishes, utensils, and pans. She gnawed her lower lip while she silently debated whether or not to leave the mess. She wanted desperately to clean for him, but she knew that wasn't her place. His kitchen wasn't her business, and she couldn't risk her reputation by being in his house alone. After all, he was a bachelor and she was a single woman. She didn't want rumors to spread about either of them.

Carolyn quickly exited the house and headed down the porch steps. Her eyes moved toward a large area she could tell had once been a bountiful garden. She imagined Hannah and her daughters had spent hours working in the dirt and harvesting vegetables for their dinner table. The rows were now overrun with weeds, and her fingers twitched at the thought of pulling them out. Carolyn enjoyed spending time in the garden at home. She could soak up the sunshine and lose herself in her thoughts.

Although she knew she was overstepping her boundaries, she couldn't bear to walk away from the need for weeding that was staring her in the face. After all, Joshua had brightened her life by giving her son a rewarding job. He worked hard every day, and he didn't have a wife to take care of all the tasks necessary to run a household. She was certain her mother would tell her it was only right to help Joshua. Cleaning up his garden was akin to helping a friend in need. She could get quite a bit done in a few minutes, and then she could head off to the market to pick up the groceries for her mother.

After she convinced herself she was making her mother proud, Carolyn hummed as she began to pull out the healthy weeds and toss them off to the side. Some of the weeds were so hardy that she had a difficult time dislodging them from the dirt. She lost herself in thoughts of her son's new job while she worked on one corner of the large area.

Carolyn heard footsteps moving up the gravel path, and when she looked up, she found an older, chubby Amish woman standing nearby with a frown creasing her unfriendly face.

"Who are you?" the woman barked.

Carolyn studied the woman for a moment, wondering why she was so rude. "I'm Carolyn Lapp."

"Lapp?" The woman studied her. "You're related to Benjamin?" She pointed toward the pasture.

Carolyn nodded, not wanting to go into details with this rude woman.

The woman gestured widely toward the garden. "Why are you weeding my son's garden?"

So this is Joshua's mother. Apparently being direct is a Glick family trait. Carolyn forced a smile in an attempt to soften the woman's mood with a little bit of kindness. "I came to deliver two pies to Josh as a thank-you for giving Ben the job. I saw how overgrown the garden is and thought I would clean up a bit as another thank-you."

"I can take care of my son's garden." The woman pointed toward her chest.

Carolyn wondered if this woman was always so outspoken and rude or if she only directed it to uninvited guests. She was both flabbergasted and insulted by the older woman's attitude. She'd never been more offended by a stranger in her life. Even the tourists who shoved cameras in her face during the summer didn't hurt her feelings as much as this woman who was supposed to be a part of her community.

"Fine." Carolyn rubbed her hands together in an attempt to clean off the dirt. "I was only trying to be nice and neighborly, but I will let you finish up. Apparently doing something nice is a foreign concept to you here in Paradise. We happen to do things like this for our neighbors frequently over in Gordonville."

The woman gasped as she continued to study Carolyn.

"It was nice meeting you." Carolyn moved past her and toward the driveway, careful not to stamp her feet even though she was still hurt by the way Joshua's mother had treated her. She looked toward the pasture as she approached her buggy and spotted the three men working together. She hoped Joshua's mother didn't treat Benjamin the way she'd just treated her. She wanted to shield her son from any more hurt, and she was willing to take more verbal insults from Joshua's mother if that was the only way to protect her precious son.

* * *

Late that afternoon, Joshua waved good-bye as Benjamin and Daniel guided their horses and buggies down the driveway toward the main road. He slowly made his way to the house, feeling physically drained after the full day's work. He remembered Carolyn had left pies in the house for him, and he quickened his steps.

Seeing her smile was the highlight of his day. Her beautiful face and lovely voice caused his heart to thump in his chest, which was confusing for him. He hadn't felt a reaction like that since he was a teenager. Why had those feelings suddenly come back to life?

Joshua pushed open the back door and shucked his muddy boots before stepping into the kitchen. The tangy smell of vinegar assaulted his nostrils as he moved toward the family room. He'd seen his mother arrive earlier in the afternoon, but he'd forgotten she was there. He'd been so busy training Benjamin that it didn't register that his mother hadn't left yet.

"*Mamm?*" he called as he headed toward the stairs. "*Mamm*, where are you?"

"I'm up here!" Her voice carried from upstairs.

Joshua climbed the steps, taking them two at a time, and found her mopping the bathroom with the vinegar he'd smelled. Guilt rained down on him. He didn't want his mother taking care of him, but he knew she felt as if she had to. After all, a man his age normally had a wife to do all the household chores.

"*Mamm*, why are you cleaning?" he asked. "I told you I would get to it later in the week. I've just been so busy training the horses that I haven't had a chance."

"I don't mind helping you." She finished mopping and then stepped out into the hallway. "Besides, I felt I had to do it after I found that *maedel* weeding your garden. If anyone works in your garden or cleans your *haus*, it should be me."

"What are you talking about? What *maedel* was weeding my garden?"

"*That maedel!*" Her voice rose with annoyance and she gestured widely with her hands. "Carolyn Lapp!"

"Wait." Joshua held up his hand, taking in what she'd said. "Carolyn Lapp was weeding my garden?"

"*Ya*, that's what I said." *Mamm* nodded with emphasis. "I came over to see if I could do any cleaning for you, and I found that *maedel* working outside."

Joshua found himself stuck on this piece of information. He was both intrigued and puzzled at the same time. "Why would she do that?"

"I had the same question." *Mamm* frowned. "She obviously has no manners at all. I don't know what they're teaching the *maed* over there in Gordonville. Doesn't she have more important things to do than come over here and stick her nose into your business?"

"Slow down." His hands were up again in his mother's face. "Yes, Carolyn does have other things to do. She works three days a week at the Lancaster Grand Hotel."

"She works at the same hotel where Hannah worked?"

Joshua nodded, and his jaw tensed at the mention of Hannah's name.

"Well, then I see why she acts the way she did. Hannah also picked up some inappropriate habits when she worked there. I guess they barge into rooms at the hotel like she barged onto your property." *Mamm* used dramatic hand gestures as she spoke to emphasize her point. "Amish women shouldn't work in an *English* hotel. It's just not proper."

"She didn't do anything wrong. I told her she could put some pies she brought in *mei haus*. She probably noticed what a mess the garden is when she was walking up the porch steps." Joshua tried to keep his tone even despite his growing provocation with his mother. "She didn't just barge onto my property."

"Still. She was inappropriate, Joshua. What *maedel* does that?" She jammed her hands on her wide hips. "And when I asked her what she was doing here, she was rather outspoken with her responses. She seemed offended that I was questioning her."

Joshua studied his mother with suspicion. He'd heard her berate Hannah more than once, so he didn't doubt she had provoked Carolyn's defensive responses.

"Why was she making pies for you? That's inappropriate too, you know," *Mamm* continued. "Does she think that will entice you to get to know her better and maybe even date her? If she wants to date you, then she should go to a singing." She wagged a pudgy finger at him. "And that's what *you* should be doing as well. How do you expect to get to know Lena if you don't go to a singing? And I don't want to hear you're too busy. No one is too busy to date. If you expect to find a *fraa*, then you really need to—"

"Hold on now." He held his hands up a third time. "I never said I wanted to date, and I never said I wanted to get to know Lena better. You're the one who wants me to get to know Lena."

"*Ya*, but—"

"Please let me finish," he interrupted her. "Carolyn never indicated she wanted to date me. She only brought the pies over to thank me for giving Ben a job. He's enjoying the job, and she said he's very *froh* to be working here. The pies were only a gesture of friendship."

"Friendship?" *Mamm* raised an eyebrow. "I don't know, Josh."

"*Mamm*, please. I've told you I'm not interested in dating right now. I'm too busy. Please don't push this issue."

"Just listen to me, Josh. Lena is perfect for you. I already told you that she likes to cook and bake. Your refrigerator and pantry are bare. You could use a *gut maedel* to cook for you. If I didn't cook for you, you would starve. If you went to a singing, you could get to know Lena better and see that she really is a lovely *maedel*. She'd be the perfect *fraa* for you."

While his mother continued to prattle on about Lena Esh, Joshua lost himself in thoughts of Carolyn Lapp. He couldn't stop thinking about her smile, and he was still surprised that she had started weeding the garden. He couldn't wait to try her pies, and he wondered when he'd be able to see her again.

He did a mental head shake and pushed away those eager thoughts. Why would he bother thinking about Carolyn when he didn't have time to date?

He knew he'd only have his heart broken again like he did when he tried to date Hannah. Besides, a woman like Carolyn would be married already if she wanted to have a husband. She was probably really picky. And maybe she didn't want to be married anyway. He was only setting himself up for heartache by thinking about her. It was better to just forget her and concentrate on running his horse farm. That was all that really mattered.

* * *

Carolyn was finishing up her vacuuming in one of the hotel rooms when she spotted Ruth standing in the doorway. She turned off the vacuum and smiled at her friend. "*Wie geht's?*"

"How are you?" Ruth stepped into the room. "How was your day off yesterday?"

"It was *gut*." Carolyn hesitated while she thought about her brief conversation with Joshua's mother. In fact, she had contemplated it most of the evening and then again while she cleaned this morning. She was still bothered by how rude the woman had been to her, though now she worried that she had done something to offend her. But she couldn't imagine what she'd done wrong.

Ruth tilted her head with curiosity. "*Was iss letz?*"

"Nothing is wrong, really." Carolyn leaned on the vacuum cleaner handle. "I just had a very odd conversation with Joshua Glick's *mamm* yesterday."

Ruth nodded with understanding in her expression. "I could see that happening. Barbie Glick is a very interesting person. What did she say?"

Carolyn shared the story of how she had delivered the two pies and had an awkward conversation with Barbie by the garden. "I was really stunned by how direct she was. She was sort of rude to me. Actually, she was really rude to me, and I'm not proud that I was sort of rude when I answered her."

"Barbie has been very abrasive at times." Ruth paused as if choosing her words carefully, which piqued Carolyn's curiosity.

"You're keeping something from me. What are you hesitating to tell me?"

"You know Hannah was married to Josh's *bruder*, right?"

Carolyn nodded. "*Ya*, of course I knew that. Hannah told me all about Gideon and how he passed away so tragically. Everyone knows Hannah left the community and that she's *English* now."

"I really don't want to gossip, but I know Hannah would confirm this if she were here." Ruth paused again. "When Hannah was married to Gideon, Barbie always had a bad habit of upsetting Hannah. She even continued to reprimand Hannah after Gideon died. Barbie constantly corrected how she raised the *kinner* and kept the *haus*. Nothing was ever *gut* enough in Barbie's eyes."

Carolyn scowled as she remembered how Barbie had spoken to her yesterday. "I could see that. She acted as if I had trespassed on private property, but Josh told me I could leave the pies in the kitchen for him. He gave me permission to be on his property, and I didn't think weeding his garden was so terribly wrong. I was only trying to help."

Ruth's expression softened as she crossed the room and stood by Carolyn. "You have to remember Barbie has been through a lot of heartache in her life. Her son died as a young man, and her daughter-in-law left the Amish church and took two of Barbie's *grandkinner* with her. I believe people sometimes change after heartache."

Carolyn grimaced. "She was very rude. It was ridiculous."

"Just remember the verse from 1 Peter, 'Live in harmony with one another; be sympathetic, love as brothers, be compassionate and humble.'" Ruth touched Carolyn's arm. "Barbie needs your understanding. She lost her son and now two of her *grandkinner* are only visitors in her home once in a while. I think she's overprotective of Josh because deep in her heart she worries that she'll lose him too. Maybe she holds on too tight because she's afraid to let go."

Carolyn sighed and guilt jabbed her in the gut. "*Ya*, I understand now. I can't imagine losing Ben."

Tears misted over Ruth's eyes. "I miss my son every moment of every day. I know Barbie is hurting like I hurt. I wish I could just know if he is still alive. Does he have enough to eat? Is he happy? Is he warm on cold nights? I don't know anything about his life, and my heart is broken every day that I don't hear from him."

Carolyn hugged Ruth. "I'm sorry."

"You don't have to be sorry." Ruth's expression brightened. "But you do need to take a break." She pointed to the digital clock next to the bed. "It's lunchtime."

Carolyn glanced at the clock and gasped with surprise. "Oh my. I didn't even realize it was noon. I'll finish this room and then meet you down in the break room."

"Okay." Ruth headed for the door.

Carolyn contemplated Barbie and Ruth while she worked. She felt sorry for Barbie's heartache, but she also wondered if there was more to her overbearing personality. She longed to get to know Joshua better, and she hoped Barbie wouldn't stand in the way of her developing a friendship with him.

NINE

Hannah pushed her shopping cart toward the produce department in the grocery store Friday afternoon. She glanced down at her list, checked off the items she'd already tossed into her cart, and then made her way to the bananas. After putting a bunch of bananas into the cart and checking her list again, she looked up to see the back of a young Amish girl. She was certain it was Lillian.

"Lily?" Hannah weaved past other shoppers, excusing herself along the way. "Lillian!"

The girl turned toward Hannah. It was Lily, and Hannah's heart skipped a beat. "Lily!" she yelled louder.

Lily's eyes widened, and she quickened her steps as she pushed her cart toward the checkout.

"Lily! Please wait." Hannah rushed toward her and grabbed the sleeve of her purple dress. "Lillian, please talk to me."

"Please stop. Just leave me alone." Lily gritted her teeth. "You're making a scene. Everyone is looking at us."

"They wouldn't stare if you stopped and talked to me." Hannah smiled, despite being hurt that Lillian rejected her. She was going to push through and make her daughter talk to her, no matter how painful it was. "It's so *gut* to see you."

"Really?" Lily shook her head. "Why do you act like everything is fine between us? Nothing is fine. You left me, remember?"

"Lily, please, just listen to me." Hannah pointed toward her shopping cart full of groceries. "I'm going to make a nice supper tonight. We have some guests arriving from New Jersey, and I'm going to make them an authentic Amish meal. Why don't you come? You can have dinner with Trey, Amanda, Andrew, and me, and you can visit the bed-and-breakfast. I'd love for you to see how I decorated it. It looks lovely. There's plenty of room if you'd like to spend the night. One of us can take you home in the morning."

Lily raised an eyebrow in disbelief. "You really want me to come and have supper with your guests? Is that so you can parade me around as your authentic Amish *dochder* to go with your authentic meal?" She folded her arms over her cloak. "Do you charge the patrons extra to meet a real Amish person?"

Hannah grimaced as hurt squeezed her heart. "Do you really think I would use you as a way to make money at my bed-and-breakfast?"

"I don't know." Lily's green eyes challenged her. "Would you? I don't know you at all anymore. I never imagined you would abandon me and tear our family apart for a man."

Hannah took a deep breath and willed herself not to cry despite her crumbling heart. "Lily, I pray every night that God will help you soften your heart toward me. Someday you will forgive me and we can be close again. Wouldn't you like to have a relationship with me?"

Lily's lip trembled. "I have to go."

Hannah watched her daughter walk away and prayed that someday she would see Lillian walking back into her life.

* * *

The scene at the grocery store repeated in Hannah's mind as she prepared the meal for the guests who would arrive at the Heart of Paradise Bed-and-Breakfast in a couple of hours. She'd cried the whole ride back to the house.

She'd been praying daily, more than once each day, that Lily would find a way to forgive her for leaving the farm and the Amish church. When she'd spotted Lily in the store, she thought maybe God had finally given her the chance to make things right with her daughter. Yet the conversation had ended just as painfully as the last time she'd spoken to her.

Hannah pulled a loaf of homemade bread out of the oven and placed it on the stove. The back door squeaked closed, and Amanda stepped into the kitchen. She dropped her backpack on the floor before swiping a banana from the counter.

"Hi, *Mamm*." Amanda kissed Hannah's cheek. "I had the best day. Guess who I ran into at the gas station on the way home? Remember my friend Mike Smithson who worked at his uncle's bookstore across from the deli? Well, he was at the next pump and he asked me if I wanted to—" She stopped speaking and her expression reflected concern. "*Mamm?* Have you been crying?"

Hannah sniffed and wiped her eyes. "*Ya.*"

"What happened?" Amanda took Hannah's hands and led her to the table, where they both sat down.

"I ran into your *schweschder* today at the grocery store." Hannah swiped the back of her hand across her cheeks as her tears started again. "I begged her to come visit, and she rejected me again."

"Oh, *Mamm.*" Amanda frowned and wiped a tear from Hannah's face. "I'm so sorry she's still not talking to you."

Hannah shared the conversation, and Amanda shook her head.

"I'll talk to her the next time I see her, okay?" Amanda hugged her and then frowned. "I don't understand why she would accuse you of using her for the business. Where does she get these crazy ideas? I wonder if *Mammi* puts them in her head. I love *Mammi*, but she says some peculiar things sometimes."

"I don't know where she gets an idea like that." Hannah shook her head. "But I would love it if you talked to her. Maybe you can make Lily see that I love her and I want to make things right. I know this isn't easy, but we can work through things and repair our relationship if she would give me a chance."

"*Ya*, I'll talk to her." Amanda handed her a napkin, and Hannah wiped her eyes. "I'll do my best to get it through her stubborn head that you do love her."

Hannah smiled. "*Danki* for understanding. I can't imagine if I had lost both of you."

"No, you won't lose me." Amanda looked at the ingredients and bowls lined up on the counter. "What's on the menu for our guests?"

Hannah cleared her throat and turned her thoughts toward her meal. "I'm making homemade chicken potpie, corn, potatoes, shoofly pie, chocolate cake, and a fruit salad."

"Oh, those are all my favorites." Amanda grinned. "How can I help?"

Hannah pointed toward the fruit. "Do you want to start cutting up the fruit for the fruit salad?"

"I'd love to." Amanda washed her hands in the sink.

"Now, tell me all about Mike Smithson." Hannah began pulling together the ingredients for the potpie.

"It was so funny, *Mamm*. I was pumping gas, and at first he didn't recognize me. He said I looked different without my prayer covering." Amanda waved her hands for emphasis while she talked. "Then he asked me if I was going to school. I told him yes. Next thing I know, he asked me out on a date. I'm so excited. He wants to take me to dinner next Friday night. Isn't that amazing?"

As Amanda detailed her encounter with her friend, Hannah silently prayed. She thanked God for her sweet Amanda. She also prayed that someday Lillian would surprise her by coming to the bed-and-breakfast and sharing everything that was going on in her life with the same enthusiasm as her twin.

* * *

On Tuesday morning, Carolyn walked out to the phone shanty she and her parents shared with Amos and Sarah Ann and checked their messages. The first two were from her mother's friends asking her to come to two separate quilting bees. She wrote down their messages for her mother.

When the last message started, a little voice spoke. "Hi, this is Emma Beiler calling for Carolyn and Sarah Ann. My *dat* and I would like to have you all over for supper tonight. *Dat* and I are going to make something special. Please call and let me know if you can come." Emma rattled off the time for supper, her phone number, and directions to their farm before disconnecting the call.

Carolyn replayed the message and then stared at her notepad. She imagined the supper invitation was Emma's idea. She had seemed like such a sweet girl, and Carolyn didn't want to hurt her feelings. She knew she should go to their house for supper instead of turning down the invitation and upsetting both Emma and Amos.

"*Gude mariye*, Carolyn." Sarah Ann approached the phone shanty. "Did you listen to the messages?"

"*Ya*, I did," Carolyn said. "There weren't any for you, except that Emma invited us all for supper tonight."

"She did?" Sarah Ann smiled. "Isn't that nice. She invited everyone?"

"*Ya*, at five thirty. Will you, Amos, and the *kinner* want to come?"

"*Ya*, Amos and I will come. The *buwe* will have chores, and Rosemary is babysitting for the *English* family up the street."

"I'll call Emma back and tell her that you, Amos, Ben, and I will be there," Carolyn said. "I'll make dessert."

"That's perfect." Sarah Ann walked back toward the house.

After dialing Emma's phone number, Carolyn cleared her throat and waited for the answering machine beep. "Hi, Emma. This is Carolyn returning your call. *Danki* for your message. Sarah Ann, Amos, Ben, and I would love to come for supper. I'll bring something for dessert. We look forward to seeing you this evening."

Carolyn hung up the phone and headed back into the house, where her mother was sitting at the kitchen table working on a shopping list.

"Were there any messages?" *Mamm* asked without looking up.

"*Ya*." Carolyn sank onto the bench beside her. "You had two and I had one." She handed her mother the piece of paper with her two messages.

Mamm examined them and then looked up at Carolyn. "Who called you?"

"Emma Beiler." Carolyn gazed toward the kitchen cabinets and contemplated what she would make for dessert.

"Emma Beiler?" Her mother raised her eyebrows. "What did she want?"

"She invited Sarah Ann, me, and our families to supper tonight."

Mamm's mouth gaped. "Really?"

"I have a feeling it was all her idea."

"Are you going to go?"

"*Ya*." Carolyn nodded. "I feel like I should go. I spoke with Sarah Ann, and she said she and Amos will go too. I'm going to make Ben come along with us. I don't want to hurt Emma's feelings. She's such a sweet *kind*. I left her a message saying I would bring dessert."

Her mother studied her for a moment. "Do you want to get to know Saul?"

"*Ya*, I think I need to give him a chance since Amos is really insistent about this." She rested her chin in her palm. "I guess I could make frosted carrot bars. I haven't made those in a while."

"You need to tread carefully here." Her mother touched her arm. "If Emma gets attached to you, you're going to break her heart if it doesn't work out. She's already lost her *mutter*. You don't want her to feel like she lost you too, do you?" Her mother frowned. "I know you're in a difficult situation, but maybe I can help. Do you want me to talk to Amos?"

"No, *danki*. That will only make it worse. I can handle this myself." Carolyn stood and moved toward the counter. "Want to help me make frosted carrot bars?"

* * *

Amos guided the horse and buggy onto the street where Saul's house was located. Carolyn sat in the back next to Ben and held the platter of frosted carrot bars. She wondered how the evening would go for the six of them.

Soon a white building came into view with a large

sign that said "Beiler's Cabinets." A two-story white house sat behind it.

"I didn't know Saul makes cabinets," Benjamin said as the buggy rattled up the rock driveway toward Saul's house.

"Saul's business is doing really well," Amos responded. "He stays busy."

"That's *gut*." Carolyn took in the large barns behind the house and the pasture.

Amos brought the horse to a stop by the first barn, and they all climbed out, walked to the front porch, and climbed the steps. Amos knocked, and Carolyn heard footsteps approach from the other side of the door.

Emma pulled the door open and beamed. "*Wie geht's!*" She made a sweeping gesture. "Please come in."

Carolyn followed Amos, Benjamin, and Sarah Ann into the house, where Amos and Benjamin hung their hats and coats on a peg by the door and then Benjamin hung Carolyn's and Sarah Ann's cloaks. They followed Emma into a large kitchen, where the aroma of ham loaf drowned Carolyn's senses.

"You made ham loaf?" Carolyn smiled at the eager girl.

"*Ya.*" Emma nodded with emphasis while gesturing toward the stove. "My *dat* helped me. I hope we got it right this time. The last time we made it, it was a little overdone. I used *mei mamm's* favorite recipe since this is a very special occasion."

"I'm certain it's perfect." Carolyn held out the platter. "I hope you like frosted carrot bars."

"*Ach!* My favorite." Emma took the platter. "*Danki.*"

Benjamin and Amos stood in the kitchen doorway and glanced around as if they didn't know what to do.

"Why don't you two have a seat?" Sarah Ann suggested. "Carolyn and I will help Emma serve the meal."

"*Mei dat* will be in soon." Emma brought a bowl of peas to the table. "He had to finish up something in his shop. He has a big order for cabinets from a local restaurant. He said it's going to help get him more business when people find out he was chosen for this job."

"That's fantastic." Carolyn made small talk while she brought a pitcher of water and four cups to the table.

"Ben, let's go see Saul." Amos motioned toward the door. "I'll show you his shop."

Ben followed Amos out the back door. Carolyn and Sarah Ann continued to help prepare the table for the meal, and soon everything was ready.

"Now, where are those men?" Sarah Ann asked with a smile.

"We could eat without them," Carolyn joked. "It all smells so delicious."

Emma laughed. "I don't think my *dat* would like that very much." She headed toward the back door. "I'll go check on them."

Sarah Ann shook her head. "Men forget what time it is when they're in a shop surrounded by tools."

"That's very true," Carolyn agreed.

The back door banged as Emma made her way into the kitchen followed by her father, Amos, and Benjamin.

"*Wie geht's*," Saul said as he hung up his hat and coat.

"Everything is ready," Emma said, pointing toward the table.

"*Gut.*" Saul sat at the head of the table.

Carolyn sat beside Benjamin and across from Emma. Saul bowed his head and everyone followed suit. Carolyn silently thanked God for the supper and asked him to bless their conversation.

When Saul shifted in his seat, everyone looked up and began to cover their plates with food.

"Everything smells *appeditlich*," Carolyn said as she reached for the peas. "You're a *gut* cook, Emma."

"*Danki.*" Emma's cheeks blushed as she cut the ham loaf.

"We're so *froh* you invited us tonight," Sarah Ann added.

"*Dat* and I talked about it and decided we wanted to have guests over. It's been a long time, right, *Dat*?" Emma asked Saul.

Carolyn was amazed as she watched Saul's expression soften. His brown eyes seemed filled with regret as he nodded. It was apparent that he deeply loved his little girl.

"*Ya*," he said. "That's true, Emma."

Carolyn cleared her throat and glanced at Benjamin, who was staring at his plate while chewing. She tried to think of something to say to start a conversation and make her son feel comfortable and included.

"Ben started a new job a few weeks ago." Carolyn sat up a little taller. "He's working for Joshua Glick. His farm isn't too far from here. It's also in Paradise."

Saul finished chewing and swallowed before he spoke to Ben. "What are you doing?"

"I'm working on Josh's horse farm." Benjamin's voice was soft and unsure. "He raises and sells Dutch Harnesses and Belgians."

"He's doing a *gut* job. Josh is really *froh* with his work." Carolyn smiled, but Saul only frowned. She wondered if the man ever smiled or if this was his usual demeanor to everyone but Emma.

"So, you're shoveling stalls and brushing horses?" Saul wiped his beard.

Benjamin shrugged. "I'm doing more than that. Josh and Danny are teaching me how to train them now."

Saul sipped his cup of water. "Have you ever wanted to learn how to make cabinets? I can teach you how to do that. My business has started booming again. I could surely use some help. The orders haven't stopped, and I don't expect that they will anytime soon. Working with horses is *gut*, but cabinetmaking is something you can do anywhere. All you need is a small shop and some tools."

Carolyn couldn't prevent her frown. Saul wasn't impressed with Benjamin's new job. She couldn't help but think that he seemed to be just as condescending and negative as Amos. It now made sense to her that Saul and Amos were good friends; they were just alike.

"Have you ever done any woodworking, Ben?" Saul asked between bites of the potatoes.

Benjamin nodded. "*Mei daadi* helped me make a little trinket box for *mei mamm* for Christmas once."

Saul shook his head. "I'm not talking about making

trinket boxes. I'm talking about real woodworking and real tools."

"I'm certain Ben could become a real carpenter, Saul." Amos gestured toward Benjamin. "Of course, Ben, you would need to get bigger and stronger before you could really help in Saul's shop. You'd have to develop quite a few muscles and look more like a grown man. The wood is heavy, and it's hard work."

Carolyn stopped chewing and stared at her brother while wondering how he could say something so hurtful to his nephew.

"Of course Ben will grow bigger and stronger, Amos," Sarah Ann said as she turned toward her husband. "He's a growing boy. He'll most likely hit a growth spurt this summer, and you may wind up having to look up at him."

Carolyn smiled at her sister-in-law and silently thanked God for Sarah Ann's quick comeback.

"*Ya*, you could be right," Amos said. "We all grow at our own pace."

Carolyn looked across the table at Emma, who was quietly eating dinner. "Everything is *appeditlich*, Emma," she told the girl. "*Danki* for having us over for supper."

"*Gern gschehne*." Emma wiped her mouth on a napkin. "I love to cook. I found my mother's favorite recipes, and I've been trying them out. Have you ever made stew?"

Carolyn nodded. "*Ya*, I have."

"I love stew." Emma cut up a piece of ham loaf. "I'll have to invite you all over to have that next."

"That would be nice." Sarah Ann reached for her cup of water. "How's school?"

"It's good." Emma told Sarah Ann and Carolyn all about school and her chores while Saul and Amos continued their discussion of cabinetmaking and farming. Benjamin looked on with a bored expression.

Soon the conversations dwindled, and they ate in silence.

Carolyn turned to Benjamin and found him still studying his plate. She needed to find a way to pull him into the conversation. "Emma, what is your favorite subject in school?"

"Oh, I love math." Emma brightened.

"Really? Ben always liked math too." Carolyn nudged Benjamin under the table to draw him into the conversation.

"*Ya*, I always loved numbers," Benjamin agreed.

"Ben likes to read too." Carolyn tried to keep the conversation going. "Do you like to read, Emma?"

"I do." Emma nodded.

"What kind of books do you like?" Sarah Ann chimed in. "Rosemary always read the Little House on the Prairie books. Do you like those books?"

Carolyn looked toward Saul, who was still talking to Amos. She wondered if she could ever find common ground with him. She wondered if his nearly constant frown was a part of how he mourned the loss of his wife. Perhaps Saul was a lonely man who didn't know how to express his feelings. She suddenly felt sorry for him. She knew in her heart that she needed to give the man a chance and try to get to know him.

Soon their plates were empty, and Carolyn helped Emma clean up the dishes and kitchen before serving her frosted carrot bars. They drank coffee and ate the bars while discussing the coming spring weather.

When dessert was gone, Sarah Ann carried the coffee cups to the sink. "Let me help you clean up," she said to Emma.

"*Danki*." Emma gathered up the plates.

Saul pushed his chair back from the table and looked at Emma. "I'll give Carolyn a tour of my shop while you and Sarah Ann clean up the kitchen."

Carolyn felt guilty for not helping with the work. She turned to Sarah Ann. "Can you and Emma handle the dishes?"

"Of course we can." Sarah Ann smiled. "Go on."

Carolyn retrieved her cloak and then followed Saul out the back and into the chilly early March air. "It's a *schee* night." She looked up at the clear sky. "Look at those stars."

"*Ya.*" He briefly gazed up at the sky and then continued toward the shop. Carolyn followed him there in an awkward silence and stood in the doorway while he turned on battery-operated lanterns. The sweet smell of stain mixed with wood dust filled her senses. Soon the shop was illuminated in the soft yellow light, and she took in an array of tools cluttering a line of workbenches. A pile of wood sat in the corner while cabinets in various stages of development sat on the benches with the tools.

She stepped over to a workbench and ran her hand over the cold, smooth wood grain of a large oak cabinet. "You do outstanding work."

"*Danki*." Saul stood near the workbench.

Another awkward silence passed between them, and Carolyn wondered what it would take to pull Saul into a conversation.

"Emma is a lovely *kind*," she said.

He nodded. "She's a *gut* girl. She works hard and tries to do as much as she can inside the *haus*."

"It must be difficult for her without a *mamm*."

His expression clouded, as if she'd hit a nerve, and she immediately regretted the statement. She needed to try to steer the conversation back to a comfortable ground between them.

Carolyn pointed at the pile of work that lined the far end of the shop. "Do you normally work with oak?"

Saul shook his head as he moved toward the pile of wood. "It depends on what the customer wants. Most prefer oak, but others want walnut or spruce. My next project will be with walnut." He talked on about his upcoming projects, and his expression relaxed.

She nodded with interest while he talked. She could tell that woodworking was his passion, and she wondered if he poured his emotions into his work. Was that how he worked through his grief?

Carolyn shivered, and Saul studied her.

"You're cold," he said.

"*Ya*, I am." She rubbed her hands over her arms.

"I don't want you to catch cold." He made a sweeping gesture toward the door. "Let's get you back inside."

"*Danki*."

Saul extinguished all but one of the lanterns and

held up the light as they walked back toward the house. She found Benjamin and Amos sitting on the porch.

"I'm going to go see if Sarah Ann and Emma need help." Carolyn climbed the steps and moved into the house, where Sarah Ann was drying dishes and Emma was sweeping. "Do you need me to do anything?"

"No, we're just about done." Sarah Ann placed a serving dish in the cabinet.

"Did you like my *dat's* shop?" Emma leaned against the counter.

"*Ya*, it's very big, and he does really nice work."

"He's the best." Emma beamed.

Carolyn looked at the clock on the wall and found it was nearly eight o'clock. "We'd better get going. *Danki* again for supper."

She picked up her empty platter before following Sarah Ann to the door, where they put on their cloaks.

"I had a lovely time," Carolyn turned and told Emma. "I hope to see you again soon." Emma gave Carolyn a quick hug and then hugged Sarah Ann.

"*Danki* for coming," Emma said. "Please come again."

The women stepped out onto the porch and made their way to the buggy where the three men were standing. They each thanked Saul before climbing in. Carolyn spent the drive back home contemplating Saul and Emma. She couldn't help but wonder if God had put them in her path for a reason. Was she meant to marry Saul and become Emma's new mother? Saul seemed like a nice man, and although he was quiet and somber, he clearly loved his daughter. He also had concern in his sad eyes when he asked Carolyn if she was cold in the shop. He could provide a good Christian home for Carolyn and Benjamin.

When they arrived home, Carolyn climbed out of the buggy and walked with Benjamin toward their house. "Did you have a nice time?" she asked.

Benjamin nodded while keeping his eyes focused on their home. "*Ya*, it was *gut*. The food was *gut*."

"What did you think of Saul's shop?"

He shrugged. "It was a nice shop. What did you think?"

"It's nice." She contemplated what life would be like if she were to marry Saul. Would Saul insist on making Benjamin his apprentice? "Do you think you want to learn how to make cabinets?"

He turned toward his mother. "No, I'd rather work on the horse farm with Josh."

Carolyn smiled. "I'm *froh* you found something you love."

As they climbed the porch steps, she wondered what God had in store for her and Benjamin, and if Saul and his daughter would play a part in that plan.

* * *

Carolyn stood at the lunch meat counter at the Bird-in-Hand farmers' market, trying to decide how much roast beef to take home for her father.

"Carolyn!" a voice behind her called.

She glanced over her shoulder as Joshua weaved his way through the crowd toward her. "Josh!" Her heart skipped a beat as he approached. "I didn't expect to see you here."

He grinned and held up a bag. "I managed to get away for a bit so I could pick up some of my favorite cheese. But I didn't expect to see you either, even though I know you don't work on Thursdays."

Her heart warmed at the sight of his smile. "What's your favorite cheese?"

"Swiss and provolone. I really like my cheese sandwiches." He gestured toward the meat counter. "Are you picking up some lunch meat?"

"*Ya. Mei dat* likes his roast beef. I'm running errands for *mei mamm* while she works on a quilt. She and my sister-in-law make quilts for a few local stores."

"Oh." He looped his thumb around his suspender. "*Danki* for the pies. They were amazing. I finished them in a few days. I didn't share, either. I hid them from Ben and Danny."

"Oh *gut*. I'm so glad you liked them. I'll have to make you a few more."

He shook his head. "That's not necessary."

"*Ya*, it is. I'm really thankful that you've given Ben something to look forward to. He can't wait to go to work every day." She studied Joshua's chiseled face and wondered why he never married.

Joshua gestured toward a quiet corner away from the food counters. "Do you have a minute to talk?"

"*Ya*." She followed him into the corner, weaving past the knot of customers. Her body tensed with worry as she wondered what Joshua was going to tell her. Was he going to fire Benjamin and break his heart?

"Ben is doing a great job," he began once they were alone. "I'm really impressed with how quickly he's learning how to work with the horses. He really has a gift."

"That's *wunderbaar*." She smiled, relishing the compliments.

"I know he's only working for me as a way to make up for what happened at the auction." Josh lifted his hat and pushed back his dark hair. "The thing is, I really need the help. My business has taken off, and I'm having a difficult time keeping up with all my chores on the farm. Danny is a great assistant, but I need someone who can work with him while I'm taking care of other things, such as reconciling the books and making appointments with customers. Hannah used to handle all of that for me, and now she's gone." His expression became hopeful. "I know your *bruder* needs Ben on his farm, but do you think there's any way he would let me hire Ben permanently? I would pay him, of course. Do you think Ben would want to work for me?"

"*Ya*." Carolyn couldn't contain her joy at the news. She nodded with emphasis. "I'm certain he would."

"Now, please don't say anything to him yet." Joshua held his hand up as if to caution her. "I'll let him finish out the time he promised me first. Once we're close to the end, we'll talk about it. Does that sound *gut*?"

"*Ya*, it's perfect." The ribbons on her prayer covering bobbed up and down as she nodded again. The news of a permanent job for Benjamin was an answered prayer. He would finally get away from the stressful situation on Amos's farm and have his own occupation to enjoy.

He gestured toward the meat counter. "What's on your shopping list besides roast beef?"

"Oh, I have to get some cheese too."

He raised his eyebrows. "Swiss and provolone, I hope."

She laughed. "*Ya*, I'll be certain to pick both of those up in case you stop by for lunch."

"I might just do that." He smiled, and her heart fluttered. Joshua nodded toward the meat counter. "I'd better let you get your groceries. The line is growing over there."

"Oh dear." Carolyn spotted a line of customers snaking toward the neighboring cheese counter. "I need to go get a place in line." She looked at him again. "I'll see you soon."

"That sounds like a *gut* plan." Joshua smiled. "I'm glad I ran into you today."

"*Ya*, I am too." Carolyn made her way over to the counter and got in line before looking back. She watched Joshua as he moved through the crowd and headed toward the exit.

She knew she could be setting herself up for heartache. After all, she hadn't told him the truth about Benjamin yet. What would he say if he knew she had a baby when she was sixteen?

TEN

Carolyn climbed out of her buggy in Joshua's driveway while holding on to the handle of Benjamin's lunch cooler with one hand. She'd spotted it sitting on the counter when she was getting ready to leave to run her errands. Since she was planning to go to a nearby grocery store, she decided to stop by Joshua's farm. Although the purpose of her trip was to deliver the lunch cooler, she also looked forward to seeing Joshua. He'd been on her mind ever since she'd seen him at the market last week. Today was Tuesday, and somehow last Thursday seemed like a long time ago.

Carolyn tented her hand over her eyes and looked toward the stables where she spotted a tall, lanky figure waving. As the figure moved out of the glare of the sunlight, Joshua's handsome face came into focus, and her pulse tripped and then accelerated through her veins.

"*Wie geht's!*" He smiled as he approached her. "It's a *schee* day."

"*Ya*, it is. I feel spring coming full force. My flowers are starting to bloom." She held up the cooler. "Ben forgot his lunch today. I was heading to the market, so I thought I'd drop it by."

"Oh, *gut*. I'll get it to him," he said as he took the cooler. "Ben and Danny went to the hardware store for some supplies, but they should be back soon. How was your weekend?"

"It was *gut*. On Saturday I helped *mei mamm* and *mei* sister-in-law finish up that quilt I told you about last week."

"Oh." He raised his eyebrows with curiosity. "You quilt? *Mei mamm* and my niece quilt."

She shook her head. "I wouldn't call myself a quilter, but I help out when I can. My stitches are never as straight as *mei mamm's*. She says I'm too impatient to do a *gut* job. I don't think my quilts would sell if I entered them into an auction or tried to sell them at a store like *mei mamm* and sister-in-law do."

"I doubt that." He leaned back against the buggy. "I'd like to see some of your quilts."

"You would?" She was surprised by his interest. "I'll have to find one to show you. I made one for Ben when he was born."

"Bring it over sometime."

"Okay." She studied him, wondering why he had such an interest in her life. Why would he want to see a quilt she made nearly sixteen years ago? She decided to change the subject. "How was your weekend?"

He shrugged. "The usual. Work and church."

"Do you ever do anything other than work and go to church?"

He paused and then laughed. "Just more work."

"Do you have any hobbies or interests other than horses?"

He shook his head. "No, I can't say that I do."

"So then what do you do for fun?"

Joshua looked toward his house. "I like to play games with friends or sometimes I like to sit on the porch and watch storms when they pass over."

Carolyn's eyes widened. "Really? I always did that with *mei daadi* when I was little, and I also shared my love of storms with Ben. We used to sit on the porch and watch the storms roll in and out."

He nodded with interest. "That definitely is one of my favorite pastimes in the summer."

Carolyn looked past him toward the horses in the pasture. "You must like being out in the sun all day."

"I do. It's one of the best parts of the job."

"What else do you like about working on the farm?"

"Hmm." He leaned to the side and balanced the small cooler on his bent knee. "I like meeting with the customers, and I like being with the horses. They're good company. I can train them and watch them grow."

"Do you ever get attached to the horses?" Carolyn asked while enjoying learning more about Joshua. "Is it ever hard to say good-bye to them?"

"Wow." His eyes widened. "No one has ever asked me that before."

"I'm sorry." She felt the tips of her ears heat with embarrassment. "I'm being too forward."

"No, you're not forward at all." He glanced back toward the horses. "I guess I try not to get too attached, but sometimes it happens." He pointed toward a chestnut gelding toward the front of the pack. "Do you see that horse there? The one standing off sort of by himself?"

"*Ya*." Carolyn held her hand above her eyes as she looked toward the horses.

"That's Huckleberry. He's my nephew's favorite horse." Joshua seemed a little melancholy. "We both were attached to Huckleberry, so he hasn't been sold."

"Really?" Carolyn studied the horse. "Huckleberry reminds me of my *daadi's* favorite horse. His horse's name was Samson."

"You were close to your *daadi*."

The comment took Carolyn off guard. "*Ya*, I was."

"You must miss him."

She nodded. "I do. I miss him terribly, and I know he would've loved Ben. It's a shame Ben never got to meet him."

Joshua sighed. "I understand. I miss Gideon every day. I think of things I wish I had said and things I would love to show him." He gestured with his free arm. "He would be so *froh* to see how much the business has grown. I know he would be a workaholic just like me." His smile was back and she enjoyed the sight. He stood up straight. "I suppose I'm keeping you from something important."

"No, not really." She longed to spend the rest of the day talking to Joshua and teasing him about his work ethic. "The grocery store isn't going anywhere, and I'm not looking forward to shopping."

"What would you rather be doing than shopping?" He wagged one of his free fingers at her.

"You got me." She absently fingered her cloak while

she contemplated the question. "Let me think. I like to read when I have time."

"When you have time?" He raised an eyebrow. "Does that mean you work too much too?"

Carolyn shrugged. "I guess maybe I do work too much, but I make time to bake and cook. I'm not the best in the church district, but I enjoy it."

"There's nothing else you like besides baking, cooking, and watching storms?"

"Sometimes I read Christian novels." She tossed that out even though she hadn't read a book other than the Bible in months.

"Sometimes?" He grinned. "Well, I guess that makes us both workaholics who like storms."

"I guess so." She smiled up at him. "At least I'm in *gut* company, *ya*?"

"If you consider me *gut* company, then I guess you are. Speaking of being a workaholic, I better get back to work." Joshua gestured toward the house. "I'll put Ben's lunch inside."

"*Danki*. Tell him I'm sorry I missed him."

"I will. I'll see you soon."

"*Ya*." *I hope so!* Carolyn blew out a sigh as she watched him walk toward the house. She hadn't felt an attraction this strong since she met Benjamin's father. Of course, back then she was much younger and naïve. She could have easily had a crush on any boy who showed interest in her.

Although she knew her feelings for Benjamin's father had been immature, she felt that same overwhelming urge to get to know Joshua that she had felt for Benjamin's father. These feelings were more mature, but that same excitement and fear surged through her. Here she was nearly thirty-two, and she was acting as if she were sixteen again. How did Joshua Glick gain this power over her?

Joshua ascended the porch steps, and Carolyn climbed into the buggy. As she guided the horse toward the road, Joshua turned and waved once before disappearing into the house.

Carolyn spent the ride to the grocery store wondering how she was going to temper these strong feelings for Joshua. She was treading on dangerous ground. She was getting to know Saul Beiler, and here she had nearly given her heart over to Joshua Glick. She needed to be careful with her feelings and her heart or she would end up hurt once again.

* * *

Barbie was wiping Joshua's kitchen counter when movement outside the window caught her eye. She peeked out the window and frowned when she found Joshua talking to Carolyn Lapp near a buggy. Joshua took a cooler from Carolyn and then they stood and talked.

Barbie's annoyance simmered as the conversation stretched beyond a few minutes. She studied their body language and watched her son smile and then relax, more than she'd seen him do in a long time. He leaned against the buggy, casually balanced the cooler on his bent knee, and behaved as if Carolyn were an old friend instead of a new acquaintance. She hardly recognized the man standing by the buggy; he didn't resemble the Joshua she knew. She'd grown used to her serious son, rarely smiling and always worrying about what was left undone on his farm. Yet now he stood as casual as a youth at a singing or at a buddy day spent with his childhood friends.

When Carolyn laughed and then fingered her cloak, Barbie gasped at the coy mannerism.

"How dare that *maedel* flirt with my son!" she exclaimed, her voice echoing throughout the empty house.

Barbie clenched her fists and studied the rest of the conversation unfolding out the window. She'd never seen her son act so casual and interested in a young lady. When Joshua was with Lena, he looked awkward and uncomfortable, and he seemed to be trying to think of things to say. From her vantage point, it looked as if the conversation between Joshua and Carolyn flowed easily between them, as if they were old friends talking in the grocery store line while awaiting their turn to pay the cashier.

Alarm surged through Barbie. She knew she had to do something to stop this relationship from progressing. She couldn't allow Joshua to get attached to someone like Carolyn. He was better suited to a more serious young woman like Lena, who could be molded into a perfect daughter-in-law and mother of her future grandchildren.

Something has to be done quickly to stop this!

Carolyn was confident and outspoken when Barbie

had questioned her. In fact, Carolyn's behavior reminded her of Hannah's. Barbie wanted to see her only living son married to a woman who would behave appropriately and not cause any more trouble for their family. Besides her personality, Carolyn also worked at the hotel that had enticed Hannah to leave the community and rip apart all that was left of Gideon's precious legacy.

Barbie considered her conversation with Eli regarding her interest in Joshua's love life. Eli had told her to back off, but Barbie still maintained that her intentions were pure in God's eyes. Despite what Eli said, Barbie knew what was best for her son. She needed to make sure Joshua married someone like Lena. She was attractive and she would be a good housekeeper. She was eager to be a good helpmate to a husband, and that was what every Amish man needed. And most importantly, Barbie could mold Lena into a good, dutiful wife and mother. She just needed to find a way to make that happen.

* * *

Joshua waved as Carolyn's buggy disappeared down the rock driveway toward the road. He was surprised at how his day perked up when she stopped by. He facetiously thought about thanking Benjamin for forgetting his lunch because he'd been hoping to see Carolyn again. He couldn't stop thinking about how much he had enjoyed running into her at the market last week. She was fun to talk to, and she always made him smile. He hadn't smiled that much in a very long time, possibly years, and it was a healthy release. He felt revived, as if she'd brought him back to life after he'd lost Gideon and Hannah.

He was surprised by how easy conversation was with Carolyn. In fact, he'd never joked around with anyone or teased anyone like he did with Carolyn. Being with her made him feel young again, something he hadn't felt since his early twenties. When he was with Carolyn, Joshua also felt as if he was able to let go of the heartache, stress, and worry he carried inside of him.

Does that mean I'm falling in love with her?

The shocking question shook him to the core. It echoed through his mind as he opened the back door and stepped into the mudroom.

"Joshua?" His mother's voice called from the kitchen. "Is that you?"

"*Ya, Mamm.* Who else would it be?" He took off his hat and coat and tossed them onto the peg on the wall. He couldn't hold back his smile. He was still thinking of Carolyn and her beautiful face, and—

His mental thoughts stopped as he stepped into the kitchen and walked right into his mother's disapproving frown.

"*Was iss letz?*" He placed the cooler on the counter.

"What was that *maedel* doing here again?" *Mamm* slammed her hands on her wide hips and glared at him.

"Her name is Carolyn, and she was delivering Ben's lunch that he forgot this morning. See?" He pointed at the red-and-white cooler. "What's wrong with that?"

"She was *flirting* with you, Josh." She stressed the

word. "Don't you see what's happening right in front of you?"

Joshua held out his hands as if to calm her. "*Mamm*, Carolyn is my *freind*. She wasn't flirting with me." He suspected that wasn't true, but his relationship with Carolyn was none of his nosy mother's business.

"*Ya*, she was. What do you think this means?" *Mamm* dramatically smiled and played with her apron while batting her eyelashes.

Joshua couldn't smother his laughter. "*Mamm*, you look *gegisch*. Please stop."

Her eyes narrowed. "Don't laugh at me. I'm trying to make a point, Joshua."

"Okay, I get it." He shook his head. "Look, Carolyn and I are *freinden*. Her nephew works here and that means Carolyn and I occasionally see each other."

Mamm shook her head and her frown deepened. "How would Lena feel if she knew you were flirting with another *maedel*?"

"We weren't flirting. Besides, what does Lena have to do with this?" Joshua grimaced and wondered when his mother would stop nagging him about a woman he didn't even know.

"I told you she likes you and wants to get to know you." She waved a finger at him. "That's why you need to attend a singing and get to know her better. You need to give her a chance. You're not getting any younger, and you need to start thinking seriously about getting married and having *kinner* while you still can."

Joshua blew out a sigh and fought the urge to tell his mother to stay out of his life. He had to find a way to redirect her attention away from him, but he didn't know how.

"Maybe you should fire Benjamin." His mother continued her tirade. "If Ben is gone, then Carolyn won't come around and ruin your chances with Lena."

"What?" Joshua leveled his gaze at her. "Did you just say I should fire Ben?"

"*Ya*." She nodded while folding her arms over her thick middle. "You and Danny are doing a *gut* job running this farm. You don't need the extra help."

"*Ya*, I do need the extra help, and Ben is a *wunderbaar* worker." Aggravation surged through Joshua, replacing the euphoria he'd felt when Carolyn was there. "I'm not going to fire Ben. I need him here." He pointed to the floor for emphasis. "I'm going to hire him on permanently. I can't keep up with the books and do my other chores now that Hannah is gone. I need Ben to help Danny so I can do other important chores to keep this farm running."

Mamm didn't look convinced. "Carolyn needs to learn her place so she doesn't ruin your chances with Lena. You need to tell her to stay away."

Joshua shook his head. It felt as though his blood pressure was spiking, bringing heat to his cheeks. "That's not going to happen either. This is my *haus* and my farm, and she's welcome here anytime she wants to come by."

His mother's expression became smug. "Actually, your *dat* and I own this land and this *haus*. And I don't want her here."

She was right. His parents owned the land, and he

paid them rent monthly. Joshua bit his lower lip to stop the angry and disrespectful words that bubbled up from his throat. He needed to walk away from his mother before he said something he regretted. "I need to get back to work."

"This conversation isn't over, Joshua." Although her words were strong, her expression was tentative, indicating she was out of arguments to support her point.

"*Ya*, it is." Joshua stalked out the door and sent up a silent prayer to God, begging him to grant him patience with his mother.

* * *

Carolyn sat on the front porch swing of her house and hugged her cloak over her nightgown. She had said good night to her parents and Benjamin and headed to her room only to find that she couldn't sleep. Her mind was still racing after the conversation she'd had with Joshua earlier in the day. She couldn't stop thinking about him.

She looked up at the clear sky and studied the stars. She couldn't help but wonder if Joshua had sat on his porch and watched some of the same storms she had over the years. She never imagined someone like Joshua would enjoy doing something as mundane as watch storms. He was much more complicated than she'd thought.

The clip-clop of a horse coming up their driveway drew her attention away from the sky. She wondered who would visit so late at night. Her stomach fluttered as she wondered if it was Joshua coming to tell her that he wanted to get to know her better, which was the tradition for the older single members of the community. Bachelors would visit their prospective girlfriends at night when they had privacy to visit without interruption. The women would sit on their porch after their family members had gone to sleep and wait for the men to arrive.

Carolyn touched her kerchief on her hair to make sure it was straight and then she smoothed her hands over her cloak. Whoever it was wouldn't be able to tell she was in her nightgown. And even with a lantern near her it was probably too dark to notice she wore slippers.

The horse and buggy stopped in front of her house, and she held her breath with anticipation. Soon the driver climbed out of the buggy and stepped into the dim light her lantern cast onto the stairs. The figure looked to be slightly too short to be Joshua, but she held on to the hope that it would be his handsome face climbing the stairs to see her. Her excitement faded and she tried to hold back her disappointment when Saul climbed the steps instead.

"Saul," she said, doing her best to appear happy to see him. "*Wie geht's?*"

"I'm doing well." He stopped at the top of the steps. "I'm surprised to see you up at this hour. I thought I would have to throw a pebble at your window."

"I couldn't sleep, so I decided I'd come out for some fresh air." She motioned toward the chair next to the swing. "Have a seat."

"*Danki.*" He lowered his body into the chair.

An awkward silence similar to what they had experienced before fell between them as they both stared straight ahead. Carolyn couldn't help but keep wishing it were Joshua sitting on her porch instead of Saul, and she felt guilty for having such negative thoughts about her visitor. After all, he'd traveled through the dark just to see her. She should feel flattered that he was there making an effort for her sake.

"Is something bothering you?" Saul's question broke through her mental tirade.

Carolyn turned toward him, worried he could read her thoughts. "What do you mean?"

"You said you were having problems sleeping. Is something weighing on your mind?"

She was silent for a moment. She'd never expected Saul to say something as thoughtful as asking her about her feelings. "No, there's nothing weighing on my mind. I'm not sure why I can't sleep." The fib rolled off her tongue as if she lied all the time. Her mother would be so disappointed in her.

"How was your day?" he asked while looking at her.

"It was busy." Carolyn told him about running errands, doing chores, and cooking dinner. She asked about his day, and he detailed the current projects in his shop.

"It sounds like your business keeps you busy."

"*Ya*, it does." His expression was pleasant. "Emma had a *wunderbaar* time last week when you, Sarah Ann, Amos, and Ben came for supper."

"Oh." She forced a smile. "I did too."

"The truth is," he said, "I had a *gut* time too." He heaved a heavy sigh that seemed to begin from his toes. "I'm not *gut* at expressing my feelings."

"That's okay. Not everyone is *gut* at that." Her shoulders tensed as she waited to hear what he was going to say next.

"Ever since I lost my *fraa*, I've had a difficult time talking about how I feel." He shook his head. "I don't even know where to begin when it comes to talking to women, except when I'm discussing cabinets." He gave a little laugh, and Carolyn smiled in response.

They were both silent for a moment. He cleared his throat and kept his eyes staring forward. "It's difficult for me to believe Emma and I have been alone for six years now. Time certainly does fly by. I wanted to find a proper *mutter* for Emma, but the time never seemed right for me to start dating again. And then Amos told me about you and Benjamin, and it seemed like God had put you in my path for a reason." He absently fingered his beard. "What I mean is that I would like to get to know you better."

Carolyn was stunned silent by Saul's openness. Although he seemed like a cold and unfriendly man at his house, she now saw him as a broken man who'd been devastated by the loss of his wife. He didn't warm her heart like Joshua did, but he was a good man. Although she wanted to marry for love, she knew it was time that she married and had a home of her own and that she had to consider settling for a man who had a kind heart. Maybe God meant for her to marry Saul.

"So, what do you say?" Saul's dark eyes were hopeful

in the dim light of the lantern. "Would you allow me to get to know you better?"

"*Ya.*" Her voice was soft.

"*Gut.*" He talked on about his current projects and then the weather while she listened in silence.

His words were only background noise to the confusing thoughts and sudden feeling of guilt that washed down on her. Carolyn knew in her heart that she would never fall in love with Saul. She felt no attraction to him. Yet here she was promising to be Saul's friend while wondering if she could ever get to know Joshua better. She hadn't dated in sixteen years, and now she was stuck in a love triangle. How did she wind up in such a predicament?

After what felt like an hour, Saul stood. "I should let you try to get some sleep. I'll come visit you again soon." He moved toward the stairs. "*Gut nacht.*"

"*Gut nacht,*" she repeated.

While she watched him drive off, she decided to give Saul a fair chance. He seemed to be the practical solution to her need for a husband and father for Benjamin. Perhaps she was the solution to his need for a wife and a mother for Emma. Yet she simultaneously wondered how she was ever going to get out of this mess without losing her heart.

ELEVEN

Carolyn arrived home from work Wednesday afternoon and picked up her pace when she spotted her parents standing on the porch. They seemed to be upset.

"*Was iss letz?*"

"Enos and Irma Bontrager's dairy barn burned down last night." *Dat* shook his head and fingered his long beard. "It was a lightning strike. I just heard the news."

"*Ach*, no." Carolyn gasped. "Is everyone all right? Did they get their cows out?"

"*Ya*, everyone is fine, but they need some fifty men to come and help frame the new barn tomorrow. Amos and I are going to help."

"We'll cook." Carolyn looked at her mother.

"*Ya*." *Mamm's* nod was emphatic. "My *dat's* shop burned down when I was five, and I still remember the men who helped rebuild it and the women who brought food."

* * *

Carolyn carried a platter of macaroni and cheese as she followed her mother, Rosemary, and Sarah Ann into

Irma Bontrager's kitchen. A crowd of women talked and moved about the kitchen while preparing lunch for the men who were working to frame the Bontragers' barn.

Carolyn greeted both familiar and unfamiliar faces as she gathered up paper cups for drinks. When she glanced across the kitchen, she spotted Barbie Glick, and her shoulders stiffened. She wondered if Barbie's presence indicated that Josh and his father had also come to help frame the barn.

"Carolyn!" Emma Beiler rushed over from the kitchen door. "I was hoping you were here."

"Hi, Emma." Carolyn smiled at the girl. *"Wie geht's?"*

"I'm doing great, thanks." She held up a platter. *"Mei dat* helped me make some whoopie pies. We made chocolate and pumpkin."

"Oh." Carolyn leaned down and breathed in the sweet aroma. "They smell *wunderbaar,* Emma. Great job."

"Hi, Emma!" Rosemary joined them. "How are you?"

The girls fell into a conversation about cooking while Carolyn helped Sarah Ann arrange food on platters that would be served outside at lunchtime. She looked up as Barbie and a young woman Carolyn didn't know came to the table and began placing lunch meat on a platter. Sarah Ann made conversation about the warm weather and vibrant blooming flowers while Carolyn kept her eyes on the food and stayed quiet. She wondered who the young woman was and noticed that she didn't speak much either. She wondered if she was also intimidated by Barbie's outspoken personality.

Once the platters were ready, Carolyn and Sarah Ann carried them outside to where Carolyn's mother and a few other ladies had set up three tables near the back porch. A sea of dishes cluttered the table, filled with bread, pickles, pretzels, casseroles, and cheese.

Carolyn placed the platter on the table and then looked toward the pasture where the wooden skeleton of the barn was taking shape. The naked wood boards stretched up toward heaven with an azure sky as a backdrop. Men lined up on the top of the structure where the roof would eventually be covered. Carolyn guessed there were at least twenty men hanging from the structure while another thirty or so were on the ground cutting boards, making plans, and looking on.

Hammers banged and voices shouted over the noise. The men worked in unison while the warm sun beat down on them. Carolyn tented her hand over her eyes and scanned the men scattered around the barn structure until she found Joshua. He was nodding and talking to an older man with a graying beard. She also spotted Daniel and Benjamin handing tools to the men who were perched on the structure. Pride swelled within her as she watched her son mingling with the men.

"They're making *gut* progress." Sarah Ann squinted while watching the workers. "I love watching barn raisings. It's always amazing to me how it comes together, and they build a *schee* barn out of a stack of boards."

"It is amazing." Carolyn folded her arms over her apron and wondered if she'd get a chance to talk to Joshua before the day was over.

"Let's go call them in to eat." Barbie motioned toward the young lady. "Come with me, Lena. We'll get these men to enjoy the delicious food we brought."

Sarah Ann stepped closer to Carolyn. "Barbie is nice, *ya*?"

Carolyn shrugged and hoped to shield her disagreeable frown. "*Ya*, she seems nice."

"She was telling me earlier that her son runs a horse farm in Paradise." Sarah Ann snapped her fingers. "Wait a minute. I just figured out the connection. Her son owns the farm where Ben works. Is that right?"

"*Ya*, that's right. Her son is Joshua Glick." Carolyn looked toward the barn and watched Barbie announce lunch to the workers before walking over to Joshua.

"Ben really likes the job," Sarah Ann continued. "I heard him telling your *dat* all about it."

Carolyn kept her eyes on Barbie and Joshua. "He does like it. Joshua has been *gut* to him. He's learning a lot." Barbie and the young woman she had called Lena stood by Joshua for a few moments, and she could see Joshua's expression change. His smile faded and his demeanor transformed. He fiddled with his suspenders and nodded while his mother spoke. Although it was none of her business, she longed to overhear their conversation and find out what his mother was saying. Was she upsetting him the way she upset Carolyn the first time they met?

"Do you think the job might become permanent?" Sarah Ann's question broke through Carolyn's thoughts.

Carolyn nodded. "Josh says so, but he asked me not to say anything to Ben just yet."

"Oh." Sarah Ann smiled. "I think that's a *gut* idea. I'm glad it's working out for him. Ben needs something beyond our farm."

"You think so?" Carolyn was surprised by the comment.

Sarah Ann gave her a knowing smile. "I'm not blind. I see what goes on. I just haven't been able to change it. I've been trying to make Amos see what our *buwe* do when he's not around, but he hasn't witnessed it yet." She looked past Carolyn. "Hello. Please help yourself. We have plenty of food."

A group of workers lined up around the table, and Sarah Ann began handing out plates. "Carolyn, would you please go get the cups and pitcher of water?"

"Oh *ya*. I had the cups in my hands earlier and forgot to bring them out." Carolyn started up the porch steps toward the kitchen. She looked back and found Joshua standing near the barn skeleton and talking to Lena alone. His mother had returned to the tables and was handing out napkins to the hungry carpenters.

Carolyn tried in vain to ignore the knot in the pit of her stomach as she continued into the house to grab the cups. She filled the pitcher with ice water and then made her way back to the tables. She spent the next several minutes handing out cups of ice water to the men as they moved through the line, covering their plates with food and commenting on how hard they were working.

She frequently looked toward Joshua and spotted him still standing with Lena. It looked as if she was doing most of the talking. Carolyn tried to ignore the green envy boiling inside of her. She knew that jealousy was a sin, but she couldn't stop the emotion from overtaking her. Why should she be jealous of her? All she was doing was talking to Joshua, and, after all, it wasn't as if Joshua was dating Carolyn. Carolyn hardly even knew Joshua. They'd only had a handful of conversations, which meant they could only honestly consider each other acquaintances and nothing more.

Yet the dream of getting to know Joshua better had haunted her more and more since she'd visited the farm to take Benjamin his lunch. She couldn't refrain from thinking about him and wondering what it would be like to spend more time with him. Joking and laughing with him was euphoria to her. When she was with Joshua, she could forget all the heartache and rejection she'd felt since Benjamin was born. It seemed as if Joshua brought out the best in her.

"Carolyn?" Sarah Ann's voice startled her from her daydream. "We're out of water. The pitcher is empty."

"*Ach!*" Carolyn's cheeks heated with embarrassment. "I didn't even realize it." She picked up the empty pitcher. "I'll go get more ice water."

Sarah Ann placed a hand on Carolyn's arm. "Are you okay?"

"*Ya!* Of course I am." She motioned toward the kitchen. "I'll be right back." She rushed into the kitchen, moving past women who were restocking the platters of food.

While she filled the pitcher with more water and ice, she tried to shake the jealousy that had seized her. She needed to focus on being Joshua's friend and not dreaming of a relationship with him. After all, he didn't know her secret, the secret that could ruin her chances of having a relationship with anyone. She knew if Joshua found out that Benjamin was her son, he most likely wouldn't want to have anything to do with her romantically.

She headed back down the porch steps with the pitcher of water and nearly ran into Saul, who was moving into the food line.

"Carolyn." He nodded and smiled. "How are you today?"

"Fine, *danki*." She groped for something to say. "The barn is coming along nicely."

"*Ya*, it is." He cleared his throat. "The food looks *gut*."

"*Ya*." She held up the pitcher as another woman moved past her with a full platter of lunch meat. "Hopefully it tastes *gut* too." She gestured toward the end of the tables where the cups sat. "I'd better get back to my post before people start complaining that there are empty cups and nothing to drink. I'll see you soon." She hurried to the last table and began pouring water into the waiting cups.

Carolyn handed out the drinks and made small talk as the men continued to move through the line. She was filling more cups when someone stopped in front of her.

"If I take a cup, will you promise not to splash any water on me?" a voice asked.

Carolyn looked up and found Joshua smiling down at her while holding a plate full of food in one hand. She laughed and then pretended to consider the question. "I can't make any promises. I've been in a splashing mood all day."

"Have you?" He grinned. "I guess that means you're having a *gut* day?"

"*Ya*." She nodded. "I'm having a really *gut* day." *Now that you're here, the day is perfect.*

"So, what do you think of our work?" He pointed at the barn with his free hand.

She rubbed her chin and scrunched her nose with feigned disapproval. "I think it might be drafty and wet if it rains."

He laughed again. "You have the best sense of humor of any *maedel* I've ever met."

"I consider that a compliment." Her heart thumped in her chest. "Are you going to help build the barn the rest of the week or are you only a framer?"

"Sadly, I'm only a framer." He frowned. "I would love to give the barn more time, but I have horses to care for. My *dat* and I are only working here today." He nodded toward the group of men eating nearby. "I brought Danny and Ben with me too. We're going to be here most of the day, but then I have to get back to my horses."

"I understand." She smiled. "It's nice that you're all helping today. It looked like Ben was enjoying helping out too. I know he enjoys being included in the work, and I'm certain Enos and Irma appreciate everything that you're all doing for them."

"Hey, Glick," another man said. "You're holding up the line. We'd all like to get a drink, you know."

"Just a minute, Silas." Joshua shook his head. "People get so grouchy at lunchtime." He picked up a cup of water and then smiled at Carolyn again. "I'll see you later."

"I look forward to it." Carolyn watched him walk

over to a large tree and sit on the grass with a group of men who were eating and talking. Although jealousy still nipped at her, she felt a renewed attraction toward Joshua. He'd complimented her when he said she had the best sense of humor of any young lady he knew. Did that mean he liked her? She held on to that tiny thread of hope.

Carolyn handed out drinks to the last of the men in line, including Ben, and then gathered up the empty cups. She was placing the cups and plates onto a platter when Barbie walked up behind her.

"Carolyn." Barbie stood close to her and lowered her voice. "I'd like to talk to you for a minute."

Carolyn pushed the ribbons from her prayer covering behind her shoulders. "Okay."

"I saw you talking to my Josh." Barbie's frown was deep in her round face. "Do you like him?"

Carolyn shrugged despite the alarm rushing through her. Why was Barbie questioning her relationship with Joshua? "We're *freinden*. I've talked to him a few times when I had to stop by his farm." She tried to keep her tone even, though she felt a growing resentment toward the woman's attitude.

"I know what you're up to." Barbie spat out the words. "And you should throw away any thoughts of dating him. He's getting to know Lena Esh, and they are going to be dating soon. You need to stay out of the way."

Carolyn frowned. "I think that's up to Josh and not you."

Barbie gasped as Carolyn picked up the platter and started toward the kitchen, moving quickly past a group of women who were setting out cakes, pies, and cookies for dessert.

Mamm caught up with Carolyn and climbed the porch steps beside her. "Is everything all right?"

"What do you mean?" Carolyn stepped into the kitchen and placed the platter on the counter.

"It looked like you were having a disagreement with Barbie Glick." Her mother's expression was full of concern.

"It was nothing." Carolyn forced a smile in an attempt to mask her anger. "Let's grab the remaining desserts and get them outside before the men start to complain."

"Wait." *Mamm* reached for Carolyn's arm and pulled her back. "You're not telling me everything. *Was iss letz?*"

Carolyn glanced toward the door as Barbie and Lena entered the kitchen. She then turned to *Mamm*. "Let's just say that Barbie reminded me of my place."

"Your place?" *Mamm* shook her head. "You're not making any sense."

"I can't tell you now." Carolyn lowered her voice. "I'll tell you later, okay?"

"Fine." *Mamm* nodded. "But you will tell me later. I'm going to remind you when we get home."

Carolyn picked up a platter of whoopie pies and headed back out to the tables. She looked over to where Joshua was sitting and found Saul beside him. She watched the men interact and wondered if Barbie's warning was a sign. Was Carolyn wrong to even think about Joshua when Saul knew about her past and was willing to accept her?

The question haunted Carolyn as she placed the platter on the table. She silently prayed for God to send her a sign to help guide her confused heart.

* * *

After the kitchen was cleaned up, Rosemary and Emma walked down the porch steps and headed toward the field to watch the men work on the barn.

"I'm so glad you could come today." Rosemary found a spot under a tree and sank down in the grass, folding her legs under her.

"*Ya*, I'm *froh* I could come too." Emma sat beside her. "I might be seeing you more often."

"What do you mean?"

"*Mei dat* likes your *aenti* Carolyn." Emma picked a piece of fuzz off her apron. "I'm hoping that means they'll be spending more time together, and we might be a family soon."

"Really?" Rosemary studied Emma with surprise. "I had no idea."

"*Ya*. Your parents, Carolyn, and Ben came over for supper last week, and we had a nice time." Emma sat up straighter. "*Mei dat* helped me make Dutch ham loaf."

"I was sorry I had to miss supper that night. I was babysitting for a neighbor." Rosemary licked her lips. "I love ham loaf."

"Maybe you can come for supper next time."

"That would be fun." Rosemary thought about her aunt. "I had no idea *Aenti* Carolyn liked your *dat*." She made a mental note to ask her aunt about that in private when she saw her again.

"*Ya*," she said. "I'm so *froh*. I would love to see *mei dat* marry someone nice so I can have a *mamm* again."

Rosemary nodded. "*Ya*, I bet you do. I hope that works out for you."

"*Danki*." Emma looked toward the barn. "I love watching barn raisings."

Rosemary squinted in the sun and looked over toward where a handsome young man stood with Benjamin. She realized he was the same handsome young man she'd spotted at the horse auction. "I love barn raisings too." She smiled.

"What are you looking at?" Emma asked.

Rosemary felt her cheeks heat. "Do you see that *bu* over there standing by Ben?"

Emma tilted her head and gazed toward Benjamin. "The tall one with the dark hair and the blue shirt?"

Rosemary nodded as her cheeks burned hotter. "*Ya*, that's him."

Emma tilted her head in question. "Who is he?"

"I don't know who he is, but he looks familiar." Rosemary studied him. He looked as if he were close to twenty, and she knew her father would never approve of her dating him.

Suddenly, the young man and Benjamin began walking toward them. She swallowed a gasp and then brushed her hands down her apron, hoping she looked presentable.

"He's coming over here!" Emma's voice was a little too loud.

Rosemary resisted the temptation to put her hand over her young friend's mouth and instead smiled as the boys approached. "Hi." She sat up straight and smoothed her dress over her legs.

"Hi." The young man smiled at Rosemary and nodded at Emma before squatting in front of them.

"Rosemary and Emma," Benjamin began, "this is Daniel—Danny. He works at Joshua Glick's farm with me."

"Hi," Rosemary said. "I've heard a lot about you and the farm from Ben. He really likes working there. He was telling me about a mare that's almost ready to give birth."

"*Ya*, that's true." Daniel ripped up a blade of grass. "Daisy hasn't foaled just yet, but it looks like she may any day now."

Although Rosemary knew he was too old for her to date, she wanted to get to know him better. Maybe they could date when she turned eighteen. An idea popped into her head and she took a breath. "Do you ever go to youth group?" she asked.

"*Ya*." He nodded. "I try to go every so often. Why?"

"You should come to mine sometime."

Daniel nodded slowly. "I might be able to do that. Is there one Sunday night?"

"*Ya*. I think it's at Eve Fisher's *haus*. We're going to play volleyball and sing. You should come."

"I think I will." He smiled, and her smile widened in response.

"Danny! Ben!" A young man yelled over to them. "We need you!"

"I'll see if I can come sometime." Daniel stood and

brushed off his trousers. "See you later." He tapped Benjamin's arm. "We'd better get back to work."

"Bye." Rosemary watched them trot back to the group of men. "He's so nice."

"*Ya*, he is nice," Emma agreed.

Rosemary watched in awe as Daniel and Ben climbed up to the roof of the barn. "I hope they're careful up there."

Rosemary held her breath as she watched them work on the barn. She couldn't wait until youth group Sunday night. She just hoped Daniel would be there.

* * *

Rosemary climbed out of the buggy and then Emma waved to Carolyn and started toward her house. She felt as if she were walking on a cloud after her earlier conversation with Daniel. She longed to see him again.

"Rosemary!" Her father's voice boomed behind her. "I want to talk to you for a minute."

"*Ya, Dat?*" She walked toward him. His frown caused her to inwardly shudder.

"I want to discuss how you behaved at the barn raising."

"What did I do?" She racked her brain, trying to remember anything she did that would have upset her father.

"I saw you talking to that *bu*." He shook a large finger at her. "You're too young to be mingling with *buwe*. You can only talk to *buwe* when you're at a chaperoned youth gathering."

Rosemary was speechless for a moment. "I don't understand. When did I act inappropriately with a *bu*?"

"You were sitting by a tree with Emma and that *bu* came over and talked to you." *Dat* shook his head. "I could tell by your body language that you were flirting with him. You like this *bu*, don't you?"

Rosemary shook her head. "I don't even know him. I met him for the first time today."

"Who is he?"

"His name is Daniel King. He works for Joshua Glick, like Ben."

"He's too old for you. Put any ideas about getting to know him out of your mind. Do you understand me?"

Rosemary nodded. It was no use arguing with her father. "*Ya*, I do."

"*Gut*. Now go do your chores."

Rosemary hurried into the house while chagrin consumed her. She knew she couldn't date Daniel King, but she wanted to be his friend. She held on to a shred of hope that maybe they could date when she was older.

She headed into the bathroom to wash and found herself smiling in the mirror. Her father told her not to see Daniel, but she couldn't stop him from going to the youth gathering Sunday night. After all, there would be a chaperone there, so they wouldn't do anything inappropriate.

Relief flooded Rosemary. She would still be able to see Daniel. Her father couldn't stop the youth gathering Sunday night. Now she had to pray that Daniel would come.

* * *

Sarah Ann changed into her nightgown and then brushed her waist-length dark brown hair as she stood in front of the mirror in her bedroom. Her feet ached from standing in Irma Bontrager's kitchen most of the day, but she had enjoyed spending time with the women from her community as well as other communities while they helped the Bontragers rebuild the barn.

Amos entered the room and closed the door. "My back hurts." He sat on the edge of the bed.

"Do you want me to rub your shoulders?" She looked back at him in the reflection from the mirror.

"No, *danki*." He pulled off his work boots and groaned.

"The barn looked *schee*." She smiled at her husband. "You and the other men did a *gut* job."

"The framing did turn out nice. We got a lot done in one day." He began to unbutton his shirt. "I'm concerned about Rosemary."

"Why?" Sarah Ann faced him while still brushing her hair.

"Her behavior at the barn raising upset me."

"What did she do?"

"She was flirting with a *bu*."

"I never saw her flirting with a *bu*." Sarah Ann was confused. "She was working in the kitchen most of the day."

"It was during the afternoon. She and Emma Beiler came outside and sat by a tree and a *bu* went over to visit with her." Amos pulled off his shirt and frowned.

"I was embarrassed by how she behaved with him. She was flirting with him in front of all the workers. I can't imagine what those other men think of her now."

"Who was the *bu*?"

"Daniel King. He works on Joshua Glick's horse farm with Ben. We need to rein her in." Amos continued to frown while he changed into his pajamas. "I'm concerned she's going to wind up like *mei schweschder*."

Sarah Ann sat next to Amos on the edge of the bed. "I think you're overreacting. You said Rosemary was only talking to the *bu*."

Amos's frown deepened. "That's how it all starts, Sarah Ann. Carolyn was only talking to the *bu* before she made her mistake."

"Rosemary is sixteen, and it's only natural for her to start noticing *buwe*. She was in a public setting with a *freind*. Anyone who thinks badly of her would be making up something that simply isn't true." Sarah Ann rubbed his shoulder in hopes of relieving his worry about their daughter. "We have to trust Rosemary. She's a smart *maedel*."

"My parents trusted Carolyn too." He stood, picked up his dirty clothes, and pitched them into the hamper. "I'm going to keep an eye on her, and I want you to also."

"Amos, I really think she'll be fine." Sarah Ann turned down the quilt and sheet on her side of the bed. "The youth gatherings are chaperoned. We also make sure the youth members are in groups and are never given the opportunity to be alone. Nothing bad is going to happen to her, and she won't do anything bad. She's never given me a reason not to trust her, and I don't believe she will now."

"It happens," he groused. "Young people don't think things through like we do. I'm concerned, and I will continue to be concerned until she's married. I told her I'm going to be watching her, and I will make sure she behaves appropriately in the future. I don't want her to embarrass me in public again."

Sarah Ann frowned and wondered how she could convince her husband not to worry. She knew, however, that Amos was stubborn and set in his ways no matter what she said.

"I'm certain she'll be fine. We didn't do anything inappropriate before we were married, and I have faith that our *dochder* will make the same decisions." Sarah Ann climbed into bed.

"She'd better not be doing anything inappropriate." Amos joined her on his side of the bed before snuffing out the lantern. "If she wound up like Carolyn, then I would send her away to my cousin in Indiana. I couldn't imagine having her here along with Carolyn. That would be too much. I never understood why *mei dat* didn't send Carolyn away. I have a feeling that *mei mamm* convinced him to let her stay."

Sarah Ann shook her head while wondering how her husband could be so cold. "I don't condone what Carolyn did, but I understand why your *mamm* supported her. I can't imagine sending my *kind* away. I would love *mei kind* no matter what happened."

Amos snorted. "You make it sound so easy."

"I didn't say it was easy, Amos. I just said I would

help her, like your *mamm* did." She rolled onto her side, facing away from him. "I don't know why we're discussing this. Rosemary will be just fine. I have faith. *Gut nacht.*"

Amos grumbled, and soon she heard him snoring.

As she fell asleep, Sarah Ann prayed that God would guide Rosemary and also grant Amos faith in their only daughter.

TWELVE

Carolyn made her way from her bedroom to the kitchen, where she placed a half-full cup of warm milk in the sink. She was hoping the warm milk would help her sleep since she'd been lying awake, thinking about her troubling conversation with Barbie earlier in the day. The milk didn't help, and she placed the lantern she'd been holding on the counter as she washed the cup while trying to think of a way to fall asleep. She considered looking for a novel to read.

"Carolyn?" *Mamm* stood in the doorway. "I thought I heard you. What are you doing up? It's the middle of the night."

"I can't sleep." Carolyn leaned against the sink.

"Sit." *Mamm* sat at the kitchen table. "Let's talk."

Carolyn sank into a chair across from her, bent her arm on the table, and lowered her chin onto her palm. "I've been trying to fall asleep for hours, but I can't turn off my thoughts. I was hoping the warm milk would help, but I'm still wide awake. I couldn't even finish the mug."

"What's bothering you?" *Mamm* reached out and took Carolyn's free hand in hers. "What is it, *mei liewe*?"

Carolyn blew out a sigh and felt tears forming. "Sometimes I get tired of feeling inferior to every other *maedel* in the community."

"What do you mean?" *Mamm* looked confused. "Why would you feel inferior?"

"I'm thirty-one and not married, and I had a *kind* out of wedlock when I was sixteen. That mistake will haunt me for the rest of my life." Carolyn sniffed and wiped a stray tear from her cheek. "I love my son with my whole heart, but sometimes the consequences of what I did are difficult to bear."

"Now wait a minute." *Mamm* tapped her fingers on the table. "You were forgiven by God and the community. In fact, you didn't even have to confess to the church because you made the mistake before you were baptized. Everything was washed clean with your baptism, so you have no reason to feel as if you're still being punished for your mistake."

Carolyn shook her head. "It's not that simple."

Her mother studied her. "What happened today?"

Carolyn paused, wondering how she could admit to her mother that she agreed to see Saul but had feelings for Joshua. Saying it out loud would make her sound like a terrible person, and she was too embarrassed to admit the truth to her mother.

"Does this have something to do with the conversation you had with Barbie Glick today? You looked upset when we were carrying in the empty plates. You promised you would tell me what she said, but we didn't get a chance to talk when we got home."

Carolyn nodded. "*Ya*, this has everything to do with

Barbie Glick. She asked me if I like her son, and she warned me to stay away from him."

Mamm's eyes widened with shock. "Why would she say that?"

Carolyn studied the tabletop. "She saw me talking to Josh. I told her we're only *freinden*, but she acted like she didn't believe me. She said Josh is seeing someone else and I need to stay away."

"And this bothers you." *Mamm* filled in the blanks.

Carolyn's tears flowed as she looked up at her mother. "*Ya*, it does, because I do like him. I like him a lot."

"What about Saul?"

"Saul is a *gut* man, and I do like him. But, at the same time, he's also an easy solution to a much deeper problem. And the problem is facing my past. I don't think Josh has realized that I'm Ben's *mamm*. I think he assumes I'm his *aenti* and Amos is his *dat*."

"Carolyn," *Mamm* began, leaning in and taking both of her hands. "Why haven't you told Josh the truth?"

"Because then he won't like me. The only people who accept me are the ones who already know the truth. I've spent my whole adult life apologizing to people when they find out. I can't imagine what Joshua would say if I told him now that we've already become *freinden*. It's too late, and it will change everything." Carolyn's voice was thick as she fought the lump forming in her throat. She longed to temper her emotion, but she couldn't fight it. She cared for Joshua and didn't want to lose him.

"Oh, *mei liewe*." *Mamm's* eyes glistened with tears, causing Carolyn's tears to sprinkle down her hot cheeks. "You're too hard on yourself. You're already forgiven. In the book of 1 John, it says, 'I write to you, dear children, because your sins have been forgiven on account of his name.' You're forgiven, Carolyn. Now you need to forgive yourself."

Carolyn shook her head. "It's not that simple. I've spent the last fifteen years of my life dealing with accusing stares and whispers. That's why I've never been able to date anyone."

"That's not true." Her mother tapped the table for emphasis. "I told you that you could go to the youth gatherings, but you refused to go. You could've gone and been with your *freinden*."

"I never would have felt right about leaving *mei boppli* with you. Ben was always my responsibility, and you've always worked hard to take care of our family."

Mamm sighed. "I've told you a thousand times that I consider Ben to be one of mine because he's yours. Your youth is gone, but you can go to the singles' group now and meet more people your age if you want to." She paused. "But, again, what about Saul? Amos told me that you're getting to know Saul better. Do you want to date him?"

Carolyn nodded. "*Ya*, I do, but it's for practical reasons. He's a *gut dat*, and he can provide for Ben and me. He knows Ben is my *kind*, and he still would consider marrying me. He'd treat me well, but I don't have feelings for him like I do for Josh."

"You're not attracted to him." Her mother completed the thought.

"Exactly."

"Sometimes love and attraction can be a product of mutual respect and friendship," her mother said.

"I've heard that before, but I want a marriage like you and *Dat* built." Carolyn gestured around the kitchen. "You love each other. I want to feel that exciting rush of new love. If I married Saul, it would only be so Emma has a *mamm* and Ben has a *dat*. Saul would want Ben to be his apprentice and work for him in his shop. Ben loves the horse farm. He doesn't want to work in a cabinet shop."

Carolyn grabbed a napkin from the holder in the middle of the table and began to shred it as she spoke. "I don't want a marriage because it is the practical thing to do. I want a marriage based on love. And I want to get to know Josh because I think I could fall in love with him. He's handsome, funny, smart, and kind. He's treated Ben with more respect in the past few weeks than Ben has ever gotten from Amos or his cousins. But now Barbie has told me to stay away from Joshua, and Saul wants me to date him. To make it even more difficult, I feel sorry for Emma. She desperately needs a *mutter*, and she seems to have latched onto me. I don't know what to do. I'm so confused." She buried her face in her hands as bewilderment stole over her.

"Carolyn, you need to calm down. You can have everything you've dreamt of. You're not too old to find love. You can't let one mistake color your whole life. Ben wasn't planned, but he's a *wunderbaar bu*. He's kind and thoughtful." *Mamm* took Carolyn's hands in hers again. "We've all forgiven you and embraced Ben. Now you need to forgive yourself."

Carolyn took another napkin and wiped her eyes. "Okay. I'll try." She paused while remembering the conversation with Barbie. "That's not all Barbie said. When she warned me to stay away from Josh, she also said that the woman he's getting to know is Lena Esh and he may date her. I couldn't help feeling jealous, but I also get the feeling that Josh likes me more than Lena. He didn't seem to want to talk to Lena today, but he talked to me and joked with me for a few minutes when he was getting his lunch."

"You should trust your instincts. And don't let Barbie Glick get to you. Josh is a grown man, and I doubt Barbie is able to convince him to do something he doesn't want to do. If you feel that Josh might like you, then see where your friendship may lead." She then frowned. "Saul is also a good man, and you need to be honest with him. You can't keep him hanging on if you're not sure."

"Okay." Carolyn yawned and then stood. "I have a lot to think about. I'm going to go pray about it."

"That's a *gut* idea." Her mother picked up the lantern and then looped an arm around Carolyn's shoulder. "*Ich liebe dich.*"

"I love you too, *Mamm. Danki.*" Carolyn made her way to her room, where she prayed for guidance and strength until she fell asleep.

*   *   *

Joshua made eggs, hash browns, and bacon for breakfast while he watched the sun rise out the kitchen window. He yawned and cupped his hand to his mouth. He'd spent a good portion of the night lying awake in bed and thinking about Carolyn. He had enjoyed their brief encounter yesterday at the barn raising. In fact, he had hoped to see her again, but the opportunity never presented itself. She was already gone when he finished helping frame the barn. He'd gone looking for her, and Ben told him that his family had already packed up and left. Joshua had longed to at least tell her good-bye, but he missed his chance to see her once more before the end of the day.

Joshua piled the delicious-smelling breakfast food on his plate, and his stomach growled. He slowly ate while contemplating the barn raising. He was irked when his mother brought Lena over to see him and forced him into a discussion with her. The conversation was awkward at best. He couldn't help but think that he enjoyed a more riveting conversation with the tabby cat that meowed incessantly whenever he went into the barn. Lena only wanted to discuss recipes, which didn't interest him at all. The only recipes he cared about were the ones he could whip up quickly himself.

When he spotted Carolyn handing out drinks, he rushed through the line, and his pulse sped up when he finally stood beside her. When he asked her if she'd splash him with the water, he prayed his attempt at humor wouldn't fall flat. He was pleasantly surprised when she responded with a witty quip in return. He was mesmerized by both her looks and her sense of humor. He wondered why his mother couldn't see how appealing Carolyn was.

Joshua sighed as he scooped more potatoes into his mouth. He knew why his mother preferred Lena. It was because she was soft-spoken and compliant, the opposite of Hannah. Yet Joshua had always admired Hannah's spark. Although Carolyn shared a similar spark, she had something more—a contagious sense of humor that kept him both laughing and guessing. He never knew what she would say next, and he enjoyed the spontaneity of their conversations. She talked about more than recipes, and she seemed to really listen to him. Carolyn seemed to be his perfect match, and his mother needed to accept that.

Joshua had to find a way to get his mother to stay out of his life without alienating her. He knew she was hurting after losing Gideon and the *grandkinner*, but it wasn't her place to choose the woman he would date and possibly marry.

He froze in his seat when he realized what he'd just been contemplating—dating and possibly getting married. For years he thought he was too busy working on the farm to date, but now he was considering getting to know a woman for whom he truly cared. The idea of getting married astounded him. For the last year, he never believed he would get married because he didn't think he'd ever love anyone the way he loved Hannah. He was surprised to find these feelings for Carolyn seemed stronger than anything he'd ever felt for Hannah. Were his feelings for Hannah real or were they more like an infatuation? She'd never reciprocated the feelings he had for her. Perhaps that meant they never were anything more than a crush. True love was reciprocated, and he had the overwhelming feeling that Carolyn cared about him as much as he cared about her.

Joshua let those ideas roll around in his mind while he finished his breakfast. After washing the dishes and placing them in the drain board, he poured himself another cup of coffee and stared out the window, considering what it would be like to have a family. He believed that his big old house would feel warm and comfortable if he weren't in it alone. As much as he loved the farm, it was lonely when Benjamin and Daniel weren't there. Sharing the house and farm with a woman whom he loved would be the answer to a prayer he'd suppressed for years. It would make his house a real home.

Joshua finished the coffee and then washed the mug. He suddenly noticed that he was cleaning up after himself, something he didn't do every day. Instead, he normally let the utensils, plates, and cups pile up and took care of them when the cabinets were bare. He knew why he was cleaning up; it was in case Carolyn came by for a visit. He didn't want her to think he was a lazy pig who ignored his housework and expected his mother to handle all the indoor chores for him.

He glanced at the calendar on the wall and wondered what Carolyn was doing. Since it was Friday, she would be working at the hotel. The idea of Carolyn working in the same place that had inspired Hannah to leave the church caused his stomach to roil. He couldn't imagine losing Carolyn the same way he lost Hannah. The idea of another heartbreak scared him. Maybe he should simply repress the feelings he had for her, let go of the crazy notion that Carolyn would date him. Even if she did, he'd run the risk of losing her to the *English* world because of her working in that hotel.

He longed to stop her from working there. He wondered how he could convince her that keeping her job at the hotel wasn't a good idea. Joshua pushed that idea aside and started toward the door. It was none of his business if she decided to work in the Lancaster Grand Hotel. After all, he couldn't act as if he owned Carolyn. They weren't even dating.

As he stepped out onto the porch, he wondered what it would be like to call Carolyn his girlfriend. However, when it came to dating, he didn't even know where to begin. He needed to ask God to guide his relationship with Carolyn and send him a sign, letting him know if he was on the right road.

* * *

Carolyn waved to Madeleine as she pushed her housekeeping cart toward the supply closet at the hotel. "Good morning. How are you?"

Madeleine smiled. "I'm doing well. Are you heading to lunch?"

"*Ya.*" Carolyn stowed the cart in the closet. "I'm actually ahead of schedule today."

"That's great." Madeleine walked beside her as they headed toward the break room.

"I didn't think I'd have much energy because I didn't sleep well last night." Carolyn shrugged. "I guess I found my second wind."

"Why did you have trouble sleeping?" Madeleine looked concerned.

Carolyn paused. She didn't know Madeleine well enough to share something so personal. Instead, she simply smiled. "I just had one of those nights when my mind was working overtime."

"Oh." Madeleine nodded. "I've had nights like that too."

Carolyn followed Madeleine into the break room, where Ruth and Linda were already unpacking their lunches. "Hello. How's your day going?" She fetched her lunch from the refrigerator.

"It's going well," Ruth said between bites.

"Mine is the same. The usual." Linda lifted her cup of water.

Carolyn sat beside Madeleine and bowed her head in silent prayer before unpacking her sandwich.

"You seem rather chipper, Carolyn." Ruth studied her.

Carolyn shrugged. "I'm just full of energy today. I spent a little extra time on my prayers last night, and I feel better about some things today."

"Oh." Linda nodded slowly. "I understand. I've experienced that too. Sometimes things are stressful at home, and I feel better after I discuss it all with God. I always feel better after I give my stress to him. He can always calm the rough seas in my heart."

Madeleine cut up an apple. "I've felt that too. I've faced some hard times in my life. Now I feel as if I'm at a crossroads, and I need to make a change for the better. I'm certain that God is leading me here. I've been lost spiritually for a long time, and coming here has given me the comfort I need. I think being in an Amish community is helping me handle some of my problems."

"Being Amish doesn't solve all your problems." Linda frowned. "I'm Amish, and I still have problems and challenges in my life."

"That's true. We've all had hard times." Ruth lifted her sandwich. "But being Amish gives you a support system. Our community is there for us when we need them."

"*Ya*, that's true." Carolyn pulled a roll out of her lunch bag. "I attended a barn raising yesterday for a family that lives outside of my church district. There were families from different church districts from across Lancaster County who came to help."

"But we still have problems." Linda's voice was soft. "The community can't solve everything."

Carolyn sighed. "That's true, but we have our deep faith, which gets us through the rough times."

"Faith is definitely a huge part of our community," Ruth said.

"I know that, and I think that's one reason I've always felt I belonged here." Madeleine sipped her cup of water. "I loved visiting my grandparents as a child, and I never wanted to leave. My grandmother used to tell me stories about growing up Amish and going to the one-room schoolhouse. I loved how she made her own clothes and used a wringer washer instead of the regular one we had in our house. The house is surrounded by Amish families."

"Where do you live?" Carolyn asked as she ripped apart her roll.

"In Paradise." Madeleine shared the street name. "My property backs up to an Amish farm. There's a sign that says Beiler's Cabinets by my driveway."

"Beiler's Cabinets?" Carolyn asked with surprise. "That's Saul Beiler's house. I'm friends with him and his daughter."

"You know my neighbor?" Madeleine looked surprised. "It's a small world."

Carolyn nodded with surprise. "*Ya*, that's very true." She bit into her roll.

Madeleine drank more water. "I always wondered what it would be like to live like an Amish person."

"Being Amish is about more than wringer washers and making our own clothes," Ruth said gently. "Some *Englishers* think it's easy to become Amish, but you have to make some big changes in your life."

Carolyn laughed. "That's right. You'll have to find a wringer washer and learn how to use it. Did you ever help your *mammi* with the wash?"

"I did." Madeleine smiled. "She taught me how to use the wringer washer and how to sew and quilt. We had a wonderful time. I guess I should say a *wunderbaar* time."

"Did you ever go to church with her?" Ruth asked.

Madeleine nodded. "Yes, I did. I couldn't understand much of it, but I was fascinated by the bishop and the minister while they spoke. I miss those times with my grandmother so much."

Carolyn nodded. "I understand how you feel. I miss my *daadi* all the time."

Madeleine began sharing more stories about the summers she'd spent at her grandparents' house, and Carolyn smiled. She was thankful that she had good friends to take her mind away from all the emotions that had haunted her throughout the night.

* * *

Sunday afternoon Carolyn carried a coffeepot toward the barn after the church service ended. Lunch was served in Amos's largest barn, where the benches were converted into tables. Carolyn smiled and greeted the members of her church district while leaning over them and filling their cups.

She looked back toward the entrance to the barn and spotted Rosemary helping Sarah Ann deliver platters covered with bowls of peanut butter spread. They talked and smiled as they approached the tables.

Emma Beiler touched the sleeve of Carolyn's purple dress. "*Wie geht's?*"

"Emma!" Carolyn smiled at her. "I was so *froh* to see you and your *dat* came to service with our district today."

"Amos invited *mei dat* and me. I was so excited that I would be able to see you and Rosemary." Emma wore a pretty pink dress.

"That's nice that Amos invited you." Carolyn nodded slowly while wondering if the invitation was a way to get Carolyn and Saul to see each other.

Emma gestured toward the entrance to the barn. "I'll go see if Rosemary needs more help bringing out the food."

"Okay. I'll see you later." Carolyn moved to the second long table and began filling more cups.

Carolyn spotted Saul sitting with Amos, and her body tensed. When she reached him, she gave him a pleasant expression as she poured coffee into his cup. He responded with a broad smile. She again found herself wondering which man was the better choice for her—Joshua or Saul. She felt caught between what she wanted, which was true love, and what she felt was more practical, which was a man who was interested in her as a housewife and who would accept her even though he knew about her past.

As she finished filling the rest of the coffee cups, Carolyn contemplated her choices once again. Which road was the best one for her and for her son?

THIRTEEN

Amanda sat on her grandmother's porch with her twin, Lillian, while their brother, Andrew, worked in the barn with their grandfather the following Saturday afternoon. Amanda couldn't stop thinking about how much her mother had cried when she last saw Lily at the grocery store. She had to find a way to bring up the subject gently without prompting Lily to turn on her as well. She was determined to bring peace between her mother and sister, and she prayed for the correct words to inspire her sister to finally forgive their mother.

"So how's school?" Amanda lifted her glass of iced tea. "Do you still like teaching?"

"I do." Lillian held her glass of iced tea in her lap. "The scholars are so smart. I love watching their eyes light up when they understand something new."

"You were born to teach. I'm so glad it's going well for you." Amanda leaned back in the swing and pushed her long braid behind her shoulder.

"Don't you miss your prayer covering?" Lillian studied her. "I can't imagine being seen in public without keeping my head covered."

Amanda considered the question for a moment before responding. "At first it felt strange, but then I got used to it. I haven't cut my hair, but I do wear it down sometimes."

"How's school going for you?"

"It's good. I've been studying hard, and so far I'm getting really good grades." Amanda smiled as she thought of Mike. "I went out on a date recently."

"You went on a date and didn't tell me?" Lillian smacked her hand on the porch swing as she moved closer to Amanda. "I want details. Who is he?"

"Do you remember Mike from the bookstore?" Amanda asked. Her sister nodded. "I ran into him at the gas station, and he asked me out. He didn't recognize me at first because of my *English* clothes. He's going to school too, and he still wants to be a doctor. He took me out to dinner and a movie. We had a really nice time."

"Wow. That's exciting." Lillian grinned. "I remember you talking about Mike last year. I'm glad you ran into him. Do you think you'll go out again?"

"I hope so." Amanda raised her eyebrows. "How's Leroy?"

"He's *gut*. I see him at youth gatherings." Lillian set down her iced tea and looked down as she swiped her hands over her apron. Amanda knew her sister was avoiding eye contact with her.

"I miss you." Amanda said the words that seemed to hang unspoken between them. "My room is too quiet without you there snoring in my ear." She tried to make a joke, but it fell flat.

Instead of smiling, Lillian responded by sniffing as tears stung her eyes. "I know what you mean, and I miss you terribly. *Zwillingbopplin* shouldn't be apart. I miss Andrew too. I love *Mammi* and *Daadi,* but it's not the same without you and Andrew."

Amanda stared out toward the pasture while trying to choose her words wisely. She knew it was time to say something about *Mamm,* but she had to be careful with how she began the conversation. She didn't want her sister to shut down and stop talking to her. "I wish you would come visit us. I think you'd like the bed-and-breakfast."

"You know I can't do that."

"Why?" Amanda faced her sister. "What's holding you back from seeing us?"

Lillian glared at her. "You know the answer to that. I can't give *Mamm* the impression I'm blessing her new marriage. She broke her vows to the church, and she left me alone. She shouldn't have left the church for that man. It's just plain wrong."

Amanda sat up straight and challenged her. "So you're saying it's your pride that's holding you back from coming to visit us?"

Lily gasped. "How dare you say that? *Mamm* abandoned me. You would feel the same way if you'd stayed."

"Lily, why do you forgive me, but you still can't forgive *Mamm?*"

Lillian stared at her for a moment. "Didn't you hear what I said? She *abandoned* me." She clearly enunciated the word.

"Andrew and I left you too, but you aren't treating

us the way you're treating *Mamm*. You're breaking her heart. Can't you see the pain you've caused her? Jesus told us to forgive and love one another. Why can't you forgive *Mamm*?" Amanda held her breath while her twin stared at her.

Soon Lily's expression softened. "I'm the one who was left behind. You have to understand that I'm grieving."

"We still love you, and we're still your family." Amanda touched her sister's hand. "Please tell me that you'll pray and try to forgive *Mamm*. Can you do that for me?"

"I don't know." Lily shook her head and cleared her throat. "I can't make any promises."

Amanda suddenly remembered a Scripture passage the minister read at church the previous week. "A verse from Ephesians really touched my heart last week at church. 'Be kind and compassionate to one another, forgiving each other, just as in Christ God forgave you.' I think that applies to this situation. You really need to forgive *Mamm*."

Lillian wiped a tear off her cheek. "I'll try. I promise."

"*Danki*." Amanda looped her arm around Lily's shoulder and hoped she would keep her promise.

* * *

Rosemary sat beside her friend Naomi on a grassy hill while they watched members of Rosemary's youth group play volleyball. Rosemary tried her best to act happy, but she was holding her true emotions inside.

Deep down, she longed to cry as disappointment drowned her. She'd been at Eve's for more than an hour, and she hadn't spotted Daniel King yet. She'd told Naomi all about her encounter with Danny at the barn raising, and she'd confided that she'd been praying that he'd come to see her today at the singing.

"He'll be here," Naomi whispered for the twentieth time since they'd arrived at Eve's house that Sunday afternoon. "Maybe he's running late because he's talking to his parents, or maybe he had to help clean up after lunch."

Rosemary grimaced at Naomi. "The *buwe* never help clean up in the kitchen after service. They just eat and leave."

"I know." Naomi sighed. "I was trying to make you feel better."

"*Danki.*" Rosemary pulled a blade of grass. "I know I'm acting *gegisch* and immature, but I can't help it."

"Rosemary—" Naomi began in a whisper.

"I just like him so much." Rosemary kept her eyes fixed on the green grass. "Have you ever had a crush that fogs your mind? It feels like you're dreaming all the time and it's the same dream. Danny is all I think about. I know it's wrong, but I can't stop how I feel."

"Rosemary, you really need to stop." Naomi moved closer to Rosemary, but she kept talking.

"I wonder if he likes me too." Rosemary sighed.

"Rosemary!" Naomi grabbed her arm. "You need to pay attention. There's a boy right over there who fits your description of Danny. Is that him?"

"What?" Rosemary looked up and found Daniel

talking to Benjamin near the row of volleyball nets. She gasped, and her heart raced. "He's actually here."

Naomi grinned. "You can stop whining and moaning now."

"I don't whine and moan." Rosemary studied Daniel. "I hope he comes over here."

"He will. Just be patient and give him a chance." Naomi squinted in the sun. "It's the perfect day for volleyball."

"*Ya*, it is." Rosemary kept her eyes trained on Daniel. When he looked over and waved, she thought her heart might explode in her chest.

Daniel and Ben began walking toward them, and Rosemary swiped her hands over her dress and then touched her prayer covering to make sure it was secure.

"They're coming this way!" Naomi said.

"I know," Rosemary responded through gritted teeth. "Stop being so obvious."

"*Wie geht's?*" Daniel sank down onto a patch of grass beside her while Benjamin sat beside Naomi.

"You made it." Rosemary smiled over at him.

"She was beginning to think you weren't coming," Naomi said, and Rosemary jabbed her elbow into Naomi's side.

"I got here as quickly as I could." Daniel turned toward Rosemary. "I have a question for you."

Her pulse raced with anticipation. "What's your question?"

Daniel pointed toward the row of volleyball nets. "Why are we sitting here when the sun is shining and volleyball nets are beckoning us?"

"Oh." Rosemary's cheeks heated.

"You want to play, Ben?" Daniel asked as he stood.

"*Ya*. I love volleyball." Benjamin started toward the net. "Come on, Ro. I know you like to play too."

"Okay." Rosemary stood up and glanced at Naomi. "Are you coming too?"

"Why not?" Naomi hopped up and walked with Rosemary toward an empty net.

Rosemary stood next to Daniel while he held up a ball and winked at her.

"Are you going to be on my team?" he asked her.

"Absolutely," she said as her heart turned over.

* * *

Rosemary rushed into her house after she and Benjamin arrived home from the youth gathering. She couldn't wait to talk to her mother and tell her all about Daniel. She rushed into the house and up the stairs to her room. After changing into her nightgown and brushing out her hair, she walked down the hallway to where her mother was reading in bed.

"Rosemary, I thought I heard you get home." Her *mamm* placed her book on her lap. "Did you have a nice time?"

"I did." Rosemary stood in the doorway. "Do you have a minute to talk?"

"Of course I do. I always have time for you." *Mamm* patted the quilt. "Come sit with me."

Rosemary climbed into the bed beside her mother, and she felt like a little girl again.

"Did your brothers come home too?" *Mamm* asked.

"I think they were dropping off a few friends. They should be here soon." Rosemary lowered her voice. "I wanted to talk to you alone. Is *Dat* gone?"

"He's out in the barn working on a project. I'm sure we have a few minutes alone, and we'll hear him when he comes up the stairs." *Mamm* placed her book on the bedside table. "What did you want to tell me?"

Rosemary paused and gnawed on her lower lip as the confidence she'd felt earlier evaporated.

"What is it?" *Mamm* asked. "You know you can tell me anything."

"I'm embarrassed now."

"You don't need to be embarrassed when you talk to me." *Mamm* smiled. "Does this have something to do with a *bu*?"

"*Ya*. He's so handsome and nice and funny." Rosemary couldn't stop a sigh from escaping her lips. "Oh, *Mamm*. I feel like I'm floating when I'm with him."

"*Mei boppli* is growing up." *Mamm* pushed Rosemary's long hair away from her face. "Tell me about this special *bu*."

"His name is Daniel King, and he works with Ben and Joshua Glick at the horse farm. He's tall and he's strong. He came to our youth group tonight. We played volleyball, and we talked and laughed. Oh, it was perfect." Rosemary flopped back on the bed and stared up at the white ceiling. "I can't wait until I can see him again. He said he'd come to youth group again next week."

"How old is he?"

Rosemary hesitated. "He's nineteen."

Mamm's smile faded a little. "He's too old for you, Rosemary. Three years is a big gap when you're a young person."

"But, *Mamm*, he's really nice and he's respectful," Rosemary said while hoping to temper her mother's concern. "You don't need to worry. I just want to get to know him. Next year I'll join the baptism class, and I won't date him until after I'm a church member. You can trust me."

Mamm nodded. "I do trust you, and he sounds like a nice young man. But I need to warn you. Your *dat* is very worried about you."

Rosemary grimaced. "He's still angry about the barn raising? All I did was talk to Danny. We were in public, and we didn't even sit next to each other. Ben introduced him to me, and then I invited him to come to the youth gathering. I don't plan on meeting him in secret or spending time alone. I just want to see him at youth gatherings. You have to believe me."

"I do believe you, and I'm glad you're telling me about him. You're not keeping any secrets from me, right?"

"I would never keep secrets from you, *Mamm*." She thought about her parents. "How old were you when you met *Dat*?"

"I was seventeen, and your *dat* was eighteen." Her mother smiled as she suddenly got a faraway look in her eyes. "It was love at first sight. I'd gone with my cousin to her youth group, which was in this community. I saw your *dat* across the barn while we were singing, and I knew I had to meet him."

Rosemary smiled. "That's so sweet."

"*Ya*, it was. He came up to talk to me after the singing, and he asked me if I wanted a ride home. We were inseparable after that. We married four years later."

"So you were only twenty-one when you were married."

"Now, now. Hold on a minute. Don't get any ideas. Not every couple is ready to be married when they are that young." *Mamm* shook her finger. "Your *dat* was already working for your *daadi* on his farm, and there was a little *haus* for us there. Don't get any ideas about running off and getting married."

"I'm not." Rosemary shook her head. "But I hope I can get to know Danny better."

"Take your time. You're young."

Her father's boots sounded on the stairs, and Rosemary jumped up.

"*Gut nacht, Mamm*." She headed for the doorway. "*Danki* for talking with me."

"I enjoyed it. *Ich liebe dich*." *Mamm* waved at her. "See you in the morning."

Rosemary jumped into her bed, snuggled under the sheets, and fell asleep dreaming about when she would see Daniel again.

FOURTEEN

The following Tuesday Carolyn was baking pies while her mother was mending a pair of her father's trousers.

"Carolyn!" Rosemary burst into the kitchen and huffed and puffed as if she'd run the length of the back pasture. "You need to come with me."

"What's going on?" *Mamm* asked. "Why are you so out of breath?"

"I just ran from the barn." Rosemary leaned on the counter and caught her breath. "*Daadi* is heading out to the hardware store, and he said he wanted to stop by to visit Ben at Josh Glick's farm on the way back. Do you want to come with us?"

"He's going to see Ben?" Carolyn wiped her hands on a towel.

"*Ya,* that's what I said." Rosemary beckoned for Carolyn to come. "He wants to leave now. He's hitching the horse to the buggy."

"*Ach.*" Carolyn looked at her mother. "I don't want to leave all this work for you. The pies—"

"Go." Her mother waved off the comment. "Have

some fun. I know you like to go to the farm." She gave Carolyn a knowing smile. "I can handle it. I've been making pies for forty years."

"Okay. Just give me one minute." Carolyn rushed to the bathroom and checked her reflection. She brushed her hands over her apron to remove any stray flour, checked to make sure her prayer covering was straight, and pinched her cheeks to give her complexion some color. She felt silly for being so worried about her appearance. After all, vanity was a sin. At the same time, she felt as giddy as a teenager who was on her way to a singing and hoping to see the boy she liked.

Carolyn met her niece in the kitchen. "I'm ready." She looked back at her mother. "I'll be home soon."

"Take your time." Her mother winked at her.

Carolyn ignored the gesture despite feeling her pulse race when she thought about seeing Joshua.

"I can't wait to see Danny," Rosemary said as they made their way toward the waiting buggy.

Carolyn smiled at her. *I know the feeling.*

* * *

Joshua stepped into the stables and found Daniel and Benjamin shoveling. "How's the work coming?" he yelled toward the back of the stable.

"It would be faster if you helped," Daniel responded from a few stalls away.

"I can't help right now. I have to balance the books." Joshua leaned on the door frame.

"Did you hear that, Ben?" Daniel asked. "Josh has to

balance the books. That sounds like a lame excuse to me. I think he just doesn't want to do the real manual labor. He leaves all the fun stuff for us."

"Isn't that what bosses always do?" Benjamin stepped out of the stall and wiped his brow with the back of his forearm. "Josh, you brought me on so you can do easier stuff, right?"

Joshua laughed at the joke and then added, "You know that's not the truth." He motioned for Benjamin to approach him. "Come here and talk to me for a moment."

"What's wrong?" Benjamin looked concerned as he walked over to Joshua.

"Nothing is wrong. Actually, I want to discuss bringing you on board permanently."

Benjamin's smile was wide. "That's fantastic. I'd love to work for you permanently."

"*Gut.* I need to discuss it with your parents. Would you mind talking with them first and then letting me know what they say?"

Benjamin paused for a moment and then nodded. "*Ya*, I'll do that."

"Great. We'll discuss the details later, and then you can talk to your folks tonight." Joshua hoped that Benjamin's parents would accept his offer. He not only appreciated having Benjamin's help, but he had also enjoyed getting to know the boy. Ben had become like a nephew to him. While he could never replace Andrew, he made the pain of that loss more bearable.

His thoughts were interrupted by the clip-clop of a horse heading up his driveway. He wasn't expecting any visitors today. No customers had called to make appointments.

"Who can that be?" he mumbled as he headed out to the driveway where a buggy came to a stop.

When his mother and Lena climbed out of the buggy, Joshua swallowed a groan.

"Hello!" His mother hurried over to him.

"Hi, *Mamm*. Lena." He nodded toward Lena and then looked at his mother as irritation nipped at him. "What brings you out here today?" The question was courteous, but his expression was pointed.

"Lena came over to visit me this morning, and we were just discussing quilting." *Mamm* motioned toward the house. "I wanted to show her the quilt your *mammi* made for you before she passed away. That quilt means so much to me." Tears prickled her eyes, and Joshua wondered if she had stood in front of a mirror and practiced her dramatic performance before she came over to visit him.

"You know where the quilt is. You can take Lena upstairs and show her."

"No, no!" *Mamm* shook her head with emphasis. "I want you to give Lena a tour of the *schee haus*."

Joshua studied his mother. "I don't have the time to give a tour right now. I need to work on the books and pay some bills so I can keep this farm running."

"That's fine," Lena said with a pleasant smile. "You can give me a tour some other time. I know your work is important to you."

"Don't be *gegisch*, Lena," *Mamm* insisted. "Josh has a few minutes. We'll go inside so Josh and I can show

you the *haus* before we look at the barns and stables."
She took Joshua's sleeve and pulled him toward the
house. "Let's go."

Joshua followed his mother and Lena into his house.
He couldn't stop wondering how he was going to get
through to his mother and make her realize she didn't
have the right to force Lena on him. He could tell Lena
was interested in him by the way she looked at him.
Although Lena was a nice young lady, she wasn't the
one who consumed his thoughts.

* * *

Carolyn sat in the front of the buggy next to her father
while he guided the horse away from the hardware
store and toward Joshua's farm.

"I can't wait to see the farm, *Daadi*," Rosemary said
while the buggy moved down the main road. "Ben
talks about it constantly. I'm certain it's just as *schee* as
he says it is."

"I can't wait either." He smiled at Rosemary, and she
returned the gesture.

Carolyn couldn't wait either. In fact, butterflies took
up residence in her abdomen when she thought about
seeing Joshua.

When they arrived, Carolyn spotted another buggy
in the driveway and wondered who was also visiting.

Dat stopped the horse behind the first buggy, and
they climbed out.

"Oh wow." Rosemary made a wide gesture. "Look at
the pasture and the stables and barns. They are so very

schee. And those horses, *Daadi.* Aren't they magnificent?"

"It's very nice." *Dat* looked at Carolyn. "Should we go out to the stables to find Joshua?"

"I think we should look in the *haus* first," Carolyn suggested.

"I'm going to go find Ben," Rosemary said before heading out toward the stables.

Carolyn started toward the porch with her father in tow. They climbed the steps, and Carolyn knocked twice before stepping into the mudroom.

"Come in!" Joshua called.

Carolyn pushed open the door, and she heard voices and laughter in the kitchen. Who was in the house with him? She walked into the kitchen and found Joshua talking with Barbie and Lena. Carolyn's mood soured as she stared at the two women. Barbie scowled at Carolyn, but Lena smiled.

"Titus. Carolyn," Joshua said, moving over to them. "What a nice surprise to see you. I'm glad you came by." His expression seemed guarded.

Barbie continued to glare at Carolyn, and Lena gazed at Joshua. Carolyn felt as if she'd interrupted a private meeting. She suddenly felt out of place and silly for pursuing Joshua. And, all at once, it became clear to Carolyn that she had no chance of winning Joshua's heart when a pretty, single woman, who certainly didn't have a sordid past, was interested in him. Lena had every right to try to get to know Joshua, while Carolyn was only kidding herself. She didn't belong with someone like Joshua, who had an entirely clean slate. She was more suited for a widower who could handle starting a blended family.

Carolyn was overwhelmed by the urge to flee. "Excuse me." She backed up toward the door. "I'm going to go see what my niece is doing."

"Carolyn? Wait a minute," Joshua called after her. "Carolyn?"

Carolyn rushed out of the house and hurried toward the barn. She found Benjamin, Daniel, and Rosemary standing near the back pasture fence talking.

Carolyn took a deep breath and tried to calm her frayed nerves as she approached them. "Hi."

Benjamin waved. "Rosemary told us you came along with *Daadi* today. Where is he?" he asked.

"He's in the kitchen with Joshua and his visitors." Carolyn pointed toward the house.

"Josh has visitors?" Daniel looked surprised. "Who's visiting?"

"His *mamm* and a young woman named Lena." Carolyn tried not to frown as she said the names.

"Oh. His *mamm* stops by a few times a week," Daniel said.

Carolyn needed to change the subject in an attempt to take her mind off Barbie and Lena. "So, what were you all talking about?"

"Youth gatherings." Rosemary's smile was wide. "I was telling Danny he should come back to one of our gatherings. We had a really *gut* time Sunday night. We played volleyball, and we sang."

Rosemary continued talking about her youth gatherings while Daniel smiled at her. Carolyn could see their friendship blossoming before her eyes. Although she was happy for her niece, she couldn't ignore her own disappointment.

She looked back toward the house and watched as Lena and Barbie stood in the doorway saying good-bye to Joshua. She longed to be the one standing on the porch talking to him. Yet she knew she had no right to be there. Joshua deserved a woman without a complicated past.

And the reality drowned Carolyn like a tidal wave—she was naïve to think that a man like Joshua could ever fall in love with her.

* * *

Joshua couldn't believe his mother's timing. Why did she have to pick this opportunity to come and visit? Perhaps it was almost predictable that she would drag Lena over to his house uninvited at the same time Carolyn would come to see him.

Carolyn had become a permanent vision in his mind since the barn raising last Thursday. But the scene had been awkward when she walked into the kitchen and found his mother and Lena there. Carolyn looked as uncomfortable as he felt.

Joshua had longed to stop her when she rushed out of the house. He felt terrible that she left so quickly, and he wanted to apologize to her. Was she angry with him? He was anxious to find out why she and Titus had come to see him, but he couldn't figure out how to get his mother to stop talking and leave. After Carolyn went out the back door, his mother prattled on and on about the weather. Titus was a gracious listener as he nodded and fingered his long beard. Joshua, however, suspected Titus, too, was wondering when *Mamm* would stop talking and leave.

"It was *gut* seeing you," Joshua began as he gestured toward the door. "I'm certain I'll see you again soon."

"*Danki* for the tour." Lena's smile was genuine. "You have a lovely *haus*."

"*Danki.*" He shook her hand. "Take care, Lena."

"Oh." *Mamm* looked surprised. "I guess we'd better go. Good-bye, Titus."

Titus nodded at the women as they disappeared through the mudroom and out the back door.

"It's *gut* to see you." Joshua motioned toward the table. "Would you like to have a seat?"

"*Danki.*" Titus sank into a chair.

"Would you like something to drink?" Joshua offered.

"No, *danki.* I'm fine." Titus folded his hands and placed them on the table. "I was in the area visiting the hardware store, so I thought I would stop by to see your farm. I invited Carolyn and Rosemary to come with me."

"*Wunderbaar.*" Joshua sat across from him. "I'm glad you came by."

"Ben really enjoys working here." Titus fingered his beard again. "I was hoping this would work out for him and he would learn some responsibility and respect."

"It's funny that you brought that up." Joshua settled back in the chair. "I've never seen a behavior problem with Ben. In fact, he's been very respectful to Danny, the animals, and me. I don't think he's a problem at all." He paused to choose his words. "To be honest with you, I don't think Ben is the one with the behavior problem. I think it's the other *buwe*."

Titus leaned forward. "What are you saying?"

"I'm saying that I don't think Ben threw that rock at my horse. I believe the other *buwe* set him up to get into trouble." He paused again, hoping he wasn't overstepping his bounds. "Ben loves the animals. He's gentle and respectful to the horses. I don't believe he would ever deliberately hurt them. Also, from what I've heard, I think they do this to him frequently."

"Who told you that?"

"Ben did."

Titus was silent for a moment as if contemplating the accusation. "I've heard this before from Carolyn, but I thought she was only making excuses for the *bu*. I'll have to look into this."

Joshua held back a sigh of relief. He was hoping he didn't upset the man by telling him two of his grandsons were trouble-makers. He was thankful Titus took the news well and also respected his opinion.

"I won't keep you long. I know you have work to do." Titus stood. "But I'd love to take a tour of your farm."

"Of course." Joshua stood. "I'll give you a tour, and we can see where everyone else is."

Joshua led Titus out to the farm, where he showed him the stables and barns before they encountered Carolyn, Daniel, Benjamin, and Rosemary talking by the fence. Joshua tried to make eye contact with

Carolyn, but she quickly looked away when she saw him approaching. His heart was breaking while he wondered what was wrong. Had he offended her? Or, even more likely, had his *mamm* offended her? He longed to talk to her alone, but he knew that wasn't possible with her father standing nearby. It would be inappropriate for an unmarried couple to be alone.

Rosemary gave Titus an eager smile. "Ben showed me around earlier. Did Josh show you the farm?"

"He did." Titus looped his thumbs in his suspenders. "It's *schee*, just like Ben said." He turned to Benjamin.

"I told you it was great." Benjamin's expression brightened.

Titus turned to Joshua. "*Danki* for the tour. I better get back home." He shook Joshua's hand. "I'll see you soon."

"Good-bye." Joshua turned to Carolyn, who gave him a quick nod before rushing past him and walking beside her father. He wanted to run after her, but he knew that would be inappropriate. Her rejection was crushing his heart, and he couldn't stand the pain. He'd never experienced anything like this, not even when Hannah rejected him.

"I better get back to work." Benjamin started up the rock path toward the stables.

Daniel climbed over the fence and started toward the horses.

"Danny. Wait." Joshua called him back.

Daniel came back to the fence. "What do you need?"

"I need advice." Joshua sighed and shook his head. "I feel *gegisch*." He turned toward the driveway and watched the buggy disappear from sight. "It's been a long time since I dated."

Daniel's eyebrows flew toward his hairline. "You need dating advice? I don't know much. I've only just started dating recently."

"But you've dated a little bit, right?"

"I have, but only a couple of *maed*." Daniel leaned on the fence and chuckled a little. "Is this about Lena?"

"No, no." Joshua waved off the question. "It's not about Lena at all."

"Then who is it?"

Joshua paused. He felt silly asking a nineteen-year-old advice about women.

"It's Carolyn!" Daniel clapped his hands. "I had a feeling you liked her. You two seem to light up when you're together."

"You're right. It's Carolyn. How do I make her see that I care about her?"

Daniel shrugged. "That's easy. You need to tell her."

"Really? That's all I need to do?"

"*Ya*." Daniel shook his head. "It's been a very long time since you've dated, hasn't it?"

"*Ya*, it has."

"In my very limited experience, I've found *maed* like to discuss their feelings. They want to talk about everything." Daniel tapped the fence. "Just tell her how you feel, and she'll realize that she can trust you. *Maed* want trust."

"*Danki*." Joshua turned to go but then faced Daniel once again. "And we never had this conversation, understand?"

Daniel laughed. "Absolutely. Your secret is safe with me."

"Back to work. I'm going to work on the books. Hopefully I won't be interrupted again." Joshua headed toward the house as a plan surfaced in his mind. He would go to Benjamin's house later in the evening with the excuse of needing to discuss the job with his parents. Although the job would be the excuse, his true purpose for the visit would be to see Carolyn and tell her how he felt about her.

He just needed to figure out how he could possibly tell her his true feelings when he'd guarded his heart for so long. He needed to pray for the words.

FIFTEEN

Carolyn stood at the stove while stirring mashed potatoes. Her mind was stuck on the vision of Lena and Barbie in Joshua's kitchen earlier in the day. Feelings of embarrassment and regret haunted her. She silently berated herself for acting like a desperate teenager by running over to Joshua's farm with lame excuses to see him. She needed to stop chasing her farfetched dreams and instead step back and wait for God to lead her to the right suitor and future husband. She couldn't stop wondering if she was missing the signs that were leading her to Saul instead of Joshua.

"Carolyn." *Mamm's* voice broke through her mental rant. "I can't stand this silence. What's bothering you, *mei liewe*?"

Carolyn kept her gaze focused on her pot of potatoes. "I'm fine. *Danki, Mamm*." Her voice was thick with emotion.

Mamm came up behind her and touched her shoulder. "Please talk to me and let me help you."

Carolyn shook her head. "Honestly, I'm okay."

"No, you're not. Look at me, *mei liewe*."

Carolyn faced her mother and her lip quivered. "I'm too embarrassed to tell you."

"Just tell me. You know you can tell me anything." Her mother gestured toward the table. "Let's talk for a minute. We have some time before your *dat* will be hungry and Ben will be home."

Carolyn sat across from her mother at the table and shared the whole story about what happened when she went to see Joshua. "I just feel so immature. I know I'm not supposed to chase after men, and I feel like I've been running after him and trying to make something out of nothing. We're just *freinden*. He doesn't even know the truth about Ben, so why am I kidding myself that he could possibly want to have a relationship with me?"

Mamm shook her head. "You're doing exactly what I told you not to. You're letting your old mistake ruin your whole life. If Josh is truly a *gut* man, he will forgive you just like God and the rest of the community have forgiven you. Don't be so hard on yourself."

"I think he's already seeing Lena, so I'm wasting my time and my emotions on a man who's already out of reach. Lena looks at Josh like he's the greatest man in the world. She has love in her eyes for him. I think I'm too late."

"If he's already seeing Lena, then you will find someone else. You're still young enough to get married and have a family. Don't rush God's plan for you." *Mamm* smiled. "Do you feel any better?"

"*Ya*." Carolyn forced a smile, but she was telling a white lie. She didn't feel any better. She still felt immature and disappointed.

"Let's finish getting ready to eat." *Mamm* moved

back to the stove. "You can set the table, and I'll check on the meat loaf."

Carolyn busied herself with preparing for supper, but her thoughts were still stuck on Joshua. Soon her father came in from helping Amos with the cows. He kissed her mother's cheek before disappearing into the bedroom. Carolyn wondered if she'd ever find a man who would kiss her every time he came into the house and smile at her from across the room. But that seemed more like a daydream than what could one day become a reality.

She set cups on the table and then placed the pot of potatoes, a bowl of carrots, and a loaf of bread on the table. She was retrieving the butter from the refrigerator when the back door opened with a squeak and Benjamin burst into the kitchen.

"Hello!" he called as he headed back to his bedroom. "Supper smells *appeditlich.*"

Carolyn looked at her mother and grinned. "He's in a *gut* mood."

"I guess that means he had a *gut* day," her mother added.

They finished their preparations just as Benjamin and Titus entered the kitchen. They each took their usual seats at the table, and after praying, they filled their plates and began to eat.

"I have *wunderbaar* news," Benjamin began as he lifted his cup of water.

"What is it?" Carolyn asked.

"Joshua wants me to stay on at the farm." Benjamin's voice was full of excitement. "He wants to hire me on permanently."

Carolyn smiled, and her mother clapped her hands.

"I'm *froh* to hear that," Titus said. "Did you tell him that you want to do it?"

Benjamin nodded as he finished chewing. "He told me to discuss it with you and *Mamm* and then give him my answer." He rattled off the salary and other details while Carolyn silently thanked God for her son's opportunity.

"That sounds *gut*," Titus said as he sliced the meat. He turned to Carolyn. "Do you approve?"

"Of course I do," she said quickly. "This is a fantastic opportunity for Ben. If he wants the job, then I support it."

"*Danki*," Benjamin told her with a wide smile. "I can't wait to tell him." He continued talking about the job while they ate.

"Do I hear a buggy?" her mother suddenly asked.

"I heard it too." Benjamin popped up from the table, crossed to the door, and stepped out onto the porch.

"I'm so thankful for this opportunity for him," Carolyn told her parents. "I've been praying—" She stopped speaking when the back door opened. She angled her body toward the door and was surprised when she saw Joshua coming into the kitchen with a cautious expression. "Josh?" Confusion flooded her. Why was he here? What did he want?

"Hi." He gave her a little wave. "I'm sorry for barging in. I didn't mean to interrupt your supper."

"Don't be *gegisch*," *Dat* said. "Have a seat and join us."

"Oh, no, I don't want to impose." Joshua took a step back toward the door. "I'll come back."

"Josh, stay for supper." Her mother pointed toward the table. "We'll set a place for you."

"Oh, no." He shook his head. "I can't let you do that."

"No, no." Her mother smiled. "I insist you stay. I've heard a lot of *wunderbaar* things about you."

I can't believe Mamm *just said that!* Carolyn hoped Joshua didn't see her cheeks heat in response to her mother's words.

"*Danki.*" Joshua hung his straw hat and coat on a peg by the back door. "I would like to wash up a little. May I use your bathroom?"

"Of course." Carolyn pointed toward the hallway off the kitchen. "The bathroom is the second door on the left."

"*Danki.*"

Carolyn retrieved a place setting for Joshua while Benjamin filled a cup with water.

Joshua soon returned and sat at the table next to Benjamin, and Carolyn sat next to her mother and across from him. After praying, he smiled at Carolyn, and her heart raced. She tried to temper her emotion by looking away, but the attraction kept her pulse racing.

"Everything is *appeditlich*," *Dat* said. "I'm *froh* you came to join us tonight, Josh. What brought you all the way out here?"

"I wanted to discuss hiring Ben on permanently." Joshua glanced at Benjamin, who smiled, then looked again at *Dat*. "I'm *froh* with his work and don't want to lose him. So I came over to see your son—Amos, right? But no one was home."

Carolyn looked up at her father and froze, and she

was sure her mother had as well. But *Dat* hesitated for only a moment before he said, "That's okay. You and I can talk about it after supper."

"That sounds *gut*," Joshua said.

Carolyn was relieved as well as grateful to her father. She needed to be the one to tell Josh about Ben, and it seemed that *Dat* agreed. Benjamin began sharing stories about the farm and Joshua joined in. Soon she found herself laughing along with them while they talked about Benjamin's mishaps while learning how to train the horses. Her father also joined in and shared stories of growing up on his father's dairy farm.

Soon the dinner was over, and Carolyn was impressed by how well Joshua fit in with her family. The dinner was very different from the one she'd shared at Saul's house, where he'd hardly spoken.

Carolyn and her mother cleared away the platters and then served coffee along with the pies Carolyn had baked earlier in the day. The conversation continued during dessert, and Carolyn noticed Joshua frequently looked over at her. Her pulse skittered every time he made eye contact with her. She tried to suppress her feelings, but the emotions were strong, stronger than anything she had ever felt for Benjamin's father.

Once dessert was finished, Carolyn and her mother took care of cleaning up the kitchen while Benjamin went out to care for the animals. Her father and Joshua excused themselves and headed to the porch to talk. Carolyn heard a horse and buggy, and she surmised her brother had returned home. She hoped nothing would come up during their conversation to make Josh wonder about Ben's parentage. She hated for her father to have to keep covering for her. She was afraid to tell Josh the truth, but tonight's close call brought home to her what she must find the courage to do.

"He's awfully nice." *Mamm* scrubbed a pot in the frothy water. "It's obvious that he likes Ben."

"*Ya.*" Carolyn wiped the crumbs from the table into her palm. "Ben enjoys working for him."

"He's quite handsome, Carolyn. I can see why you like him. And I think he likes you."

"*Mamm!*" Carolyn faced her and frowned. "Keep your voice down. They're right outside that window."

"I doubt they can hear me." *Mamm* shrugged. "I'm just telling you how I feel."

"He's seeing Lena." Carolyn stopped wiping the table and looked over her shoulder at her mother. She couldn't help her curiosity. She had to find out what her mother was thinking. "Why do you think he likes me?"

Mamm walked over to her and lowered her voice. "It's obvious by the way he looks at you."

Carolyn's eyes widened. "What do you mean?"

"He looks at you like he cares about you." Her mother touched her arm. "Just trust me. I know that look when I see it."

Carolyn studied her mother as a sliver of hope swelled inside her. "That can't be possible. His mother told me he's seeing Lena, and Lena was at his house today."

"He hasn't married her yet, has he?"

"No, but—"

"Carolyn, trust me," her mother began, interrupting her, "I know what I'm talking about. Besides, from what you've told me, I have the distinct impression Barbie is a constant meddler in her son's life."

"Maybe." Carolyn let the idea swirl in her head while she finished cleaning up the table and then swept the floor. She was putting the broom away when her father and Joshua came in from outside.

"It's official," *Dat* said with a smile. "Amos, Josh, and I just finished discussing it. Benjamin is going to work full-time at the farm and earn a fair wage beginning this summer."

"That's *wunderbaar!*" *Mamm* said.

"*Ya*, it is." Carolyn studied Joshua. She took in his handsome face and wondered if he was truly dating Lena.

Her father shook Joshua's hand. "*Danki* for giving Ben the opportunity."

"I'm glad he wants to continue working for me. I need the help." He looked at Carolyn's mother and then Carolyn. "*Danki* for supper. I better head home now." His eyes lingered on Carolyn, and she held her breath. "*Gut nacht*," he finally said.

He started out the door, and Carolyn released the breath she'd been holding.

"Go." Her mother bumped her with her elbow.

"What?" Carolyn asked.

"He wanted you to follow him. Couldn't you see it in his expression?" Her mother's voice was full of exasperation.

"What's going on?" *Dat* asked.

Her mother waved off her father's question. "I'll tell you later. Go, Carolyn. Catch up with him before he leaves. *Dummle!*"

Carolyn rushed out the door and caught up to Joshua as he stood by his buggy. Her heart thumped in her chest as she approached him. "Josh! Wait."

"I was hoping you'd come out to say good-bye to me." He smiled, and her pulse accelerated once again.

How did Mamm *know that?* Carolyn pushed the thought away and thought about the scene at his house earlier. She had to discuss it with him, or it would eat her alive. She swallowed a deep breath. "I'm sorry for showing up at your *haus* today uninvited. Rosemary asked me to come with her. I realize now I should've just stayed home."

"Actually, I wanted to talk to you about that alone. Coming over here to talk to Amos was just an excuse to see you." He leaned back against the buggy, and it shifted under his weight. "I felt bad when you left in a hurry. Why did you run off so quickly?"

The direct question surprised Carolyn and stumped her for a moment. "I thought I was interrupting something."

He tilted his head. "Why would you think that?"

"Your *mamm* and Lena were there, and I felt out of place."

"You weren't out of place." He shook his head. "You had as much right to be there as they did."

"*Danki.*" She contemplated her mother's words and wondered if he cared for her. She longed to be as certain as her mother was about his feelings for her.

"I noticed Rosemary and Danny were talking by the fence." He crossed his arms over his wide chest.

"*Ya*. They seem to be becoming friends. Rosemary convinced Danny to go to one of her youth gatherings Sunday night, and it sounds like they had a nice time." Carolyn smiled. "She's hoping he'll keep coming to them so she can see him more often."

"*Ya*. Young love is easy, isn't it? Things weren't so complicated when we were teenagers."

"Sometimes it's easy. Sometimes it gets complicated." She stopped speaking before she shared the secret from her youth. She longed to tell him the truth, but the fear of losing his friendship held back the words.

"That's true," he continued, apparently not noticing her apprehension. "But then life gets even more complicated the older we grow, and as a result, love gets more complicated."

"*Ya*." Carolyn had to know the truth, but she wasn't sure how to ask about Lena. She decided to take an indirect approach. "Lena is nice."

"*Ya*, she is." He rubbed his chin and paused as if choosing his words. "*Mei mamm* thinks Lena is the right person for me. I love *mei mamm*, but sometimes I get tired of her trying to run my life."

"Your *mamm* is pushing you to date Lena?" Carolyn felt the worry lift from her heart when she said the words out loud. *Mamm* was right again!

"*Ya*." His expression softened. "But it's not as bad as it sounds. Her heart is in the right place. I know she means well, and she's made it her goal to marry me

off and have more *grandkinner*. I know she misses my
niece and nephew. In fact, I miss having my nephew by
my side every day when I work at the farm, but I don't
think I can fill that hole in her heart. Those feelings are
too deep to just disappear."

"That makes sense." Carolyn nodded slowly while
marveling how Joshua was baring his soul in front of
her as if they were old friends.

"I just feel I will find the right woman in my own
time. You can't rush God's plan."

"No, you can't. *Mei mamm* reminds me about that
all the time." She fingered her apron while thinking
about her brother. "I know how you feel."

"You do?" He looked surprised. "How?"

"Amos has been pressuring me to marry Saul."

"Who's Saul?"

"Saul Beiler. You had lunch with him at the barn
raising."

"Oh, I remember Saul. He didn't say much that day.
He seems to be very reserved." Joshua continued to
look surprised. "Isn't he a widower?"

"He is. Amos thinks it's time for me to get married
and move out of the *daadi haus*." She pointed toward
the house behind her. "Saul is nice, and I really like his
dochder. But I think the decision about who I marry
needs to be mine."

"Absolutely." Joshua looked concerned. "Have you
ever tried to talk to Amos about this and tell him how
you feel?"

She nodded. "I have, but he's set in his ways. He

believes it's time for me to be married, and he doesn't understand that I want to marry for love. Saul seems awfully serious, though. I don't think we're a *gut* match."

"Well, don't do anything that makes you uncomfortable." He bent his leg and rested his hand on his knee. "Life is too short to be unhappy."

"That's true." She studied his eyes and longed to know what he was thinking. Did he enjoy talking to her as much as she enjoyed talking to him?

"Our lives are similar, aren't they?" He smiled. "We seem to have the same experiences."

Carolyn laughed. "*Ya*, we do."

Except I have a child.

His smile faded slightly just as hers did. "How do you like working in the hotel?"

"I enjoy working there." She leaned on the fence behind her. "I love talking to new people. Sometimes it's nice to get away from the community and just experience the world without being a part of the world."

His expression hardened slightly, and she wondered what he was thinking.

"I like being out in the world, but I'm not planning on leaving the Amish community," Carolyn continued. "I was baptized when I was seventeen because I knew that I belonged here. I have no interest in being *English*."

"That's *gut*." He then stood up and jammed a thumb toward the buggy. "I'd better get home. The horses are waiting to be fed again. *Danki* again for supper. I had a nice time."

"*Gern gschehne*." She waved as he climbed into the buggy.

"I'll see you soon." He guided the horse toward the road.

Carolyn waved again before he disappeared onto the main road. She walked slowly toward the porch while thinking about their conversation. She was surprised how many personal things he had shared with her. Her heart soared with happiness when she found he wasn't dating Lena. Maybe she had a chance with him! She was certain she was falling in love with him, and she couldn't wait to see him again.

She spotted Benjamin coming out of the barn after feeding the horses, donkey, and chickens, and her smile faded again. She'd had the perfect opportunity to tell Joshua the truth about Benjamin, but she'd been a coward.

She knew the truth was the one issue that could cause Joshua to back away, and the longer she waited to tell him, the more damage the truth would cause, especially after Joshua had shared personal feelings with her.

Carolyn smiled as Benjamin approached. "Are you ready to head inside?"

"*Ya*." He moved toward the porch steps, and Carolyn touched his shoulder.

As they headed toward the house, her thoughts turned back to Joshua. She had to find a way to tell him about her son. Tonight she could pray about it and ask God to give her the right words that would convey the truth without causing her to lose her special friendship with Joshua.

*   *   *

Joshua smiled as he guided the horse toward his farm. He'd had a wonderful evening. He'd enjoyed a delicious and satisfying supper, and he'd relished the tasty pies for dessert. He'd also confirmed Benjamin's employment at his farm.

The highlight of the evening, however, was his long discussion with Carolyn. He'd been mesmerized with her during supper, and he had a difficult time keeping his eyes off her. He'd hoped that she would follow him outside to say good night in person.

Once she did come outside, their conversation was easy and time flew by quickly. In fact, he was amazed how easy it was for him to open up to Carolyn and share feelings he'd never said aloud to anyone. When he was with her, he felt compelled to share all the thoughts and feelings he'd kept locked deep inside himself for years. He'd longed to talk to her all evening, but he had to get back home and take care of his horses.

He stared out the windshield while contemplating Carolyn. She seemed to be everything he'd always wanted in a woman. She was intelligent, beautiful, and funny. His feelings for her were becoming stronger every time he saw her. He was certain he was falling in love with her. His emotions were much deeper than anything he'd ever felt for Hannah. This love was real and palpable, and he still had a feeling Carolyn shared similar emotions for him.

As he guided the horse onto the road leading to his farm, he admitted there was one issue weighing on his mind. He was still concerned about her employment at the hotel. He couldn't stop worrying that her experience with the *English* world might cause her to want to leave the community just as Hannah had. When he asked Carolyn about the job, he was hoping she would say that it was temporary and she planned to quit soon. His stomach plummeted when she told him that she liked experiencing the *English* world. He prayed she wouldn't find herself on the same road that Hannah followed. The worry crept into his soul, and he prayed she was solid in her faith and wouldn't even entertain the thought of leaving the church. He couldn't stand the thought of losing her.

The horse pulled the buggy up the driveway leading to his barn, and Joshua climbed out and began to unhitch it. He looked toward his lonely farmhouse and wondered what it would be like to bring Carolyn home as his wife. He smiled when he thought of starting a family with her and growing old with her. It was a far-fetched notion, but he hoped that Carolyn was in God's plan for him.

Maybe, just maybe, Joshua could finally find the happiness his lonely heart craved.

SIXTEEN

Joshua fed the animals and then walked back into his house and sat in an easy chair by the window. Since today was an off Sunday, there wasn't a church service to attend. His thoughts had been stuck on Carolyn since he'd visited her Tuesday evening. He'd hoped she would come and visit him at the farm during the week, but she hadn't. He considered going to visit her in the evenings, but he couldn't find the courage to go over again without an invitation.

Joshua looked toward the stack of ledgers sitting on the coffee table in front of him and considered losing himself in the numbers that ran his farm. He needed something to keep his mind busy and mute the constant thoughts of Carolyn, but he wasn't permitted to do any work on Sunday. He couldn't work on the books or do unnecessary farmwork without committing a sin.

He stood and walked to the window while considering what to do to try to stay busy. His house seemed too big and quiet today. He longed to go visit Carolyn, but he didn't know if she was at church or if it was an off Sunday for her district too.

Instead of spending the day moping, he decided

to go visit his parents. After hitching the horse to the buggy, he headed over to their house, where he found another buggy parked by the barn.

Joshua started up the porch steps and was greeted by his mother, who pushed the door open wide.

"Josh!" She sang his name. "I was hoping you'd come over today. We have visitors. Lena is here with her *schweschder* and parents."

Joshua frowned and stopped climbing the steps. *I should've gone to see if Carolyn was home.*

"What are you waiting for?" *Mamm* beckoned him. "Come in, come in. Lena and her family would love to see you."

Joshua slowly climbed the stairs, his steps bogged down by his growing agitation with his mother's meddling. When he reached the kitchen, he found Lena, her sister, and her parents sitting around the table drinking coffee. Lena met his gaze with a warm smile. He gave her a halfhearted wave.

"Where's *Dat*?" Joshua asked his mother while standing beside her near the back door.

"He had to go out to the stable to check on Molly. She's the mare we're expecting to give birth soon." She'd kept her voice low. Lena's father was sharing a story with his family and Lillian.

"I'm going to go see him." Joshua started out the door and down the porch steps.

"Josh!" His mother ran down the stairs and trailed him. "Where are you going?"

"I told you." He adjusted his hat on his head. "I'm going to see *Dat*."

"But what about Lena?" *Mamm* looked confused. "I invited her and her family over hoping that you would come."

"I'm glad you were finally honest about their visit. I knew you were trying to set this up for me." Joshua's smile was wry. "When are you going to realize that you can't make me interested in someone I am not interested in? We Amish don't believe in arranged marriages, but you're acting as if this behavior is common and acceptable."

His mother stared at him and blinked, but no words escaped her mouth. For once in his life, Joshua had rendered his mother speechless. He made a mental note to write down this day in a book somewhere.

"I'm going to see *Dat*." Joshua turned and stalked toward the stable, where he found his father watching a mare pace in her stall. "*Wie geht's?*"

"Hi, Josh," *Dat* said. "Your *mamm* was hoping you'd come over."

Joshua sighed with a frown. "*Ya*, I know." He reached over a stall and rubbed a nearby horse's neck. "How's Molly doing?"

"She's frustrated." *Dat* fingered his long, graying beard. "I think it may be soon."

"I have one that's close too. I think Daisy may give birth this week." Joshua continued to rub the horse's neck. "When it's Molly's time, you can call me if you need help."

"*Danki*. I'm going to put her in a secluded stall today. The horses like their privacy when they get to this point." *Dat* motioned toward the entrance to the barn. "I think I'll enjoy the privacy and quiet with her. I was tired of sitting at the table and listening to Joe's stories about his hardware store and his wife's bakery. Am I bad because I don't want to sit there and pretend I'm interested?" He chuckled.

"No, you're not bad. I feel the same way." Joshua squatted and leaned against the stall door. "I was hoping to escape the quiet of *mei haus* today, but I wasn't expecting to have to try to make conversation with Lena. *Mamm's* been pushing me to date her, and I'm really not interested."

"We'll hide out here together then."

"Sounds *gut* to me." Joshua grinned at his father.

They discussed horses, their farms, and his father's woodworking projects for the next couple of hours. Joshua then helped his father lead the mare to a secluded stall at the very back of the stable before they started toward the house to see if lunch was ready.

When Joshua stepped out of the stable, he spotted Lena coming toward them. Although he'd been relaxed while he spoke to his father, he felt his body stiffen and anxiety resurface as she approached him.

"Hi, Josh," she said. "I was coming to see where you were."

"I was helping *mei dat* with a mare that's going to give birth soon." He motioned toward the stable.

"Oh." Her eyes widened. "I bet you have a lot of experience with horses that give birth."

"*Ya*, I do. I run a horse farm."

"Did you have a *gut* week?" she asked.

"I did. Did you have a *gut* week?"

"*Ya.* I did a lot of baking. I brought some chocolate chip oatmeal *kichlin*." She pointed toward the house. "You'll have to try one. It's a new recipe I created myself. I like to invent recipes."

"That's interesting." He nodded and wondered what else to say. They stood in awkward silence for what felt like a lifetime, and he began to wonder what Carolyn was doing. Was she thinking of him?

"You should come to the singles gathering tonight," she finally said. "We're going to sing for a couple over in Bird-in-Hand who lost their son recently. He died in an accident. His buggy was hit by a truck that ran a red light."

"Oh. That's *bedauerlich*." He had to think of an excuse not to go. He racked his mind for a believable reason.

"*Ya,* it's really *bedauerlich*." She shook her head. "My heart breaks for his family. It's always hard to lose someone, but we have to remember that God has the perfect plan for all of us." She was silent for a moment and then her expression brightened. "What kind of pies do you like?"

Joshua was stumped by the question. "I like all pies."

"But which one is your most favorite?" She raised her eyebrows in anticipation.

"I can't say I have one favorite."

"You have to have one favorite."

Joshua paused and thought about the dinner he'd enjoyed at Carolyn's house. She'd made a pie, and it was delicious. "Lemon meringue."

"I can make you a lemon meringue pie." Lena wagged her finger for emphasis. "In fact, I don't mean

to be prideful, but *mei mamm* says I make the best pies
in the bakery. Come see me at the bakery one day, and
I'll have a special one waiting for you. Just call before
you come. Did you know that I make most of the pies
at the bakery?"

Lena prattled on about pies and cookies for several
minutes, and Joshua longed for someone to come and
save him. Where was his father when he needed him?

"With all of this food talk, I'm actually getting hungry," he finally interrupted.

"Oh? I am too." She turned toward the house. "I
should go help Barbie serve lunch."

"That's a fantastic idea," he agreed. "Let's go see if
we can convince *mei mamm* that it's time to eat."

Lena continued talking about the bakery as they
made their way to the house. Joshua tuned her out and
thought of Carolyn. He hoped she was thinking about
him, and he also hoped she was having a better day
than he was.

* * *

After lunch, Joshua said good-bye to his parents, Lena,
and her family before heading out to his buggy. He'd
just finished hitching the horse when he spotted Lena
coming toward him.

"Josh," she called. "May I speak to you alone for a
moment?"

He swallowed a groan as he faced her. "Of course.
What can I do for you?"

"I wanted to tell you that I really like you. You're a

nice man." Her smile faded a bit. "I can tell that your *mamm* really wants us to get together."

He leaned against the buggy and grinned. "Is it that obvious?"

She laughed. "Your *mamm* doesn't hold her feelings back."

"No, she doesn't."

"Listen, Josh, I don't want to hurt your feelings, but I was doing some thinking while we were eating lunch. I don't think this can work between us."

"You don't?" He felt his smile brighten.

"Like I said, you're nice, but you're too reserved for me." She shook her head. "And, sadly, I don't think we have anything in common."

"Really?" He bit his lower lip to stop his smile from getting any bigger.

"I hope I'm not hurting your feelings, but I'd like to just be *freinden*. I don't think we should date. Does that sound okay to you?"

He stood up straight. "That sounds perfect to me. *Danki*, Lena."

"I'm so glad you agree." She gave him a little wave. "I'll see you at church."

"Take care." He climbed into the buggy and started for the road. As he guided the horse, he let out a satisfied laugh. His mother's attempts to marry him off had failed, and the tension released from his shoulders. He could stop feeling pressured by his mother to date Lena, and instead he could concentrate on the woman he preferred—Carolyn Lapp.

* * *

Carolyn finished cleaning the rooms on the second floor of the hotel late Monday morning and then went looking for Ruth. She'd been reflecting on her feelings for Joshua since she'd last seen him, and she needed to get some advice on how to handle telling him the truth about Benjamin.

She found Ruth vacuuming a conference room. She waited until the vacuum cleaner stopped before she got Ruth's attention.

"Carolyn." Ruth faced her while coiling the vacuum cleaner cord. "Is it lunchtime already?"

"No." Carolyn began putting the chairs back under the table. "We have an hour yet. I just was hoping to talk to you."

"Oh." Ruth pointed to the chairs. "You don't need to help with the chairs."

"I don't mind helping. Besides, I don't want to set you behind with your work. I finished my rooms early." Carolyn pushed chairs as she spoke. "I wanted to ask you something."

"I'm listening." Ruth moved chairs on the other side of the room.

"I'm falling in love with Joshua Glick." Carolyn shivered as she said the words aloud. "And I'm scared."

Ruth gasped. "Carolyn, that's wonderful."

"No, it's not." Carolyn pushed another chair and shook her head. "I can't fall in love with him because he doesn't know the truth about Ben."

"You haven't told him yet?" Ruth stopped pushing a chair and faced Carolyn. "Why haven't you?"

Carolyn moved the last chair under the table and

then walked over to Ruth. "I'm afraid he'll be upset that I haven't told him the truth."

"*Ya*, he will be." Ruth sat in a chair and then patted the one beside her. "Sit."

Carolyn sank onto the chair beside Ruth and frowned. "He and I had a long talk last Tuesday night. He came over to see *mei bruder* and stayed for supper. We talked outside before he left. It was the perfect opportunity to tell him, but I was a coward. I couldn't do it. I was afraid of ruining the moment." She hid her head in her hands. "He's going to find out eventually, and I'm going to lose him."

"Now wait a minute. You can make this right."

"How?" Carolyn looked up at Ruth.

"By telling him the truth."

Carolyn sighed. "I don't know how to do it. *Mei mamm* said I need to remember I'm worthy of love. She also said God has forgiven me for my mistake, and my community has forgiven me. I didn't have to confess to the church because I had Benjamin before I was baptized. *Mei mamm* says that the baptism washed away my sin."

"Your *mamm* is right, and that's why Josh will understand and forgive you too." Ruth smiled. "But you have to tell him the truth. He needs to know."

"But I've waited too long." Carolyn gestured widely with her hands. "He's opened up to me about his feelings. I've gotten the impression that he doesn't do that often. He's going to be upset when I tell him because I wasn't up front with the truth."

"That's right." Ruth's smile faded. "I've told you already that Josh has been hurt. He was devastated when Hannah left the community because she had rejected him. He proposed to her. He wanted to marry her and help her raise her *kinner.*"

"*Ach*, I had no idea." Carolyn shook her head. "I knew he cared for her, but I didn't know she rejected his proposal. I can't imagine how much that hurt."

"*Ya*, he's been through a lot since he also lost his *bruder.* I'm certain he has a difficult time trusting people. If he's already opened up to you, that means he cares for you. He's going to expect you to be open and honest with him."

"Are you saying it's too late?" Her shoulders tensed at the thought of losing him.

"No." Ruth shook her head. "I'm saying that the longer you wait, the harder it will be to tell him, and the more hurt he'll be. Just explain to him that you wanted to tell him a long time ago, but you were afraid. Explain that you've had people look down on you your whole adult life, and it's a difficult mistake for you to admit. I'm certain he'll understand. He's been through a lot in his life, and he'll understand that you have too. I have faith that he'll forgive you."

Carolyn nodded. "*Danki.*"

"Pray about it." Ruth touched Carolyn's arm. "Remember what the scriptures say in 1 John: 'Dear children, let us not love with words or tongue but with actions and in truth.' You'll show Joshua how much you care for him when you tell him the truth."

"I know you're right, but it's more complicated than that." Carolyn stared down at her apron as she spoke. "Saul has been coming to see me at night."

"He has?"

Carolyn nodded. "He came last night, and we sat on the porch together. He said he wants to continue getting to know me. I feel so stuck because he knows about Ben, but he's still willing to marry me. I know he's only interested in marrying me so that he has a mother for young Emma. But I feel like I should think about marrying him to give Ben a real family."

"Do you love Saul?"

"No."

"Carolyn, look at me."

She looked up at Ruth.

"You know the answer to this," Ruth began. "Ben has a real family. He has you, your parents, and your extended family. You don't need to settle for a loveless marriage just to satisfy some notion you have about what family is. Ben is a *gut bu*. You and your parents have given him enough love to last him a lifetime. You need to find a marriage that makes you *froh*."

"I know, but I don't feel worthy of a marriage based on love." Carolyn sniffed as tears stung her eyes.

"You're worthy, Carolyn. Everyone is worthy of a happy life."

The truth drowned Carolyn. She wanted to be with Joshua, not Saul.

"Now you need to tell Saul you aren't interested in marrying him, and then you need to tell Joshua the truth. You're a strong *maedel*. You've raised your son without worrying about what people thought up until this point. Now you need to trust your instincts and go forward. Follow your heart and pray." Ruth squeezed Carolyn's hand. "Tell me that you're going to do what's right."

"I will." Carolyn's voice was soft and hesitant.

"Say it like you mean it, Carolyn." Ruth smiled. "Come on now. You've never been shy before."

"You're right, Ruth. I'll do the right thing." Carolyn forced a smile despite the worry overtaking her. "*Danki*. I knew you would give me *gut* advice."

Now she needed to find a way to tell Joshua the truth without losing him.

* * *

Ruth studied Carolyn and a question rang through her mind. She'd been thinking of her son constantly, ever since Carolyn mentioned that she'd had a baby when she was sixteen. "Carolyn," she began. "How old is Benjamin?"

Carolyn looked over at her. "He's fifteen."

"And when will he be sixteen?"

"In June." Carolyn moved another chair under the table.

Ruth needed to know more. She couldn't stop the feeling that Aaron could be Benjamin's father. "Carolyn, may I ask you how you met Benjamin's father?"

Carolyn stopped pushing a chair and faced Ruth. "He worked at the market in Philadelphia with me. I was completely blinded by young love, and I didn't think straight when he was around." Carolyn's expression clouded as if she were reliving the memories. "He was so handsome and I felt so blessed that he even noticed me. He was so confident. Looking back, I see how irresponsible and immature I was."

Ruth's memories took her back to when Aaron was a teenager. He also worked at the Philadelphia market with a few of his friends. The coincidence was almost too much for Ruth to bear.

"He told me that he loved me," Carolyn continued. "I was stupid and irresponsible, and I gave in to his constant pressure." She shook her head. "I'm not proud of my mistakes, but I love my son."

"I know you love him, Carolyn. You don't have to apologize to me." Ruth paused and then asked, "Why did your boyfriend leave the community?"

"He told me that he had a terrible argument with his father over his strictness. He couldn't stand the restriction of our culture anymore, and he decided he had to leave. He wanted me to go with him, but I couldn't leave my family. He left before I even knew I was going to have a *boppli*." Carolyn gave Ruth a curious expression. "What do you want to ask me, Ruth?"

Ruth forced a smile. "Nothing, nothing. I was just wondering. Let's finish up and then we can go enjoy our lunch."

They both continued moving the chairs.

While she worked, Ruth contemplated her son, Aaron, and her mind raced with confusion. He had left a note saying he never felt as if he fit into the community and the Amish culture was too restrictive.

Now she couldn't stop wondering if Aaron had been Carolyn's boyfriend.

Could Benjamin Lapp be my grandson?

The thought caused a chill to dance up Ruth's spine. At first the idea seemed preposterous, but then it began to resonate when Carolyn said that she had worked at the market in Philadelphia. There was a chance that Aaron and Carolyn had met and even fallen in love.

Ruth pushed the thoughts away. She couldn't spend her life drawing conclusions about Aaron when she didn't know if they were true. She could only pray that he was healthy and safe.

And someday, maybe someday, she'd have the chance to see him again.

Those thoughts continued to percolate in her mind as they finished straightening the conference room. As they moved to the break room, Ruth sent up a prayer to God, asking him to someday bring her Aaron home to her and heal her broken heart.

SEVENTEEN

As Joshua climbed up his porch steps the following Monday morning, his eyes moved to the over-grown mess of weeds that had once been Hannah's glorious garden. His house had once been a beautiful home surrounded by vegetables and flowers that Hannah and his nieces had cultivated with love and hard work. He longed to transform his house back to the beautiful property it once was.

His thoughts turned to the day Carolyn had begun to clean out the weeds, and he wondered if she would consider taking care of the garden for him. If she agreed, then they not only could have an opportunity to see each other, but they could also share any profits if she wanted to sell vegetables at the market.

Excitement swelled within him as the plan took shape. First he had to talk to her and see if she'd be willing to work in his garden. He knew that she worked at the hotel on Mondays. He'd already planned to go to the hardware store today, and since he needed some bulky supplies, he'd arranged for a driver. He'd ask his driver to stop by the hotel on their way back to the farm.

As he made his way to the large barn, Joshua quickened his steps. He couldn't wait to see Carolyn. He prayed that he'd get to the hotel in time to see her, and if so, that she would also be open to the idea of working on the garden.

* * *

The elevator door opened with a whoosh, and Carolyn pushed her supply cart out onto the second floor. She hummed to herself as she moved to the end of the long hallway to start cleaning one of the rooms. She knocked on the door and yelled, "Housekeeping!" After receiving no answer, she used her master card key to unlock the door and stepped inside the large, fancy room.

Carolyn was gathering up the used towels in the bathroom when she heard someone call her name. She moved to the hallway while holding an armload of damp towels.

"Carolyn! I've been looking for you." Madeleine hurried down the hall toward her. "Stacey sent me to get you. You have a visitor in the lobby."

"A visitor?" Carolyn dropped the towels into the supply cart. "Who is it?"

Madeleine shrugged. "I didn't get his name, but he's Amish."

"An Amish man?" Carolyn's curiosity was piqued. Who would come to visit her at work?

"Go on." Madeleine shooed her toward the elevator. "I just finished up my work, so I'll take over for you."

"Are you certain you don't mind?" Carolyn brushed her hands over her apron.

"I don't mind at all. Take your time."

"Thank you." Carolyn rushed toward the elevator.

When she stepped into the lobby, she spotted a tall, muscular Amish man standing with his back to the reception desk while looking out the front windows. The man turned and faced her, and her heart turned over when she realized it was Joshua. He was clad in a dark blue work shirt, and his eyes somehow seemed a deeper shade of blue. He fingered his straw hat and gave her a tentative smile.

"Josh," she said as she hurried across the lobby to him. She hadn't seen him for almost two weeks, and although she missed him, she was waiting for him to make the first move. Saul had also been absent from her life for the past several days, and her instinct told her to let both men come to her. She was thankful that Joshua had finally reached out, and seeing him in person was a special treat.

"Carolyn." He made a sweeping gesture toward a quiet corner away from the hustle and bustle of the lobby. "May I speak with you for a moment?"

"*Ya,* of course." She followed him over to the corner. Alarm stole over Carolyn as she suddenly wondered if something had happened to Benjamin. "*Was iss letz?*"

"Nothing is wrong." He stood close to her, and, as she might have predicted by now, her pulse increased. "I needed to talk to you, and I was out running errands this morning. I hope it's okay that I came to see you here."

"*Ya,* I have a couple of minutes." Carolyn studied his

expression, which seemed nervous as he continued to absently spin his hat in his hands.

"I came up with an idea this morning. I know you've seen the weeds that have taken over the garden that Hannah used to maintain. I've wanted to clean up my garden, but I don't have the time."

"I understand. You're running a business."

"Exactly. I just don't have time to do it all. I was wondering. If I bought the seeds, would you take care of the garden for me?" His expression was hopeful. "You could keep half the vegetables and sell them if you want."

"Oh." Surprised by the idea, Carolyn was speechless for a moment.

"It would be a partnership," he continued. "And I know you're busy, but you could come over and garden whenever it's convenient for you."

Carolyn turned the idea over in her mind, and excitement filled her. Not only could she use the extra money to give to her parents, but she also was enticed by the opportunity to work on Joshua's farm and spend more time with him.

"I like the idea," she finally said. "I could talk to Amos and Sarah Ann and see if they would let Rosemary help me."

"Fantastic!" Joshua's expression brightened. "If you're certain, then I can pick up seeds today. I'll stop by Amishtown General Store. You just tell me what you'd like me to pick up."

"Oh, I should give you money." She reached for her wallet in her apron pocket.

"No, that's not necessary." He reached out as if to

stop her from retrieving her money. When his hand brushed hers, the heat of his skin sent her senses spinning. "I'll pay for the seeds."

"That's not right," she disagreed while trying to ignore how much she'd enjoyed the brief contact of his skin. "If we're going to split the profits, then I should help pay for the seeds."

"This is my idea, so I should pay. Just let me know what you'd like me to get."

"Since spring is here, why don't you get cucumbers, broccoli, and lettuce?" she suggested.

"I'll do that." He smiled. "*Danki*, Carolyn."

Carolyn glanced over her shoulder and spotted her supervisor, Gregg, standing by the reception desk. "I need to go, but I can come over tomorrow and start on the garden. And I'm going to ask if Amos and Sarah Ann will let me bring my niece, Rosemary, to help."

"I look forward to it." He nodded and then put on his straw hat.

Carolyn said good-bye and then watched him walk outside and climb into a waiting pickup truck. She couldn't wait to start working on the garden—*their* garden.

* * *

Joshua grinned with delight as he filled a basket with seeds. He'd prayed that Carolyn would agree to manage his garden, but he'd been worried she'd say no. Not only had she agreed, but she offered to bring her niece over to help. The garden would be a wonderful success for certain, and he would have the opportunity to enjoy her company more often.

He paid for the seeds and walked toward the exit. As he pulled the door open, he nearly walked into his niece Amanda.

"*Onkel* Josh?" she asked, her pretty face bright with a warm smile.

"Amanda!" he exclaimed. "It's so *gut* to see you. *Wie geht's?*"

They moved to the side to allow other customers to pass by.

"I'm doing great. College is amazing. My classes are tough, but I'm loving it." She pushed her long blonde braid over her shoulder. She wore blue jeans and a long-sleeve pink blouse. Although it was strange to see her in *Englisher* clothes, he still recognized his sweet-natured niece. "How are you?"

"I'm doing fine. The farm is busy. I have a new employee. Huckleberry misses Andrew. You two need to come by to visit sometime." His thoughts turned to Hannah. "How's your *mamm*?"

"She's doing really well." Amanda's smile faded a bit. "But she really misses Lily."

"Lily is still angry?"

Amanda nodded. "*Ya*, she is. I've tried to talk to her, and I've begged her to give *Mamm* a chance. So far it hasn't worked. She refuses to accept *Mamm's* decision to marry Trey and leave the community. She won't come over to visit us. *Mamm* is heartbroken."

Joshua shook his head, and sympathy flooded him. "I'm sorry to hear that. I'm certain she misses the close relationship they had. Please tell Hannah I'm thinking of her."

"Why don't you tell her yourself?" Amanda asked.

"Excuse me?" Joshua was stunned to hear Amanda say something so bold. He wondered if that *English* college had changed his once respectful niece.

"I didn't mean to sound so rude." Amanda pointed toward a car in the parking lot. "I meant to say that *Mamm* is sitting in my car over there. It's the blue Ford. Why don't you go talk to her?"

"Oh." Joshua lifted the bag of seeds and turned toward the small blue sedan. He immediately spotted Hannah sitting in the front passenger seat. For the first time since she'd abandoned the farm, he realized his broken heart was healed and he was ready to be her friend.

"I'm certain she'd love to talk to you." Amanda prodded him with a gentle nudge.

Joshua looked down at his niece. "*Ya*, I think I need to speak with her too."

"Go on." Amanda pointed toward the car. "I need to run in and get a few things for her."

"It was *gut* seeing you, Amanda. Please tell Andrew that Huckleberry and I miss him."

Amanda smiled. "I will."

Joshua crossed the parking lot and approached the car as Hannah climbed out. "Hi, Hannah."

"Joshua." Hannah's expression was tentative. Her prayer covering was missing, her red hair was arranged in a bun, and she was clad in a denim dress. "You look well."

"You do too." He nodded toward the car. "I see Amanda is driving."

"*Ya.*" Hannah smiled. "She's studying biology, and she's driving like an *Englisher.* But she's still my sweet Amanda."

"I'm glad she's doing well." He set his bag on the hood of the car. "How's Andrew?"

"He's fine. He loves school. He's made a lot of new friends." She ran her fingers over the car door. "He talks about the farm a lot."

"I was telling Amanda that they should both come by to see Huckleberry. You should come by too, and bring Trey."

"*Ya?*" She looked surprised.

"*Ya,* of course." It felt strange to invite Hannah and her new husband over, but the invitation was genuine. He was ready to accept her new life and her happiness. "How is your bed-and-breakfast?"

"It's going well. We've stayed busy with visitors. How's the farm?"

"It's busy also. Amanda told me that you haven't been able to fix things with Lily."

Hannah's expression clouded as she shook her head.

"I'm sorry to hear that. I hope that God helps her forgive you."

"Thank you."

He held up the bag. "I'm getting ready to work on the garden."

"Oh yeah?" Her smile was back. "You're going to plant some vegetables?"

"Actually a friend is going to garden for me." His smile deepened.

"That's *gut*." She gestured toward the store. "Amanda is picking up some seeds for me. You know I can't shop in there since I'm shunned."

He nodded. "It was *gut* seeing you. I better get back to the farm."

"Take care, Josh." She reached her arm out toward him, and he shook her hand.

"You too." As Joshua made his way back to the pickup truck, he felt a weight lift from his shoulders. He was thankful the Lord had helped him to finally release his hurt and anger toward Hannah. He was ready to let someone new into his heart, and he couldn't wait to see what the Lord had in store for his future.

* * *

Carolyn found Amos and Sarah Ann walking from the barn toward the house. She'd spent most of the day thinking about Joshua's garden partnership proposal, and she was eager to ask Amos and Sarah Ann if Rosemary could help her. Having Rosemary's assistance would not only be fun but also make the work go faster and mean that she and Joshua would not be inappropriately alone at the farm.

"*Wie geht's*," Carolyn said as she approached them. "I wanted to discuss something with you. I've been thinking about this all day long. How would you feel about Rosemary working on a project with me?"

"What type of project?" Amos asked as he folded his arms over his chest.

Carolyn explained Joshua's idea about the garden. Her brother's expression remained stoic while Sarah Ann nodded with interest.

When Carolyn finished her explanation, Sarah Ann smiled. "I think it's a *gut* idea. Rosemary is eager to make a contribution to the family, and this would be the perfect job."

Amos continued to frown. "I don't know. Doesn't that *bu* that she spoke to at the barn raising work at the Glick farm?"

Carolyn's excitement faded. "*Ya*, he does, but Rosemary will be with me. She will be chaperoned. She will be there to work, not socialize."

Sarah Ann sighed with exasperation. "Amos, we've discussed this. It's time for you to trust Rosemary. She's a smart *maedel*, and Carolyn won't let anything inappropriate happen. Please, Amos. Let Rosemary do this. Let's give her some responsibility and let her prove how mature she is."

"I'll let her go, but there will be rules," Amos said. "Sarah Ann and I will discuss what time she can go and when she needs to be home."

Carolyn smiled. "That sounds perfect. We'll discuss the schedule tomorrow morning before we go." She said good night and then headed into the house. She couldn't wait to get to Joshua's farm and start on their garden.

* * *

Rosemary stood in the doorway to Carolyn's kitchen. "*Aenti* Carolyn, I'm so excited! We're going to work at Joshua's farm."

Carolyn looked over from the sink where she was washing the breakfast dishes and raised her eyebrows. "I knew you'd be excited. I'm happy we can work on the project together."

"Are you ready to go?" Rosemary stepped into the kitchen and wrung her hands together. "I can't wait."

"I'll be ready in a few minutes. I'm just finishing cleaning up after breakfast."

"I can't wait to see Danny." Rosemary picked up a dish towel and began drying dishes. "I miss him. I haven't seen him since youth group Sunday night."

Carolyn frowned. "*Ach*, you have to remember that he's nineteen, and you're only sixteen. You shouldn't get so wrapped up in him. You're too young to date, and he's too old for you. Believe me, I know what the consequences can be."

"I know that, but I can't help how I feel." Rosemary placed a stack of dry dishes in the cabinet. "I want to be his friend."

"Just be careful. You can be his friend, but keep some distance between you and him."

"I'll try." Rosemary's expression brightened. "I have a great idea! We can make lunch and take it over there for everyone. We can eat at the picnic table by the porch."

Carolyn considered the idea. If they ate outside, then no one would say that they were behaving inappropriately. After all, they would have to eat lunch, so they might as well eat together and enjoy the spring weather. "I think that's a nice idea."

"Great! I'll go get lunch together. I'll meet you outside." Rosemary started for the door, but then she suddenly stopped, turned around, and hugged Carolyn. "*Danki* for asking me to work on the garden with you." She then rushed out before Carolyn could respond.

Carolyn laughed and shook her head as her niece disappeared.

* * *

An hour later, Rosemary sat next to Carolyn and held a large picnic basket on her lap as they made their way to Joshua's farm.

"We're going to have so much fun working on the garden," Rosemary said for probably the twentieth time. "I know we're there to work, but it will be fun to see Danny too. I mean, even though we're only friends," she added quickly.

"We'll have a lot of fun."

"Oh, I've been meaning to ask you something." Rosemary angled her body toward Carolyn. "Do you remember when we were at the barn raising a few weeks ago?"

"*Ya*, of course I do."

"I talked to Emma, and she mentioned that her *dat* wanted to date you. She was so excited. She said that if you married her *dat* then she and I would be family. She's so sweet. I would love to be her cousin. So are you going to marry Saul?"

Carolyn swallowed a groan. She didn't want to lie to her niece, but she also didn't want to hurt Emma in the process of telling the truth.

"Did I say something wrong?" Rosemary frowned. "I'm sorry if I did."

"No, no. You haven't said anything wrong. It's just complicated." Carolyn glanced toward Rosemary. "Saul and I are getting to know each other right now. He hasn't asked me to marry him. If he did, I'd need to consider not only how it would affect my life, but also how it would affect Ben's."

"Oh. Right." Rosemary gnawed on her lip. "That makes sense."

"Please don't tell Emma what I said, okay? I don't want to hurt her feelings or make her think I don't like her. I like her a lot, but I need to figure out what's best for Ben and me."

"I understand." Rosemary changed the subject and talked about Daniel for the rest of their ride to the farm.

When they arrived, Benjamin and Daniel came out of the barn and walked over to meet them.

"We brought you lunch." Rosemary held up the basket as she stood in front of Daniel. "We can all eat together at the picnic table later."

"*Danki.* I'll have to leave soon after lunch today. I need to help *mei daadi* finish a project at his *haus.*" Daniel reached for the basket. "Let me carry that for you."

Rosemary turned to Carolyn. "I'm going to start weeding."

"Okay," Carolyn said. "I'll be there in a few minutes. I need to talk to Josh and get the seeds."

Rosemary and Daniel started toward the house.

"How's your day going?" Carolyn asked Benjamin.

"*Gut*." He pointed toward the stable. "Josh has a mare in labor right now. She keeps stopping and starting the contractions. Josh is with her."

"Oh." Carolyn looked toward the stable. "I'm going to let him know we're here and ready to work on the garden."

"Maybe you can convince him to leave the mare for a little while." Benjamin frowned. "I've been telling him to walk away and give her some space, but he's really worried about her. He loves his horses."

The comment warmed Carolyn's heart. "That's sweet."

Benjamin pointed toward the large barn. "I'll go find the rake, watering can, and the other supplies you'll need."

"*Danki*, Ben." Carolyn padded toward the stable and found Joshua in the back, standing by a stall where a horse paced back and forth. "Hi."

Joshua looked over his shoulder and smiled. "Hi. I'm glad you made it."

"I promised you I'd come." She crossed her arms over her apron. "Did you think I wouldn't keep my promise?"

He leaned against the stall and grinned. "No, I knew you'd keep it. Did Rosemary come too?"

"*Ya*, she did. She insisted that we bring lunch for everyone. She couldn't wait to get here." Carolyn looked at the mare to avoid the way his smile caused her pulse to race. "It looks like she's almost ready to have her *boppli*."

"I think it's going to be soon." He gestured toward her. "You can see Daisy's milk is ready. That's one of the signs that it's almost time."

Carolyn watched the horse pace. "She looks uncomfortable. Poor thing."

"I hope it's over for her today." He turned toward her. "So, you say you brought lunch?"

"*Ya*, but it was Rosemary's idea."

"Sure it was. You just couldn't wait to see me again," he teased.

"Why would I want to see you?" she countered with a smile.

"I was just asking myself the same question." His expression became tender, and he suddenly reached down and pushed back a wisp of her hair that had fallen loose from beneath her prayer covering.

The gentle touch of his fingertips caught her off guard. Her mouth dried, and she had to work against her raging emotions to regain her composure.

"I was wondering where the seeds were," she said, her words coming out in a rush. "Ben went to the barn to get the tools we'll need to start weeding and planting."

"Oh, right. You need the seeds." Joshua started for the door. "I put them in the kitchen. I'll run in and get them for you."

Carolyn followed Joshua to the house and waited on the porch. Thoughts of his tender touch continued to assault her mind while she stared at the back door. He soon returned and held out the bag of seed packets to her. She gave him a quick nod, took the bag of seeds, and then moved to the garden, where Rosemary was already crouched and filling a bucket with weeds.

Carolyn tried to engross herself in the garden, but her mind kept slipping back to the memory of Joshua's fingers on her cheek. The intimacy of his gesture confused her. Did he want to be more than friends? If so, then what would happen when he found out the truth about Benjamin?

"Are you all right, *Aenti*?" Rosemary asked while she pulled another handful of bright green weeds.

"*Ya*," Carolyn said as she crouched beside her. "It's a *schee* day, *ya*?"

"*Ya*, it is."

By noon, Carolyn's back was sore, and her stomach was growling. She and Rosemary served lunch to the men at the picnic table. After lunch, Daniel left to help his grandfather with a project, Benjamin and Joshua returned to the stables, and Carolyn and Rosemary continued working in the garden for the remainder of the afternoon.

"It looks like it might rain." Carolyn brushed the back of her hand over her chin as she looked up at the large gray clouds clogging the sky. "I wanted to get those seeds planted before we left."

"I wonder what time it is." Rosemary angled her face toward the back porch. "I'll run into the kitchen and see."

Carolyn grabbed another handful of weeds and marveled at how much they'd accomplished in one day. The garden was almost ready to be tilled and then seeded.

"*Aenti*." Rosemary rushed back onto the porch. "It's after four."

"*Ach*, you'd better go." Carolyn stood. "It's almost time to make supper. Your *dat* will be upset if you're not home by five. He made it clear that you had to be home on time or you couldn't help me with the garden."

"Fine." Rosemary frowned. "I'll pick up the picnic basket." She disappeared into the house. When Rosemary returned, she and Carolyn headed out to the buggy, and the men were nowhere in sight.

"I wonder where Ben and Josh went," Rosemary said as she placed the basket in the buggy.

"They might be with Daisy." Carolyn gestured for Rosemary to follow her to the stable. They found Benjamin and Joshua standing by the stall and watching the horse.

"It's getting late." Carolyn sidled up to Joshua. "Rosemary needs to get home, but I want to stay and finish the garden. I'd like to get it seeded before the storm hits." She turned to Benjamin. "Rosemary needs to be home by five."

"It's time for you to go too, Ben." Joshua turned toward Benjamin. "You can go hitch your horse."

"Would you please take Rosemary home?" Carolyn asked Benjamin. "I'll head home after I finish planting."

"Okay." He disappeared from the barn, leaving Carolyn and Joshua there alone.

"I think she's getting ready," Joshua said, nodding toward the horse. "She seems really uncomfortable. I hope it's her time now. She's been suffering for a while now."

"I hope it's soon for her too." Carolyn grimaced while watching the horse move back and forth. "I feel so bad for her."

Joshua faced her. "I'm glad you and Rosemary started on the garden. *Danki* for lunch."

"*Gern gschehne.*" Carolyn nodded.

His expression softened. "Even though it was really Rosemary's idea, not yours." He winked at her.

Carolyn laughed. "*Ya*, it was. I didn't want to come at all."

"Now you tell me the truth." Joshua shook his head. "You're something else, Carolyn Lapp."

Carolyn looked into his blue eyes and again remembered the tenderness of his touch earlier in the day. She knew at that moment that she loved him, and she prayed he'd someday return that love despite her past.

She pulled herself back to reality. "I better get back to the garden. I'm certain that storm will be here soon." She jammed a thumb toward the door.

"I'm going to stay here with Daisy. I'm worried about her." Joshua leaned on the stall door. "Be sure to say good-bye before you leave."

Carolyn stepped out of the barn and waved to Rosemary as she and Benjamin rode in the buggy toward the road. She then returned to the garden and finished up the weeding. She tilled the dirt and then began to plant the cucumbers, broccoli, and lettuce seeds. She was finishing up when the wind picked up and the sun began to set.

"Carolyn!" Joshua's voice bellowed from the stable. "Carolyn, I need help!"

"Okay!" Carolyn's heart thudded in her chest as she jogged toward the stable. "*Was iss letz?*"

"Daisy is struggling," Joshua yelled toward her, his face full of fear. "Something is wrong. I need some help."

"What can I do?" She moved toward him, wringing her hands.

"A vet named Cameron Wood lives in the blue house directly across the street." He pointed toward the road. "Would you please go get him? I think Daisy and her foal are in trouble!"

"*Ya*, I'll go. You stay with her." Carolyn ran down the rock driveway and crossed the street. When she reached the blue house, she found the driveway empty and a note stuck to the front door. She climbed the steps and read the note, which said, "Out of town. Be back Sunday night." The date for his return was listed, and it was nearly a week away.

"*Ach*, no." Panic seized Carolyn as she rushed back to Joshua's farm.

She found Joshua in the stable, watching the horse pace.

"Cameron isn't home." Her words came in short bursts as she worked to get her breath back. "A note on his door said he'll be gone until Sunday."

"I was afraid of that. He'd mentioned to me that he planned to visit some family out in Michigan." Joshua shook his head. "*Danki* for checking. She was just straining and then it stopped again. I'm worried that the foal is in trouble." He blew out a sigh. "I would call *mei dat*, but he went to his cousin's *haus* in western Pennsylvania today and won't be home until late tonight."

"I'll stay." Carolyn walked toward him.

"No." Joshua shook his head. "I can't ask you to do that."

"I can help."

"You can?" He looked surprised.

"*Ya*, I helped *mei daadi* deliver a foal once. The horse was in trouble, just like Daisy, and I was the only one home. I can help you."

Joshua walked over to her and touched her arm. "You don't have to do this."

"But I want to help." She looked up at him. "I *want* to."

"This could go on well into the night. Horses can stop the contractions at any time and then start again."

"I know. I've been through this before. I'll stay."

Joshua paused and then nodded. "All right. You can stay, but I will take you home. I don't want you driving yourself home in the dark."

"That's fine." Carolyn said a silent prayer for Daisy.

* * *

Rosemary held the picnic basket on her lap while Benjamin guided the horse down the road. She and Benjamin talked about their day as they made their way toward the dairy farm. When they arrived, she helped Benjamin unhitch and guide the horse into the stall before stowing the buggy.

Rosemary headed out of the barn with her cousin and found her father waiting for her with a frown creasing his face. She prayed that his anger wasn't directed at her. To try to brighten his mood, she forced a smile as she approached him. "Hi, *Dat*."

Dat looked at Benjamin. "You need to go into your *haus*. I want to talk to Rosemary alone."

"Okay. Bye, Ro." Benjamin gave Rosemary a sympathetic expression before rushing toward his house.

"What did you want to talk about, *Dat*?" Worry gripped Rosemary as she looked up at her father. She felt like a small child facing a giant as he glared down at her. "I'm on time, right?"

"You're almost thirty minutes late." He shook his head. "You were supposed to be home by five."

"I'm sorry. It won't happen again. We were trying to get the garden seeded before the rain came, and we lost track of time."

"Don't let it happen again."

"I won't," she promised.

"Where's Carolyn?"

"She was going to finish planting before the rain comes. She said she'd be home as soon as she was finished."

Her father nodded. "Go help your *mamm* with supper."

"*Ya, Dat*." As Rosemary made her way to the house, she felt a cold drop of rain sprinkle her nose. She hoped her aunt would have a safe trip home despite the storm.

EIGHTEEN

Carolyn stood beside Joshua as they studied Daisy and rain pounded the stable roof. The horse lay down on her side, rolled over, and then stood up. Joshua explained the horse was trying to make the birth happen. For more than an hour, they stood and watched the horse struggle while the rain beat a steady cadence in the background.

Carolyn glanced toward the barn door and realized it was getting dark. She lit three battery-powered lanterns and hung them on hooks around the stall. Joshua left the stable for a moment and returned with a pile of blankets and a box of surgical gloves. She could tell he was consumed with worry about Daisy.

"Tell me about your childhood on your *dat's* farm, Josh," she said in an effort to help him relax. She knew they could be there for hours yet. "My brother did a lot of hunting and fishing with our *dat* and *daadi*. Was it like that for you and Gideon too?"

Josh didn't take his eyes off Daisy as he answered. "*Ya*, we did a lot of hunting and fishing."

"And were you any good at it?" she teased. This time he looked at her and grinned.

"Was I good at it? Let me tell you about the time I beat all the men in my family in a fishing contest."

Her effort to distract him worked. They both shared stories from their childhood, but Carolyn was careful to avoid her teen years. Even if she found the courage to finally tell Josh about Ben, this was not the time or place.

When Daisy began to snort and seemed to be straining, Carolyn was surprised to see on the clock in the stable that two hours had gone by. Her heart thumped in her chest as she watched Joshua approach Daisy.

"It's okay, girl," Joshua whispered to the horse. "Everything will be all right. Just relax. It will all be okay. I promise you, girl." He rubbed her neck as he murmured encouragement to her.

Carolyn was overwhelmed with admiration for Joshua as she watched his gentle hand move over the horse while he mumbled sweet words into her ear. It was clear Daisy trusted him. The scene was so heart-warming that it caused tears to sting Carolyn's eyes.

As another hour passed, Carolyn crossed her arms around her middle and wondered how she could help. She felt useless, but she knew she had to stay in case Joshua needed her.

While she watched Joshua soothe the horse, Carolyn wondered how her family was at home. She prayed Rosemary was able to make it home before five. Carolyn silently berated herself for not getting Rosemary home sooner. She should've watched the clock instead of worrying about planting the garden before the rain came.

Then Carolyn noticed the foal was showing. "Joshua," she said, pointing. "Look!"

"It's time," Joshua said. He stood by Carolyn for a

few minutes and then his eyes widened. "Oh no." He moved toward Daisy. "It's red bagging."

"What do you mean?" Carolyn asked as her heart raced with worry. "What's wrong?"

"The placenta detached." He looked closer. "And the foal is backward. This isn't how it's supposed to happen. This could be bad. Really bad."

Carolyn motioned toward the door. "What should we do?"

He rolled up his sleeves. "I'm going to have to help her. I have to turn the foal the right way or Daisy could be injured." He washed his hands and arms at a nearby sink and then pulled on a pair of the surgical gloves. He slathered lubricant from a tube onto the gloves and then rushed back into Daisy's stall.

Carolyn held her breath as Joshua reached into the mare and turned the foal.

"Get the blanket ready," Joshua said.

"Okay." Carolyn stepped closer and held up a blanket. She held her breath again and prayed for the foal and Daisy.

Joshua assisted Daisy with the birth, and when the sack didn't open on its own, Joshua had to open it. The foal lay motionless.

"Go ahead and cover it," Joshua said, his eyes fixed on the foal.

As she did, Carolyn wiped away some of the blood. The creature still remained motionless. Her blood ran cold and worry filled her. *No, no. It can't be!*

"Josh?" She looked up into his concerned eyes. "Something isn't right. Shouldn't the foal be moving?"

Joshua lifted the foal into his arms. "I'm going to have to do CPR." He covered the horse's nose and mouth with his and then blew three times.

Carolyn silently prayed the foal would make it while she held the blanket against its tiny body. *Please, God, breathe life into this* boppli. *Please, God. Place your healing hand on this poor little creature.*

"Please," Joshua whispered, his voice shaky and his eyes wide. "Please live." He tried CPR once more.

Suddenly, the foal jumped up and wobbled.

"Hallelujah!" Carolyn clapped her hands together as Josh hooted, quickly removed the gloves, and wiped his hands on a towel.

Then he pulled Carolyn into his arms. She lost herself in the warmth of his hug. She felt as if she belonged in his strong, muscular arms. His body was warm, and she could feel his heart beating close to hers.

"It's a miracle," he whispered into her ear, his voice sending electric pulses through her body. "That's what we'll name him!" He looked into her eyes. "Miracle." His soft voice mixed with his body heat sent electric throbs dancing up her spine.

"That's a great name." Her voice was soft and full of her overwhelming emotion.

Joshua suddenly jumped up, and taking her hand into his, he pulled her to her feet.

"Watch." Joshua rested his hand on her shoulder as Miracle made his way over to Daisy and began to suckle. "Isn't that a miracle?"

Carolyn nodded. "*Ya*, it is." Her heart swelled with renewed love and admiration as she watched Joshua study the horses with love in his eyes. She marveled at how caring and gentle he was with his horses. He treated the animals as if they were his own children.

As they silently watched Miracle suckle from Daisy, Carolyn considered the beauty of God's creation. She was thankful she could help Joshua and witness the amazing beginning of new life.

"It stopped raining," Carolyn said as she glanced toward the stable doors. She shivered, and Joshua turned toward her.

"You're cold." He picked up a blanket from the pile and hung it over her shoulders like a shawl. He leaned down close to her, and Carolyn held her breath. She braced herself for a kiss, but he quickly stood up straight.

His eyes scanned her, and he grimaced. "You're a mess. I shouldn't have hugged you."

"It's okay." She glanced down at her soiled apron. "That's what an assistant is supposed to do, right? I'm supposed to get dirty."

He laughed as he examined his stained shirt. "And I'm a mess too."

"Aren't we a pair?" Carolyn glanced toward Miracle and Daisy and then noticed the mess on the ground. She motioned toward the hay. "I'll help you clean this up."

"Okay." He nodded. "But after we're done, I'll change and then take you home. It's late, and I can feel the chill in the air getting colder. I don't want you to wind up sick because of this."

Carolyn grabbed some rags and they cleaned up

together before heading into the house. She washed her hands and wiped off her apron at the kitchen sink while Joshua disappeared toward the back of the house. She scanned the kitchen and then stepped into the doorway separating it from the family room. Her thoughts wandered as she took in the sofa, coffee table, chairs, and grandfather clock. She wondered what it would be like to live there as Joshua's wife. The idea sent her insides flipping with excitement.

Carolyn thought back to the hug he'd given her in the barn. The feeling of his arms around her had left her breathless. His body was warm and his arms were muscular. His sweet voice in her ear nearly made her dizzy. She was falling deeper and deeper in love with him, and she prayed their friendship would continue to blossom.

Joshua appeared in the doorway. "Are you ready?"

"*Ya.*" She stood up straight and smoothed her hands over her damp apron. "Is it a little cleaner?"

He grinned and shook his head. "Not really. I'm sorry about the mess."

"It's okay. That's what happens when babies are born."

He raised his eyebrows. "I can say I've only witnessed horse births."

Her cheeks heated, and she turned toward the kitchen. "We'd better go. It's nearly eleven."

"Uh-oh." Joshua headed toward the back door and then held it open for her. "I hope your *dat* isn't upset with me."

"I'm sure he'll understand when I explain what happened." Carolyn clasped her hands together and hoped she was right that her father and, more importantly, her brother would understand why she'd been out so late.

* * *

Joshua quickly hitched the horse to the buggy while Carolyn talked about how beautiful the experience of watching Miracle's birth had been. He guided the horse down the driveway. As he steered onto the main road he passed another buggy and waved.

While Carolyn talked, he glanced over at her and smiled. She was even more strikingly beautiful in the low glow of the streetlights. He was captivated not only by her beauty but by her strength and helpfulness when the foal was born. He'd never met a woman who was so comfortable around nature. She didn't shy away or say the process was revolting. Instead, she stood beside him and helped him when he asked.

Joshua had been so overwhelmed when Miracle responded to the CPR that he had lost himself in the moment and hugged her. Holding her close was like paradise. He'd never experienced such an emotional rush, and he hoped it would last forever. He'd felt her respond to the touch and move closer while holding on to him. Although he knew it was inappropriate for him to touch her, he didn't want to let go. He caught himself before he almost kissed her. He'd been close to giving in to temptation, but he didn't want to ruin his chances with her by being too forward.

He was captivated by her as she talked, occasionally responding to her questions about the horses. He longed to remember every detail of her. He attempted to memorize her voice, her dark chocolate eyes, and her beautiful round face. He felt himself falling deeply in love with her. His thoughts drifted as he realized he wanted to spend all night talking to her and learning more about her. He wanted to know everything about her, and he wanted to make her his.

"Joshua?" Her voice broke through his trance as he guided the horse up the rock driveway toward her house. "Are you listening to me?"

"*Ya.*" He gave her a sideways glance. "You were talking about Miracle and how beautiful he is."

She laughed. "No, I wasn't. I was asking you how many mares you've foaled before. I knew you weren't listening to me for the last few minutes. You're in your own little world." She swatted at his arm, and he was thankful that she felt comfortable enough to tease him.

He grinned at her. "I heard you. I was just testing you to see if you remembered what you said."

"That doesn't even make sense." She sighed. "You're not very *gut* at fibbing."

"That's a *gut* thing, right? You'll always know you can catch me in a fib. So If I tell you I was working in the barn, and I really went fishing, you'll know the truth just by looking at me." He raised his eyebrows, and she shook her head while gracing him with another beautiful smile.

She tilted her head. "Does that mean you're not going to answer my question?"

"What question?"

Carolyn blew out another frustrated sigh. "I asked you how many mares you've foaled before."

"Oh." He considered her question. "Honestly, I'm not certain how many horses I've foaled because I've helped *mei dat* with a few also. I'd say probably two dozen or so."

"Wow. That's a lot."

"*Ya*. It is." Joshua stopped the buggy near her brother's barn and then turned to face her. "I guess it's time to say *gut nacht*." Sadness consumed him as he spoke the words. He didn't want the evening to end even though he knew it had to. He felt like a teenager again, and the realization astounded him.

"*Ya*," she said with his disappointment reflected in her eyes. Was she just as disappointed as he was that their evening together was over?

Joshua climbed out of the buggy and met her in front of the horse. "*Danki* for your help tonight. You were a *wunderbaar* assistant." He touched her hand. "*Gut nacht*."

"*Gut nacht*." She gazed up at him, and for the second time tonight, he was overpowered by the urge to kiss her. He had to get out of there before he gave in to that urge and crossed a line that could cause her to push him away. He had to take this slow despite his longing to ask her to marry him.

Marry?

The word coursed through him and it felt right. The idea of marrying Carolyn Lapp felt right.

"I hope to see you soon," Carolyn said.

"You will," Joshua promised before heading to the

buggy. He waved as he guided the horse back down her driveway. He spent the ride home smiling and thanking God for leading him to Carolyn Lapp.

. . .

Carolyn waved as Joshua's buggy disappeared into the darkness of her driveway. She sighed and hugged her middle while contemplating her wonderful evening with him.

"Carolyn!" Her brother's voice bellowed from the porch behind her.

She gasped as she spun to face the house. "Amos?" She made her way to the porch and found his silhouette sitting there. She stepped into the light glowing from two lanterns. Amos had been waiting for her. "Why are you still up?"

"Rosemary was worried about you. She said you were going to be home shortly after she arrived." Amos's stare hardened. "She said you wanted to finish planting before the rain. It seems it would be difficult to plant in the dark."

"It's not how it looks," Carolyn insisted as she climbed the porch steps. "Josh had a mare that was having trouble giving birth. The veterinarian who lives across the street from him was out of town, and Joshua needed help. I only stayed because Daniel and Benjamin had already left when the mare took a turn for the worse. I offered to help him because I once helped *Daadi* with a foal when you and *Dat* were gone. That's it. There was nothing inappropriate going on between us."

"You were alone with a man, Carolyn. You're both unmarried. It looks bad no matter how many excuses you list." Amos shook his head. "This isn't *gut* at all. Do you know how this makes *Mamm* and *Dat* look? They've already had to defend you once. How will they feel if they have to make excuses for you again?"

Carolyn's annoyance boiled into anger. "I never asked anyone to make excuses for me. I made a mistake, one mistake, and I faced raising Benjamin alone head-on, without his father to help me." She shook a finger at her brother. "And everyone forgave me except for you. You've never let me forget it. In fact, you've reminded me about the mistake every moment you've had a chance to throw it in my face."

Amos glared at her.

"I'm going to bed now. *Gut nacht.*" She started to open the front door.

"Wait." Amos stood. "I'm not done talking to you."

She faced him, hoping to finally get an apology from him after fifteen years of listening to his criticism.

"You do realize that you could ruin your chances with Saul if you're not careful. He came to visit you tonight." He gestured to where Saul had apparently been sitting. "When I went out to check on the animals, I found him waiting on the porch for you. He asked where you were, and I told him you were at Joshua Glick's farm."

"*Danki* for telling him the truth." She pushed the door open. "I've done nothing wrong. I was helping Josh with his mare."

"You have feelings for Joshua, don't you?"

She nodded. "I do, but Saul is a *gut* man too."

"Does Joshua know about Benjamin?"

"I'm going to tell him." Carolyn's voice was hesitant.

"You need to tell him the truth." He stood and started toward the porch steps.

"I will in my own time. It's my business when I tell him." She hoped her voice was confident this time, despite her frayed nerves.

As she watched Amos walk to his house, Carolyn leaned against the door frame. She was emotionally and physically exhausted after helping with the foal, hugging Joshua, and then coming home to her judgmental brother and his accusations. Her mind was swimming with excitement for Joshua and agitation toward Amos. She needed to rest and sort through all the confusing feelings. She found herself torn by her love for Joshua and the practicality and kindness Saul could offer her. With which man did she belong?

Despite all the confusion, Carolyn knew one thing for certain—she was falling head over heels in love with Joshua Glick, and she prayed he felt the same way about her.

* * *

Joshua was checking on Daisy and Miracle the following afternoon when his mother marched into the stable.

Mamm slammed her hands on her wide hips and glared at him. "What's this I hear about Carolyn Lapp staying here all night with you?"

"Hi, *Mamm. Wie geht's?*" He leaned against the stall door and deliberately ignored her question. Nothing was going to ruin his good mood. He was still flying high after his evening with Carolyn.

"Don't get sarcastic with me, Joshua!" She eyed him with discontentment. "I heard from neighbors that you took Carolyn home very late last night. Apparently she was over here with you alone. What happened?"

Her accusatory tone caused resentment to heat up inside him despite his determination to hold on to his good mood. "Do you see that *schee* foal?" He pointed toward Miracle.

"*Ya.*" She shrugged. "I've seen many *schee* foals in my lifetime. You're avoiding my question, Joshua, and I'm getting impatient. I want to know what happened."

"I'm telling you what happened. You need to be quiet and listen for once."

She flinched.

"That foal was in trouble last night while Daisy was trying to give birth. Cameron Wood, the veterinarian who lives across the road, wasn't home, and Danny and Ben had already gone home. Carolyn was here working on my garden—at my request." He gestured toward Daisy as Miracle suckled. "I had no help, and Carolyn was gracious enough to stay and help me with Daisy."

"Do I look stupid?" *Mamm* looked unconvinced. "You've helped many mares foal over the years. Why would you need that *maedel* to help you?"

Joshua took a step toward her. "*Mamm*, I had to turn Miracle, and then he wasn't breathing when he was born. I had to do CPR. I needed help. Stop assuming the worst about Carolyn Lapp. She means a lot to me."

His mother gasped. "You have no right to talk to me that way, Joshua."

"And you have no right to make accusations about Carolyn. She was a wonderful help to me. Nothing inappropriate happened here last night. We both witnessed a birth. She helped me clean up, and then I took her home. That's all that happened, and I was thankful she was here."

Mamm lifted her chin and studied him. "You need to be careful about perception. People get the wrong idea sometimes."

"I can't stop what people say or what they think. I can only tell you the truth." He turned back toward the horses.

"I guess you're interested in this Carolyn Lapp then." Her voice brimmed with disappointment.

He looked back over his shoulder at her. "*Ya*, I am."

"Have you told her that you care about her?"

"Not yet, but I think she knows." He studied her expression. "Why are you asking me about her?"

"I know Lena cares for you." Her expression became hopeful. "You know she's waiting for you, right? She would make a much better wife for you."

"Actually, that's not true." He sighed and ran his hand down his face. "*Mamm*, I've told you more than once that I'm not interested in Lena. I don't know how else I can make you understand this."

"I understand, but Lena is going to be crushed."

"No, she's not. Lena told me that she's not interested in dating me." Joshua shook his head. "She already said she only wants to be friends."

"She did?" His mother looked stunned.

"I'm surprised she didn't tell you that. She's probably dating someone else."

"Well, I'm surprised to hear this," *Mamm* said, obviously struggling to take in this new information. After a moment she said, "I'm going back into the house to start supper for you."

"*Mamm*, you don't need to make me supper. I can fend for myself."

"No, no." She smiled at him. "I don't mind."

Mamm hurried out of the stable, and he stared after her, pondering why her mood had suddenly brightened. He shrugged and then looked back at the mare and foal while remembering the previous evening. He smiled as he thought of the hug and almost kiss he'd shared with Carolyn. He couldn't wait to see her again.

* * *

Barbie headed toward the house. Although she'd tried to act as if she was fine, she was fuming on the inside. She'd hoped the gossip wasn't true when her neighbor told her that she'd seen Joshua taking Carolyn home late last night. Barbie believed her son when he said nothing inappropriate happened, but she knew the gossip would probably spread throughout the community. She needed to find a way to convince Joshua that Carolyn wasn't the right woman for him. She wasn't certain what that would take, but she believed she still had a chance. After all, Joshua and Carolyn weren't married yet!

She climbed the porch steps while trying to think of a plan. She would find a way to keep them apart. She was determined to get a more compliant daughter-in-law this time. Somehow she would make that happen.

NINETEEN

Carolyn smiled as she worked in her garden at home on a Thursday morning. The warm April sun warmed the back of her neck and the colorful flowers seemed to smile back at her.

For the past two weeks, in keeping with the Amish dating tradition for older singles, Joshua had come to visit her multiple times in the evening after her parents were asleep. He had also come for supper and stayed to play games with her parents, Benjamin, and her. And she'd spent time over at his farm tending to the garden with Rosemary's assistance. The vegetables were starting to sprout, just like their relationship.

Her family approved of him, and even though he hadn't officially asked her, it seemed as if he wanted to date her. She was so happy that she found herself humming and smiling constantly. She had never been so happy. She was so thankful she'd found someone who shared similar hopes and dreams. Joshua seemed perfect. He was funny and sweet, and most importantly, he was kind to Benjamin. He was the man she'd been praying she'd meet her whole adult life.

Yet one problem remained—she hadn't yet confessed

to him that Benjamin was her son. She needed to tell
him soon, but it never seemed like the appropriate time.

Her smile disappeared as she admitted her excuse
wasn't the truth. She'd had plenty of opportunities to
tell Joshua about Benjamin, but she was terrified the
revelation would scare him away and she'd be back to
where she started—alone. He hadn't even clearly indicated he thought she was Benjamin's aunt so that it
would only be right to correct him.

She felt like a coward when she realized she'd been
almost hoping her being Ben's mother would come up
if, in Joshua's presence, Benjamin called her *Mamm* or
her parents referred to her as his mother. With other
people around, he'd be forced to take it in calmly and
think about how much Ben meant to her. Hopefully he
would be more likely to forgive her for waiting so long to
tell him with her family supporting her and less inclined
to immediately dismiss their growing relationship. But
her family seemed to be waiting for her to do the right
thing—tell him herself. And telling him herself was the
right thing. It was what Joshua deserved.

Carolyn pulled another weed while she contemplated
the problem. She promised herself that she would tell
him as soon as she could. She'd instructed Benjamin
to ask Joshua to follow him home and stay for supper
tonight.

Tonight would be the night when she opened up
and told Joshua the truth about her childhood and the
truth about her son. She planned to tell him after supper. She'd get him alone and then she'd break the news.
She held on to her faith that Joshua would understand

and forgive her just like her mother had. Surely his love was strong enough to see past her faults.

While she finished up her weeding, she sent up a special prayer to God, asking him to guide her words when she confessed the truth, and she prayed for the strength to find the right opportunity tonight.

* * *

Carolyn sat across from Joshua while they ate roast beef, potatoes, and carrots. She laughed while he and her father traded stories about funny farm mishaps.

She couldn't stop thinking how perfectly Joshua fit into her family. She dreamed of marrying Joshua and living on the farm with him and Benjamin. They would invite her parents over for supper and also come back to visit her parents while they continued to live in the *daadi haus* on her brother's farm. Life would be perfect, especially if they were blessed with more children.

Carolyn allowed that fantasy to play through her mind while they ate chocolate cake and later played Scrabble with Benjamin. The evening was perfect, and she couldn't keep herself from smiling.

After the second round of Scrabble, Carolyn put the game away and then walked Joshua to the door. "I had a nice evening."

"I did too." He took her hand in his, and her heart turned over in her chest. "Would you like to take a walk with me?"

"*Ya.*" She grabbed her cloak while he pulled on his hat.

They walked out toward the barn, and he continued to hold her hand. She looked up at the bright stars twinkling in the clear sky.

"It's a *schee* night," she said.

"*Ya*, it is." He stopped by a bench near the barn. "Want to sit for a minute?"

"That would be nice." She sank onto the bench beside him.

He looked up at the sky. "Did I ever tell you about Hannah?"

"No." She shook her head and looked down at their hands, fingers still intertwined. "You haven't."

"I saw her at a singing when we were teenagers," he began. "Well, we grew up together, but I didn't really notice her until we were older. I thought I saw her first, but *mei bruder* was the one who asked her to date him before I had a chance."

He kept his eyes focused on the sky, and Carolyn assumed it was difficult for him to open up to her. She studied his chiseled profile and admired how attractive he was.

"I loved her," he continued. "At least, I thought I did, but I wasn't angry when she and Gideon fell in love with each other. I wasn't jealous when they were married or when they had their three *kinner*." He turned toward her, and she spotted sadness in his powder blue eyes. "I was heartbroken when Gideon died. I felt like someone had punched a hole in my heart."

"I'm so sorry," Carolyn whispered as tears threatened her vision.

"I thought I would never recover. He was my best

friend all my life, and then he was gone." Joshua's voice was thick with emotion. "It was like everything changed in only a few hours. I was running a business by myself. Hannah still owned his half, but she could only take care of the books. She couldn't actually help me with the horses and all the chores he used to do."

She nodded.

"And then I thought that maybe I could finally have a chance with Hannah. I still loved her, and I loved her *kinner* as if they were my own. I thought we could be a family." He turned back toward the house. "But that was a silly idea. Hannah never loved me, and then she met that *Englisher* at the hotel and fell in love with him. When she moved out of the *haus*, I lost her and my niece and nephew. My other niece, Lillian, lives with my parents now. She's the teacher at the school near their *haus*. I see Lily all the time, but I rarely see Amanda or Andrew now that they're *English*."

"That has to be so difficult," Carolyn said while marveling at how much he was sharing with her. She felt as if he were opening his soul and letting her in.

"It is." He gave her hand a gentle squeeze. "My nephew, Andrew, used to work with me on the farm, and he said he wanted to be my partner someday just like his *dat* was. Now he lives with Hannah and her new husband. I see him when he visits my *mamm's haus*, but he rarely comes to the farm."

He stared at their hands and was silent for a moment. "I was heartbroken when Hannah left. Until I met you."

Joshua looked up at her, and the intensity in his eyes caused her pulse to race. "You changed everything,

Carolyn. You made my heart beat again. You gave me hope. You brought me back to life." He ran his thumb down her cheekbone, and she couldn't breathe for a moment. "You're the reason I can smile again. *Danki*, Carolyn, for teaching me how to smile again."

"*Gern gschehne*," she whispered with emotion choking back her words. She knew she had to tell him the truth now. This was the perfect time. Yet she hesitated as the words escaped her. She didn't know how to confess to him that she was a mother.

Carolyn knew she had to just say it. She had to tell him that Benjamin was her son. It was now or never. She opened her mouth to speak just as her brother walked toward the barn.

"Carolyn?" Amos asked.

"Amos." Carolyn let go of Joshua's hand and jumped up to her feet as worry coursed through her. She'd been caught with Joshua again. She was certain Amos was going to tell her father they'd been holding hands. "Josh and I were talking. He came for supper and then stayed to play a few games."

"Oh." Amos rubbed his long beard.

"You have a few beautiful horses on your farm," Joshua said. "I was admiring them the last time I was here."

"*Danki*. I've heard you have some *schee* horses as well," Amos said. "Benjamin likes to talk about your farm all the time."

"*Danki*." Joshua crossed his arms over his wide chest.

The men fell into an easy conversation about horses

while Carolyn stood beside them. She hoped this meant Amos would accept Joshua and not criticize her for sitting alone with him.

Amos and Joshua talked for several minutes before her brother started toward the barn.

"Well, it was *gut* talking to you," Amos said. "*Gut nacht*."

"*Gut nacht*." Joshua waved toward him. He turned back to Carolyn and studied her. "You look nervous, but I don't think he's upset with you."

"I'm okay." She forced a smile despite her anxiety. "I just didn't expect anyone to walk out here."

He touched her hand again. "I better get going."

"*Ya*, it's getting late." She walked him toward the buggy and contemplated telling him about Benjamin. Although she knew she needed to be honest with him, the moment had passed, and her courage had disappeared as soon as her brother had walked around the corner.

They stood together in front of his buggy.

"*Gut nacht, mei* Carolyn," he said softly. "I'll see you again soon."

"I look forward to it." She smiled up at him. "*Gut nacht*."

Carolyn waved as Joshua's buggy moved toward the road.

Amos came up behind her. "Did you tell him about Benjamin?"

"No." Carolyn faced her brother. "I was going to, but you interrupted us."

"It's a *gut* thing I did. You two were getting too cozy

out here." He frowned. "I saw he was holding your hand. You know it's against our beliefs to touch before marriage."

Carolyn blew out an irritated sigh. "Of course I know that. I was reminded over and over again after I made my mistake. You don't need to keep reminding me, Amos."

"People are going to talk about you if they find out you're breaking the rules with Joshua." He paused and his expression softened as if he truly cared about her. "You do realize Joshua is going to find out the truth eventually. Don't you think he should find out from you and not someone else?"

She nodded. "I know you're right."

"You need to tell him now." Amos turned and started back toward the barn.

Carolyn stared after her brother while regret drowned her. She may have messed everything up by not telling him the truth tonight when she had the chance.

She walked slowly toward the house and found her mother standing at the counter while a pot warmed on the stove.

"*Mamm?*" she asked, crossing the kitchen. "I thought you and *Dat* were in bed."

"I'm trying your trick." *Mamm* pointed toward the pot. "Warm milk."

"You can't sleep?" Carolyn leaned against the counter.

"No, I can't." Her mother studied her. "Is something wrong? You looked so *froh* earlier. Did Josh do something to upset you?"

"No, it's not Josh." Carolyn sighed. "Josh is wonderful. I think he almost told me he loves me tonight. He said I'm the reason he can smile again, and he called me his Carolyn."

Mamm hugged her. "That's *wunderbaar*! That means he's in love with you, Carolyn. That's the best news!"

"No, it's not." Carolyn shook her head as tears filled her eyes.

"Why are you crying? I thought you loved Joshua."

"I do love him." She wiped her eyes. "But I haven't told him the truth. He still thinks Benjamin is my nephew." Carolyn sniffed. "I was going to tell him the truth tonight, but Amos walked out back and found us sitting together. After Amos left, the perfect opportunity was gone. I couldn't bring myself to say the words."

Mamm smiled. "You can still tell him. You'll find the right words and the right time. Have faith."

Carolyn shook her head. "I'm afraid it's too late now. He shared some really private feelings tonight. It was as if he let me into his heart. I should've told him about Ben while he was sharing his secrets with me. He's going to think I deliberately kept my secrets to myself."

"No, he won't think that. If he really loves you, he'll understand why you waited." *Mamm* touched her shoulder. "He loves you, Carolyn. I can see it in his eyes when he looks at you. He will understand. Just have faith. Trust your heart."

Carolyn nodded, even though she doubted her mother's words.

"You're a *schee maedel* inside and out, and you're

worthy of love, Carolyn. Trust me. God has waited for the perfect time to bring love into your life. Embrace it. Tell Joshua about Benjamin when the time is right, and everything will turn out just fine." She turned back to the pot, poured some of the warm milk into a mug, and held it out to Carolyn. "Would you like some?"

"No, *danki*." Carolyn cupped her hand over her mouth to stifle a yawn. "I'm going to head to bed."

"*Gut nacht*."

"*Gut nacht*," Carolyn repeated. As she walked toward her room, she prayed her mother was right about Joshua. Yet deep in her heart, she couldn't help worrying that she could lose him as soon as he found out the truth about Benjamin.

* * *

Joshua stopped his horse in front of his father's barn. He jumped out of the buggy and headed back to where he spotted a dim light spilling out from under the door of his father's woodworking shop.

He pushed the door open and found his father sanding a small piece of wood. Tools cluttered the small workbench while several battery-operated lanterns hung on hooks around the shop.

"*Dat!*" he said, his heart thumping against his rib cage. "*Dat*, I need to talk to you."

"Josh. What a pleasant surprise." *Dat* patted a bench beside him. "Have a seat. What brings you out here so late?"

"I need to tell you something." Joshua grinned with

excitement. "*Dat*, I'm in love, and I think I'm ready to ask her to marry me."

"Really?" His father's eyes widened. "This is exciting news. Who is this special *maedel*?"

"Carolyn Lapp." Joshua's smile deepened as he spoke. "I'm so *froh*. I've never been this *froh* in my life. I thought I was in love with Hannah, but this is different. It's different than anything I've ever felt. I thought I was going to be alone for the rest of my life, but I was wrong. I was so very wrong."

"I'm so *froh* to hear you say this." *Dat* clapped. "Your *mamm* will be thrilled."

"Actually, no. She won't." Joshua grimaced. "*Mamm* doesn't like Carolyn for some reason. She's been pushing me to date Lena Esh."

"Are you certain she doesn't like Carolyn?" *Dat* looked surprised.

"*Ya*, I'm completely certain. She's made it clear." Joshua ran his finger over the workbench as he spoke. "She's not going to be *froh* when she finds out I plan to ask Carolyn to marry me."

"Well, don't you worry about your *mamm*. I'll handle her."

Joshua's courage wavered as he considered his next question. "How do I ask Carolyn to marry me?"

His father laughed. "What do you mean? You just come out and say, 'Will you marry me?'"

"Right." Joshua laughed, despite his anxiety. "I just need to ask her."

"That's right. Just ask her."

"I hope so." Joshua gnawed his lower lip. "I was so

confident when I rode over here. I was certain I could ask her, and she would say yes. Now I'm *naerfich*. Is that normal?"

"Of course it is, son. It's very normal. But I have a feeling she *will* say yes." His father smiled. "You'll do just fine. I guess we'll be planning a wedding in the fall, *ya*?"

"That's a possibility. We'll see what happens when I ask her." Joshua stood. "I guess I better get home. I have work to do in the morning."

"You have a *gut nacht*." His father winked at him. "I'm thrilled for you, Joshua. Your *mamm* will be too."

"*Danki, Dat. Gut nacht*." Joshua headed back out to the buggy and looked up at the sky. He prayed Carolyn would say yes and his lonely house would finally become a home.

* * *

Barbie was climbing into bed when Eli came into the bedroom. She scowled at him. "I was wondering when you were going to come in from your shop."

"I had a visitor." Eli began to take off his work clothes.

"A visitor? Who would come and visit this late at night?" Barbie asked.

"Your son."

"Joshua?" She sat up straight. "Why did he come by? *Was iss letz*?"

"Nothing's wrong. He had *gut* news." He fished his pajamas from his bureau. "He's in love."

She studied her husband. "What do you mean?"

"He's going to ask her to marry him."

"Who is he going to ask to marry him?" She knew the answer, but she asked the question anyway.

"Carolyn Lapp." Eli laughed as he pulled up his pajama pants.

"I've never seen our *bu* so *froh*, Barbie. It's a true blessing. He's smitten. He asked me what to say when he asks her. I remember being that *naerfich*."

She forced a smile as disappointment built up inside of her. "That's *wunderbaar* news."

Eli buttoned his pajama top and climbed into the bed beside her. "You're going to get your prayers answered now. You'll have more *grandkinner* to love." He reached over and flipped off the lantern.

"*Ya*, I will." She smiled at Eli through the dark. "The Lord is *gut*."

"*Ya*, he is." Eli kissed her cheek. "*Gut nacht*."

"*Gut nacht*." Barbie stared at the ceiling while Eli snored loudly beside her. She needed to find a way to stop Carolyn from marrying Joshua. She didn't know how, but she would find a way before it was too late.

TWENTY

Barbie was standing in line at the market the next day when she glanced behind her and spotted Sarah Ann Lapp. She paid for her groceries and then took her time putting her money back in her purse.

"Barbie?" Sarah Ann came up behind her, just as Barbie hoped she would.

"Oh, Sarah Ann!" Barbie feigned surprise. "*Wie geht's?*"

"I thought that was you." Sarah Ann smiled as she pushed her grocery cart up to Barbie. "How are you doing?"

"I'm fine." Barbie moved her cart over to the wall so shoppers could walk past them. "How are you? How's your family?"

"We're doing well." Sarah Ann sidled up to her. "It's been busy. Ben has enjoyed working at your son's farm. That's a *wunderbaar* opportunity for him." She lowered her voice. "I think it was *gut* for him to get away from Robert and David. I love my *kinner*, but they were constantly getting Ben in trouble. It's *gut* for him to work somewhere else."

"Oh really? I didn't realize that." Barbie suppressed

a smile as she hoped Sarah Ann would spill some more family secrets. "Ben has had a hard time on your farm?"

"Well, it hasn't been all bad." Sarah Ann smiled. "It's just been difficult for Carolyn. She was so excited when Joshua hired Ben on permanently. Things have always been difficult for her given her situation."

"I'm sorry to hear that. Carolyn seems like such a strong *maedel*." Barbie tried to look empathetic as she hoped Sarah Ann would keep talking.

"I'm sure you already know she had Ben when she was very young. She was really a *kind* herself when she simply made a bad decision." Sarah Ann gestured with her hands. "We've all just wanted the best for Benjamin. He's a *gut bu*, and Carolyn has done a fantastic job raising him without a husband."

Barbie couldn't stop her gasp. *Benjamin is Carolyn's son! Carolyn was a teenage mother!* This was just the information she needed to stop Joshua from marrying her.

Sarah Ann's eyes widened. "You didn't know Carolyn had Benjamin when she was sixteen?"

Barbie shook her head and then smiled. "I didn't know, but your secret is safe with me."

"It's not really a secret, but I guess our church district is protective of her and Benjamin." Sarah Ann spoke quickly. "We don't really talk about it because everyone accepted Benjamin after he was born. Carolyn joined the church when she was seventeen, and she was forgiven. Her parents helped her raise Ben, and they've done a wonderful job."

"What happened to Benjamin's father?" Barbie wanted to know everything.

"He left the community before she found out she was pregnant." Sarah Ann shook her head and frowned. "It was so *bedauerlich*. He really broke her heart. She won't talk about him. I think she was certain she'd be alone the rest of her life because of that one mistake, but I told her that she'd find true love. I think she has. She's really *froh* with your son. It's so sweet how they met."

Barbie forced a smile. "*Ya*, it certainly is."

"I better let you go. I have to run to the farmers' market next." Sarah Ann pushed her grocery cart ahead. "It was *gut* seeing you."

"*Ya*, it was *gut* seeing you." Barbie grinned as she pushed her cart behind Sarah Ann. She had the information she needed to stop Joshua from making the biggest mistake of his life. She couldn't wait to tell him. Once he knew the truth about Carolyn, she could convince him that he needed to find someone else and not marry the woman who had a sordid past.

* * *

Carolyn climbed the porch steps later that afternoon. Her feet were sore after cleaning an extra floor of rooms for Linda, who had called in sick today. She couldn't wait to sit down and have a cup of coffee with her mother. She stepped into the kitchen and found Sarah Ann and her mother sitting at the table together.

"*Wie geht's?*" Carolyn kicked off her shoes and then

turned around to see that her sister-in-law and mother were frowning. "What's going on?"

"Have a seat." *Mamm* pulled the chair out beside her. "We need to talk."

Carolyn sat beside her mother and looked at Sarah Ann, who was wiping a tear from her cheek. "Sarah Ann, what happened?"

"I think I did something wrong. I'm so sorry, Carolyn." Sarah Ann sniffed. "I'm so sorry."

"I don't understand." Carolyn looked at her mother. "Please tell me what's going on."

"Sarah Ann ran into Barbie Glick at the grocery store this afternoon." Her mother's voice was calm. "She talked to her for a few minutes, and Barbie asked how our family was doing."

"I started talking about Ben." Sarah Ann's voice was thin and shaky. "I told her how much he likes working at the farm."

Carolyn's heart thudded in her chest and alarm caused the hair on the back of her neck to stand up. "What did you tell her?" She studied Sarah Ann.

Mamm touched Carolyn's shoulder, and she jumped with a start. "Sarah Ann didn't know."

"What are you saying?" Carolyn's voice rose as anguish overcame her. "What did you tell her, Sarah Ann?"

"I mentioned that Ben was your son." Sarah Ann wiped her cheeks with a napkin as more tears poured from her eyes. "I didn't know that you hadn't told Josh yet. Your *mamm* told me that you were going to tell him soon, and I assumed he already knew."

"Oh no." Carolyn stood up and started for the door. "I have to go see him." She pushed open the front door and found Ben and Amos standing near the porch.

"Wait!" Sarah Ann rushed after her. "Carolyn, please. You have to forgive me. I thought Josh already knew. Then the more I thought about my conversation with Barbie . . . and then your mother and I talked about it . . . I'm so sorry."

"I'm not angry with you. This was bound to happen eventually." Carolyn took a deep breath, hoping to calm her racing heart. "I was going to tell him, but it never seemed like the right time. Now Barbie is going to beat me to it. She's going to tell Josh, and everything is going to fall apart."

"I thought he knew already," Sarah Ann said again, pointing toward Benjamin, who was watching with his eyes full of confusion. "I thought maybe Ben had told him. I'm so sorry."

"Told Josh what?" Benjamin asked. "What did you want to tell Joshua?"

"That you're my son." Carolyn sighed as she looked at him. "I haven't told Josh the truth about you."

"It hasn't really come up, so I haven't mentioned it to him." Benjamin shrugged.

"I'm so sorry." Sarah Ann's voice was still thin. "I really thought Barbie knew, and I didn't think it mattered."

"Stop apologizing." Carolyn touched Sarah Ann's arm and tried to calm her sister-in-law. "It will be okay." Although she said the words, she didn't think it was okay, or that it would ever be okay again.

"Did you really believe you could keep it a secret forever, Carolyn?" Amos asked. "You knew this was going to happen eventually. Maybe Sarah Ann did you a favor. Now you don't have to tell Joshua because his *mamm* will tell him for you."

Carolyn felt something inside her snap and white-hot fury seized her. "Amos, I'm tired of your comments about my life. You need to just stay out of my life and keep your unkind and judgmental criticisms to yourself. I'm doing just fine, and Ben is too. We don't need you butting in and telling us how to run our lives." She marched down the steps past him and headed toward Benjamin's buggy.

"Carolyn!" *Mamm* ran after her. "Wait."

Carolyn climbed into the buggy and took the reins. "*Mamm*, I have to go talk to Joshua. I know exactly what Barbie is going to do. She's trying to keep us apart, and this is her perfect opportunity."

"Do you want me to go with you?" her mother offered.

"No, *danki*. I have to do this myself." She directed the horse to move forward.

"Be careful!" *Mamm* yelled after her.

Carolyn guided the horse toward the road while praying she could somehow beat Barbie to Joshua's farm.

* * *

Joshua stood at the stove and poured some macaroni and cheese from a pot into a bowl. He glanced at the clock on the wall and wondered if Carolyn was home from the hotel yet. He planned to eat supper and then head over to her house to visit with her this evening. And if he felt confident enough, he might just ask her to marry him. The idea caused his pulse to skitter. He couldn't wait to hear her response, and he prayed it was positive.

"Joshua, we need to talk." *Mamm* appeared in the doorway wearing a deep frown.

"Hi, *Mamm*." He carried his bowl of macaroni and cheese to the table. "Would you like something to eat?" He sat at the table and bowed his head in prayer.

When he finished, *Mamm* sat beside him and shook her head. "You're not going to feel like eating after I share the news I heard today. You have to listen to me."

Joshua gave in to her dramatic expression and pushed his bowl away. "You have my attention. I'm listening."

"Your *dat* told me you're in love with Carolyn Lapp and you're going to ask her to marry you."

"That's right." He nodded his head. "I'm going to ask her tonight."

"I need to tell you something before you do that."

"You're not going to change my mind." Joshua frowned at her. "If you're here to talk me out of it, then you can just forget it."

"Just listen to me, Josh." *Mamm* paused and took a deep breath. "Did you know that Benjamin isn't Carolyn's nephew?"

"What are you saying?"

"Benjamin is Carolyn's son." His mother said the words slowly. "She had him when she was only sixteen. Carolyn is an unwed *mutter*."

Joshua stared at her as the words soaked through him. "That can't be true."

Mamm nodded. "*Ya*, it is. I ran into Sarah Ann today at the grocery store, and she told me. I know it's true."

His mouth gaped, and he felt as if the world were spinning out of control. "That can't be true. It just can't be true."

"Sarah Ann thought you already knew." *Mamm* shook her head. "She thought Carolyn told you."

"Why didn't she tell me?" He whispered the question as he raked his fingers through his hair.

"Carolyn isn't the *maedel* you thought she was. She hasn't been truthful with you, Josh. She's not *gut* for you."

"I don't understand." Joshua shook his head. "I trusted her. I told her everything. Why wouldn't she tell me something so important?" He felt all of his dreams crumbling around him while the happiness that had been blossoming inside him disappeared in an instant.

How could everything go so wrong so quickly?

* * *

Carolyn guided the horse up the driveway, where she spotted Barbie standing by a horse and buggy. Joshua stood on the porch and stared toward her. Carolyn's blood ran cold. She stopped the horse, climbed out, and faced Barbie, who gave her a smug smile.

"You're too late," Barbie said as she approached her. "Joshua knows the truth about you. Your sister-in-law told me all about how you had Benjamin when you were a teenager and your boyfriend left you. I shared everything with Joshua and now he doesn't want you."

Carolyn stood up straighter as confidence mixed with fury surged through her. "I don't think it's your place to decide what's best for Joshua."

Barbie shook her head slowly. "No, it's not my place, but I know my son. He's devastated that you never told him the truth. Were you too ashamed to tell him about your past? Is that why you let him think Benjamin was your nephew instead of your son?"

"No, I'm not ashamed." Carolyn took a step closer to her. "*Ya*, I made a mistake, but I was young, and my family and my community forgave me. God forgave me. And I'm tired of having to justify something that happened to me nearly sixteen years ago. Not you or anyone else is going to make me keep feeling bad about it."

"Carolyn," Joshua said as he walked up behind her. "Is it true?" His sad, wilted expression caused Carolyn's heart to crumble. "Is Benjamin your son?" he asked, his voice hoarse and thick with emotion.

"*Ya*, he is." Carolyn nodded as a lump swelled in her throat and her stomach began to churn. "Can we talk alone?"

"Is that really necessary now that the truth is out?" Barbie rested her hands on her wide hips and glared at Carolyn.

"That's enough, *Mamm*," Joshua said. He turned to Carolyn. "*Ya*, we can talk in there." He gestured toward the barn, and they walked toward it together. Almost inside, Carolyn tried to explain.

"I wanted to tell you." Carolyn hoped she could temper her growing sadness. "I was going to the other night, but Amos interrupted us."

He stopped just inside the door and faced her, his expression transforming from hurt to anger. "I don't understand why you weren't honest with me. I told you everything. I poured my heart out to you, but you couldn't tell me the one most important secret of all, that you're a *mamm*."

"You have to believe that I wanted to tell you, Josh." She laced her fingers together as if she were praying. "But you have to understand that I've dealt with so much hurt. I've spent my whole adult life trying to protect Ben from the judgment I've faced nearly every day since I was sixteen. I made one mistake that changed my whole life, and people feel it's their right to talk about me behind my back and call me names that aren't even true."

"But I'm not other people, Carolyn." He pointed to his chest. "I care about you. I care about Ben, but you couldn't have the decency to tell me the whole truth."

"I was going to tell you."

"When, Carolyn?" His voice rose. "When were you going to tell me?"

"Soon. I was planning to tell you the next time I saw you." When his expression remained unchanged, Carolyn shook her head. "Why isn't that *gut* enough for you?"

"I don't know." He let his hands hit his thighs. "This changes everything."

"Why does it have to change everything? I'm being

honest with you right now, Josh. I'm telling you the whole truth." She studied his eyes. "It's her, isn't it? It's your *mamm*."

"No." He shook his head. "That's not true."

"*Ya*, it is. She told you to reject me because I made one mistake." Her voice wavered as she realized she was losing him even though she'd thought he loved her. "It's people like your *mamm* who judge me and my precious son for my one mistake—they're the ones I've had to protect Benjamin from. Ben is a *gut bu*. He doesn't deserve to be treated differently because of the way he came into this world. He deserves to be treated with the same respect as anyone else. But there are still people like her who enjoy criticizing Ben and me."

"I'm not one of those people." Joshua shook his head. "I'm hurt because you didn't tell me." He paused for a moment as if contemplating something. "I thought he spent a lot of time at the *daadi haus* because he was close to you and his grandparents, but now it all makes sense. When I told Ben to talk to his parents about working full-time here, he hesitated. He didn't correct me, so I guess he's used to lying about all this."

"No, he didn't lie to you, and he's not used to lying either. I told him he could let people believe what they wanted as long as it didn't hurt him. His biological *dat* was a *bu* I met and thought I loved when I worked at a market in Philadelphia. He pressured me into being with him. He wanted me to go to Missouri with him, but I couldn't do it. I found out I was going to have Ben after his *dat* left me. My parents were my biggest supporters. They stood by Ben and me despite what some other members of our community said. I was baptized into the faith after I had Ben, and I've been true to my Amish vows." She stood up straighter as a surge of confidence overtook her despite her growing heartache. "Your problem is that you let your *mamm* run your life."

"This isn't about *mei mamm*. This is about us." Joshua gestured at her and then back at him. "This is about you telling me the truth. I told you everything about me. I told you things I had never said aloud to anyone before. You have it backward. You couldn't trust me."

"You forgive me for making a mistake as a teenager but you won't forgive me for being too afraid I'd lose you to tell you the truth about Ben weeks ago?"

"I don't know what to say, Carolyn." Joshua shook his head. "I'm really hurt that you didn't have the courage to tell me after I poured my heart out to you more than once."

They stared at each other as an awkward moment passed. Carolyn could see his eyes hardening as the stubborn, cold man she'd met at the auction replaced the warm, funny man who had hugged her after his miracle foal was born.

"So where does this leave us?" he finally asked, his voice sharp and cold.

"I guess it's over," she whispered, her words choking on her heartbreak. "Good-bye, Joshua."

"Good-bye, Carolyn." He looked toward the pasture.

She started toward her buggy and then stopped and faced him. "Joshua," she called, and he faced her. "You once asked me why I liked working at the hotel. The truth is that I like working at the hotel because it gives me a chance to get away from judgmental members of the community like your mother."

Joshua stared at her, and she was almost certain she saw a tear in his eye. When he didn't respond to her comment, she knew it was time to leave and go back to her lonely life at her brother's farm.

Carolyn kept her head high as she stalked past Barbie and climbed into the buggy. She held back her tears until the horse pulled onto the main road, then she cried all the way home until she ran out of tears.

* * *

Joshua felt as if his hopes, dreams, and future were slipping away from him as Carolyn's buggy headed toward the main road. He wanted to run after her and tell her that he loved her and wanted to marry her. He longed to beg her to come back and then hug and kiss her until she was breathless.

Instead, he stood cemented in place as his pride held him back.

His mother's voice broke through his thoughts. "You're better off without her. I know it hurts, but it's best you found out the truth before you married her. It would've been terrible if you'd taken her as your *fraa* and then found out that she had a son. Trust me, it's better this way. In fact, I'm certain you'll meet someone who will be a better match for you."

Joshua glared at his mother. "You need to go home."

She gasped. "What? You don't mean that."

"*Ya*, I do. Please go home. You've done enough damage." He turned and walked toward the barn. He looked over his shoulder a few minutes later and spotted his mother's buggy traveling toward the road.

Once he was certain his mother was gone, Joshua stepped into the barn, dropped to his knees, and covered his face with his hands. He leaned forward and closed his eyes as tears flooded them.

He felt as if the walls were crumbling in on him and all his plans were flittering away like pieces of paper caught in a tornado. All the dreams he'd had for a life with Carolyn were gone in the blink of an eye. He'd found someone to love, and the loneliness that had haunted him since Gideon died and Hannah left had finally disappeared. Yet now Carolyn was gone, and the loneliness was strangling him, consuming him, tighter and stronger than ever before.

Feeling as if he'd reached rock bottom, Joshua opened his heart and began to pray.

"God, please show me the right path," he whispered, his voice sounding weak and foreign to him. "I thought Carolyn was the one, but now I'm confused. In my heart, I still believe she is my true love, but I don't understand why she didn't tell me the truth. Am I supposed to be with Carolyn or am I supposed to be alone? What is the right plan for me, God? What am I missing? Please tell me, God. Send me a sign."

Joshua stayed in the barn for some time and listened to the birds in the distance and the horses nickering nearby. With tears in his eyes, he waited for a sign.

TWENTY-ONE

Carolyn entered her house and hurried past her parents and Benjamin, who were sitting at the kitchen table eating supper. She tried her best to shield her raw emotion from her son as she headed straight to her room at the back of the house. After closing the door, she threw herself onto her bed and buried her face in her pillow. She thought she'd cried out all her tears during the ride home, but more came when she hit the pillow. She sobbed and sobbed as desolation flooded her soul.

She heard the door squeak open and then close again.

"Carolyn? Are you all right?" her mother asked.

Carolyn couldn't respond. Any words were stuck in her throat.

"Please, Carolyn." Her mother's voice was soothing to her ear. "Talk to me, *mei liewe*." She rubbed Carolyn's back, but the touch gave her little comfort. "Tell me what happened."

Carolyn rolled onto her side and looked up at *Mamm* as she wiped away her tears. She cleared her throat. "Barbie was there when I got to the farm. She had already told him, and she looked so *froh*. It was as if she was searching for something that would convince Josh not to be with me."

Mamm shook her head. "That is so wrong."

"I told Josh I wanted to talk to him alone, and we walked to the barn. I explained I was going to tell him the truth the next time I saw him, but that wasn't *gut* enough for him." She detailed the conversation, and her mother listened while rubbing her arm.

"Josh just couldn't accept that I hadn't told him the truth from the beginning, even though I tried to explain how hard it was for me. No matter what I said, he wouldn't accept it." Carolyn sniffed. "He was exactly like everyone else who judged me when Ben was born. He wouldn't listen. He let everything we had disappear because of that one issue."

"I'm so sorry, *mei liewe.*" *Mamm* sighed. "I had hoped you'd finally found happiness."

"*Ya*, I did too." Carolyn crossed her arms over her middle as her abdomen knotted. "It hurts so much, *Mamm*. I can't believe how much this hurts."

"Oh, Carolyn. I wish I could take the pain away." *Mamm's* eyes shimmered with tears. "I'm so sorry things turned out this way."

"I thought he was the one, *Mamm*. I thought I'd finally found my future husband, but I guess that doesn't exist for me. I'm supposed to be alone. Maybe that really is the punishment for my mistake." Carolyn choked back tears as regret stole her words.

"No, no." *Mamm* shook her head. "Don't say that. God has already forgiven you. You know that. We've talked about this."

"I know he has, but when am I going to find some-one who will love me completely, despite my past? Does that exist for me or should I settle for someone like Saul who will take me just to have someone to call his *fraa*?" Carolyn couldn't stop her tears as they flowed once again.

"You will find true love, Carolyn. Someday you will. I promise." *Mamm* gently squeezed her hand.

＊ ＊ ＊

Benjamin leaned against his mother's door and listened while she cried. He knew he shouldn't, but he couldn't stop himself. He hated hearing her cry, especially when he knew from the conversation that her pain was because he existed. His whole life he'd watched his mother face judgmental people who called themselves Christians, and he was tired of listening to her make excuses and watching her endure criticism. He couldn't take it anymore, and he couldn't stand there in silence while she suffered.

He walked down the hall and found his grandfather slurping coffee from a mug. "I'm going to go see *Onkel* Amos."

Daadi nodded. "Don't be too late."

He headed to the barn and got his horse. Once the horse was hitched to a buggy, he climbed in and guided the horse toward the road. He knew he shouldn't have lied, but his grandfather would never agree to let him hitch up the horse and head back to Paradise to talk to Joshua Glick, man to man.

Benjamin spent the trip to Paradise considering what he was going to say, but by the time he arrived at the farm where he spent his weekdays working, he'd forgotten his speech. Instead, he left his horse and buggy by the barn and climbed the back porch steps as his indignation and disappointment with his mentor surged through him. He knocked on the door, and a few minutes later Joshua wrenched open the door and gave him a surprised look.

"Ben?" Joshua stepped outside. "Did you forget something?"

"No, I need to talk to you, man to man." Benjamin gestured to the house. "May I come in?"

"Of course." Joshua motioned for him to follow him. "Would you like a drink or a snack? I have some left-over pie *mei mamm* brought over earlier."

"No, *danki*. I just want to talk." Benjamin took a deep breath and prayed he could remember some of the things he'd considered during the ride over. "I should've told you that Carolyn was *mei mamm*, but I thought she'd want to tell you, and I hoped it wouldn't matter to you."

Joshua shook his head and held his hand up to dismiss him. "Please. This whole situation is between Carolyn and me, and it doesn't concern you."

"*Ya*, it does." Irritation boiled in Benjamin. "Don't treat me like a *kind*. I'm not a *kind*. I've grown up quickly, even though I'm small for my age. My whole life I've watched *mei mamm* suffer because she had me. I've heard people call me a mistake and call her promiscuous. She's spent half of her life being judged because she made a mistake. Well, that may have been a mistake, but without that one bad choice, I wouldn't be standing here talking to you."

Joshua's expression softened.

"*Mei mamm* is heartbroken now, and it's tearing me apart. I've always hoped she could find some happiness. And when she was with you, she finally did. I'd never seen her as *froh* as she was the past couple of months. She would walk around humming, and she actually told *mei mammi* she was falling in love for the first time in her life." Benjamin shook his head.

Joshua sighed, and Benjamin thought he saw tears glistening in his eyes.

"You have no idea what she has gone through," Benjamin continued, his voice seeping with resentment. "*Mei onkel* Amos told her that she brought shame on her family, and that's why he wanted her to marry Saul. It was as if she would finally be forgiven and I would be legitimized if a man would marry her and pretend to be *mei dat*. I don't need a *dat*. I have *mei daadi,* and he has been all the father I've ever needed."

Benjamin shook his finger at Joshua. "I know why she didn't tell you about me, and it's the real reason I never told you she was *mei mamm*. We're tired of being judged. It doesn't matter if anyone knows what circumstances brought me into this world. All that matters is that I have a family, and no one has the right to judge my family."

"You're right," Joshua finally said.

"If you reject *mei mamm*, then you're throwing away a *wunderbaar maedel*. I pray someday she can find someone who will truly love her and accept me. I'm tired of watching her suffer. I have to stand up for her because she's done the same for me for the past sixteen years. Now it's time for me to tell the community she's a wonderful Christian woman despite the way she's been persecuted." Benjamin threw his hands up with disgust. "I can't work for you anymore. If I continue to come here and work, that means I'm accepting how you treated her. I can't do that."

Benjamin started for the door. He looked back over his shoulder to where Joshua was staring at him wide eyed. "I quit."

Benjamin rushed down the porch steps and climbed into the buggy. During the ride home, he prayed to God, begging him to heal his mother's broken heart.

* * *

Joshua stared at the back door after Benjamin left. He was speechless. He'd never expected Benjamin to come and visit him. He sank into a kitchen chair while contemplating what the young man had said. He couldn't stop wondering if this was the sign he'd asked God to send him. Was this the sign he needed to realize that Carolyn was the one for him?

The question echoed through his mind as he headed to bed, and it haunted his dreams.

* * *

Carolyn hugged her cloak to her body, grabbed a battery-powered lantern, and made her way out to the porch later that evening. Although she'd tried to shut down her thoughts to sleep, she couldn't stop her swirling emotions. She'd pulled on her robe and slippers, grabbed her cloak by the door, and then padded out to the porch for some fresh air, hoping to clear her mind so sleep could overtake her.

She settled onto the porch swing just as a buggy made its way up the driveway toward her house. She held her breath while wondering if it was Joshua or Saul. But she knew it was unlikely that Joshua would ever speak to her again, and she quickly trumped any hope that he would come to visit her.

When the man climbed from the buggy, she knew it was Saul. He walked up the porch steps, and she forced a smile as he stepped into the warm glow of the lantern.

"Saul," she said. "*Wie geht's?*"

"How are you, Carolyn?" He pointed toward a rocking chair next to the swing. "May I have a seat?"

"Please, join me." She looked up at the bright stars in the clear sky and couldn't help but think that they mocked her bleak mood.

"It's a *schee* evening, *ya*?" he asked.

"It is." The air was crisp, and she pulled her cloak closer. "I haven't seen you in a while."

"I've wanted to come visit you, but I've been overrun with cabinet orders. I can hardly keep up." He folded his arms over his coat. "I've wanted to expand my business, but I just haven't had the money. I'm hoping I can soon."

He talked on about his projects, and she nodded while trying her best to look interested. Instead, her thoughts were lost on her heartbreaking conversation with Joshua. She wondered if things would've ended differently if she had been honest about Benjamin from the beginning.

"So that's why I came over tonight." Saul said her name, and she snapped back to reality. "Did you hear me, Carolyn?"

"I'm sorry, Saul. What did you say?"

His dark eyes pleaded with her. "Carolyn, I asked you if you would consider being my *fraa*. Will you marry me?"

She swallowed a gasp. She'd never expected him to ask her the direct question. She stared at him, not knowing what to say. The question hung suspended between them, and an awkward silence covered them. For a few moments, she considered marrying him and accepting his offer for a practical, safe marriage. Yet the more she considered the idea, the more she rejected it. In the end, she knew she'd rather be alone than be stuck for the rest of her life in a loveless marriage.

"I'm sorry," he finally said as his expression clouded. "It's too soon."

"Saul," she began, "I'm so honored that you asked me. You're a *gut* man, and Emma is a lovely *kind*. I've really enjoyed getting to know you."

He frowned, and she held up her hand.

"Wait. Let me finish. I know that someday you'll find a *maedel* who will love you completely. Unfortunately, I'm not that *maedel*. I'm honored that you considered me, but I know I'm not right for you. Please forgive me for saying no."

He nodded as he stood. "*Danki* for visiting with me."

"*Gut nacht*, Saul," she called as he walked toward his buggy. She watched him drive off and wondered if she would spend the rest of her life sitting on her parents' porch, hoping to find a man to love. Someone who wasn't Josh.

. . .

Joshua jumped out of bed. He was certain Benjamin's visit last night was the sign that he'd been waiting to receive from God. He had to go see Carolyn and apologize. He had to make things right before it was too late, before he lost her for good.

He quickly fed the animals, rushed back inside to eat breakfast, and then hurried out to the barn and called Aiden Monroe, his parents' usual driver.

"Aiden, how soon can you give me a ride? I need to go somewhere as soon as possible." Aiden was able to come right away, and Joshua was anxiously awaiting the ride when Daniel arrived. He had hoped he would get there before Aiden did so he wouldn't have to leave a note.

"Danny." Joshua dashed out to meet the young man. "I need you to run things for me today. Can you handle it alone?"

"Sure." Daniel studied him. "What's going on?"

"Ben quit last night."

"Why did he quit? I thought he loved working here."

"He does love working here." Joshua shook his head. "I can't explain it all now, but I'm going to try to make things right. Hopefully Ben will be back here Monday."

"What's going on?" Daniel asked. "You look upset."

"I am." Joshua glanced toward the road as Aiden's pickup truck steered into the driveway. "I have to go out for a few hours. I promise I'll explain everything when I get back, okay?"

"All right. I hope everything turns out okay." Daniel looked suspicious. "See you later."

Joshua rushed toward the pickup truck and climbed in the front seat. "Thanks for helping me at the last minute."

"It was good to hear from you, Josh." Aiden glanced over at Joshua. "Where can I take you first?"

"I need to talk to my mother, and then I was hoping you could take me to Gordonville."

"No problem." Aiden backed out of the driveway and then drove up the street to Josh's parents' farm. He parked in the driveway, and Joshua walked swiftly up to the house.

He found his mother standing at the sink washing dishes.

"Joshua?" She wiped her hands on a dish towel. "I wasn't expecting to see you today. You normally have customers visiting on Saturdays. Would you like something to eat?"

"No, *danki*." He cleared his throat. "I need to talk to you."

"What's wrong?" She took a step toward him. "You look upset."

"I've done a lot of thinking, and a fifteen-year-old talked some sense into me last night."

"Which fifteen-year-old are you talking about?"

"Benjamin Lapp came to see me. He made me realize I've been wrong about a lot of things, mostly how I treated his *mamm* yesterday."

His mother frowned, and his temper flared.

"*Mamm*, I'm in love with Carolyn Lapp, and nothing is going to change that. God led me to her so I could finally find happiness after spending so many years alone. I know you don't approve of her, but this is my life, not yours." He pointed toward his chest. "I'm going to marry her if she'll forgive me. I was wrong to be upset with her for not telling me the truth about Ben from the beginning. Ben made me realize Carolyn has been persecuted for years over making one mistake. I was just as bad as the other judgmental people in this community who call themselves Christians."

Mamm shook her head. "No, you weren't bad. You were right, and she was wrong to keep that secret from you. She lied to you."

Joshua swallowed a deep breath and closed his eyes while trying to hold back his boiling fury. "*Mamm*, I need you to listen to me for once. You need to stop meddling in my life and let me make my own decisions. I know you miss Gideon, and I know you're hurting because Hannah left the church. But you need to concentrate on living your own life, and let me live mine."

Mamm blanched as her eyes gleamed with tears.

"*Ich liebe dich*, but if you can't accept Carolyn, then you're going to have to stay away from us. I can't allow you to interfere in this relationship. It's too important to me. I need you to respect my decisions and back off." He couldn't stand to see his mother cry, but he had to stay firm with her or she would never cease butting into his life.

"I'm sorry." Her voice was tiny and unsure, which he'd never heard before. "I'm sorry, Joshua. I will respect your decision. I promise to back away and let you live your life."

She hugged him, and he breathed a sigh of relief.

"*Danki*." Joshua started for the door. "Now I'm going to see if Carolyn will forgive me." He rushed out the door and climbed into the truck. As the pickup bounced down the driveway, Joshua prayed that Carolyn would indeed forgive him.

TWENTY-TWO

Carolyn hung up the phone in the phone shanty and then walked back toward the house. She found her mother in the kitchen making a shopping list.

Mamm looked up from her list. "Did you check the messages?"

"*Ya*, there weren't any." She craned her neck and examined the list. "Can I help you with that?"

"Sure. Why don't you go over to the pantry and see if we have any flour." *Mamm* gestured toward the other side of the kitchen. "I think we were low the last time I checked."

Carolyn opened the pantry door and peeked inside the flour canister. "*Ya*, we're low. I'd say we have about half a cup left."

The back door opened, and Benjamin walked in.

"What are you up to today?" Carolyn asked.

"I'm helping *Daadi* with chores." He crossed the kitchen and disappeared into the hallway.

Mamm pointed toward the door. "Why don't you go work in the garden? I can handle the shopping list, and I know being out in the sun makes you *froh*."

"Are you sure you don't need help?"

"Carolyn, I can handle it."

"Okay." Carolyn started toward the back door. "Call me if you need me."

Mamm smiled. "I promise I will."

As Carolyn walked toward her garden, she wondered if Joshua missed her as much as she missed him. She had spent most of last night crying and asking God to bring Josh back to her.

When she awoke this morning, however, she felt a strange sense of peace come over her. It was as if God had laid his healing hand on her and helped her realize that things would be okay somehow. She was thankful to have parents and a son who loved her.

But despite all her blessings, she still missed the happiness she'd felt when Joshua smiled at her. He had left a gaping hole in her heart, and she hoped somehow time would heal it.

* * *

Joshua turned to Aiden as he turned onto the road. "Now I need to go to the Lapp farm in Gordonville."

"Okay." Aiden merged into traffic, wondering what was causing Josh so much anxiety. "Do you know the address?"

"*Ya.*" Joshua rattled it off. "I just hope she's home."

Aiden smiled over at his passenger. "She will be, Josh. Have faith."

* * *

Carolyn was crouching in her garden pulling weeds when she heard someone call her name. She stood and turned just as Joshua rushed toward her. Her heartbeat tripped and then raced double-time, and her shoulders tightened at the sight of him. She felt her defenses stiffen, like a cat arching its back to ready itself for a fight.

"Carolyn!" He approached her, his expression full of anguish. "I've been so worried about you."

"You were worried about me?" She studied him with confusion while wiping her hands down her apron, trying to remove some of the dirt.

"*Ya.*" He stood in front of her. "I had to see you."

"Why?" Suspicion nipped at her.

He reached for her hands, and she took a step back, not wanting him to get too close and deepen her heartache.

"Carolyn, *Ich liebe dich.*" His blue eyes sparkled with tears in the bright sunlight. "You're the love of my life. I was so wrong to reject you, and I want to make it up to you. You had every right to keep your secret until you were ready to tell me. I'm sorry for being just as judgmental as everyone else who has hurt you all these years. I've been praying you could find it in your heart to forgive me and give me a second chance."

Her heart turned over. She studied his eyes, wondering if she was dreaming or if he was truly saying these beautiful words.

"Please, Carolyn, please forgive me." His eyes pleaded with her. "I can't imagine living without you. These past couple of months have been the happiest of my life because God led me to you."

She wanted to believe him, but her heart reminded her to be cautious. "What made you change your mind?"

"Your son."

"Benjamin?"

Joshua nodded. "Ben came to see me last night, and he talked some sense into me. He made me realize how wrong I've been."

Carolyn gasped and cupped a hand to her mouth. "Ben went to see you?"

"*Ya*," he said with a nod. "He told me I acted like all the other so-called Christians who have judged you and persecuted you since he was born. He made me realize I was prideful and stubborn."

She wiped a tear from her eyes. "My son said that?" She was overwhelmed with love and admiration for Benjamin.

"*Ya*, he did. He also quit. He said he couldn't work for someone who treated his *mamm* so badly. He was right. I don't blame him at all."

Carolyn wiped a tear from her cheek. "He quit?"

He took her hand in his. "Carolyn, I love you. Please tell me you'll give me a second chance. I can't stand this heartache."

"*Ya*," Carolyn said. "I forgive you."

Joshua leaned down and brushed his lips over hers, sending the pit of her stomach into a wild swirl. Her heart rate surged, pounding fast in her ears. *Yes, this is true love, and it is amazing!*

"Marry me, Carolyn," Joshua whispered close to her ear, his breath sending shivers dancing down her back. "Marry me. I want to live with you and Benjamin on the farm. I want to spend the rest of my life with you."

The words were like a sweet melody to Carolyn's ears. For a moment she was sure she was dreaming, but when Joshua touched her cheek, she knew she was awake. Her dream had finally come true. She was going to marry for love!

"I'll marry you." Carolyn looked up at him and grinned as her sense of humor nipped at her. "But Benjamin quit. I don't know if he'll want to live there if he refuses to work for you."

Joshua laughed and hugged her while lifting her off her feet. "This is why I fell in love with you, Carolyn Lapp. You have the craziest sense of humor I've ever known."

She giggled as he kissed her cheek. "I love you too, Joshua." She took his hand. "Let's go tell my parents."

"That's a *gut* idea. And maybe I can apologize to Ben and ask him to come back to work for me. I need to make sure things are *gut* between my future stepson and me."

"*Ya.*" She laughed. "That's a *gut* idea too."

Joshua held her hand as he led her back toward the house. They were climbing the steps when Amos appeared.

"Carolyn," he said. "I need to talk to you."

Carolyn glanced at Joshua, who looked concerned. "It's okay," she said as she released her hand from Joshua's grip and went back down the steps to face her brother. "Joshua and I are getting married."

"I know," Amos said. "I heard you talking. I'm *froh* for you." He looked up at Joshua standing at the top of the steps. "You're a *gut* man, and I'm *froh* you chose my *schweschder.*"

Amos's gaze met Carolyn's. "I owe you an apology. I've been very un-Christlike. I've treated you badly for years, and I'm sorry. We all need to follow Jesus' example and forgive one another. You made a mistake, but I never let you forget it. None of us are perfect, and we all fall short of the glory of God. That doesn't excuse me, but I hope you can forgive me."

"Of course I can." Carolyn smiled. "I forgive you, Amos. *Danki*."

Amos cleared his throat. "I also found out you were right about my sons all along. Robert admitted to *Dat* and me that he threw the rock at Joshua's horse at the auction. He said he and David lied to get Benjamin in trouble. Apparently they've been victimizing Benjamin for years. I'm sorry I never believed you or Benjamin."

"*Danki*, Amos." Carolyn sniffed as a tear trickled down her cheek. "I can forgive you for that too."

"I'm going to have my *buwe* apologize to Ben, and I will apologize to him also." Amos shook his head and frowned. "I've been wrong for a long time. I need to be careful how I treat others, especially my family. *Danki* for forgiving me and giving me a second chance." He nodded and then walked back toward the barn.

Carolyn climbed the steps, took Joshua's hand in hers, and looked into his eyes and into her future. She silently thanked God for answering her prayer, leading her to her soul mate, and giving Benjamin the chance to have a father. She knew the power of her secret had finally been overcome, and that she was loved and cherished by the man who now stood by her side.

DISCUSSION QUESTIONS

1. Carolyn feels stuck between agreeing to a marriage of convenience and risking her heart by pursuing true love. Which path did you think was the right one for her? Which is the best for her son? Take a walk in her shoes. Which path would you have chosen if you were Carolyn? Share this with the group.

2. By the end of the book, Joshua finally stands up to his mother and tells her to stop meddling in his life. Do you think Joshua should forgive his mother for trying to come between him and Carolyn? Why or why not? Have you ever been asked to forgive someone whose actions changed your life negatively? Did you forgive this person? Why or why not? What Bible verses would help with this situation?

3. Ruth quotes 1 John 3:18, which speaks about how we should love one another. "Dear children, let us not love with words or speech but with actions and in truth." What does this verse mean to you?

4. By the end of the book, Amos realizes he was wrong to criticize Carolyn and treat Benjamin badly. He believed he was helping his sister by being hard on

her, but he realized his behavior was un-Christlike. What do you think caused him to realize he was wrong?

5. Benjamin stands up for his mother when he hears her suffering. He knows she's struggled to be the best mother she could be despite her circumstances, and he's tired of how people treat her. Have you ever taken a stand for someone you loved? Where did you find your strength? What Bible verses would help with this situation?

6. Due to a mistake she made when she was sixteen, Carolyn feels she's been judged much of her life by her community that is supposed to be Christlike. Do you think we do this in our own church communities—judge and gossip about our fellow Christians without considering the consequences? Why do you think that is?

7. "Finally, all of you, be like-minded, be sympathetic, love one another, be compassionate and humble" 1 Peter 3:8. This verse speaks about how we should treat one another. What does this verse mean to you? How does this verse apply to the story? Share this with the group.

8. In *A Hopeful Heart,* the first book in this series, Lillian is convinced her mother, Hannah, is being selfish and is betraying her by leaving the Amish community. In this book, we see Lillian still struggling to forgive her mother. Do you agree with Lillian's feelings? Or do you believe Hannah

was justified in her decision to leave and pursue a new life outside of the Amish faith when she fell in love with an Englisher? Do you think it's time for Lillian to forgive her mother and move on? Share this with the group.

9. Which character can you identify with the most? Which character seemed to carry the most emotional stake in the story? Was it Joshua, Carolyn, Benjamin, or someone else?

10. Carolyn is irritated by her brother's constant criticism and reminders about the mistake she made when she was sixteen. Have you ever been criticized by a close family member for a choice you've made? If so, how did you handle the criticism? Share this with the group.

11. What did you know about the Amish before reading this book? What did you learn?

Acknowledgments

As always, I'm thankful for my loving family, including my mother, Lola Goebelbecker; my husband, Joe; and my sons, Zac and Matt. I realize I'm absolutely no fun when I'm stressed, especially when I'm on deadline. Thank you for not throwing me out or changing the locks on the doors when I'm in the midst of a book project. You're all saints for dealing with me, and I'm so blessed to have such an awesome and tolerant family.

I'm more grateful than words can express to my patient friends who critique for me, including Stacey Barbalace, Amy Lillard, Janet Pecorella, Lauran Rodriguez, and, of course, my mother. I truly appreciate the time you take out of your busy lives to help me polish my books. Thanks to your hard work, my editor thinks I'm actually capable of writing without many typos or missing words. (Please continue to keep the truth a secret!) Thank you for always making me look good!

I'm so thankful for the people who helped me with the horse research, including Jim and Mary Frazier, Andy and Lucia Hunter, Bobbi Kendrick, and Michelle Melton. You were lifesavers since the only animal I can say I'm an expert in knowing anything about would be the common spoiled house cat. Special thanks also to Stacey Barbalace for helping with research and also for tolerating my constant emails with strange questions.

Special thanks to my special Amish friends who patiently answer my endless stream of questions. You're a blessing in my life.

Thank you to my wonderful church family at Morning Star Lutheran in Matthews, North Carolina, for your encouragement, prayers, love, and friendship. You all mean so much to my family and me.

To my agent, Mary Sue Seymour—I am grateful for your friendship, support, and guidance in my writing career. Thank you for all you do!

Thank you to my amazing editor, Sue Brower. I appreciate your guidance and friendship. Thank you also to editor Becky Philpott for your friendship and guidance. And thank you to Jean Bloom for her amazing edits and help with this book. I also would like to thank Laura Dickerson for tirelessly working to promote my books. I'm grateful to each and every person at HarperCollins Christian Publishing who helped make this book a reality.

To my readers—thank you for choosing my novels. My books are a blessing in my life for many reasons, including the special friendships I've formed with my readers. Thank you for your email messages, Facebook notes, and letters.

Thank you most of all to God—for giving me the inspiration and the words to glorify you. I'm so grateful and humbled you've chosen this path for me.

ABOUT THE AUTHOR

Amy Clipston is the award-winning and bestselling author of more than a dozen novels, including the Kauffman Amish Bakery series and the Hearts of the Lancaster Grand Hotel series. Her novels have hit multiple bestseller lists including CBD, CBA, and ECPA. Amy holds a degree in communication from Virginia Wesleyan College and works full-time for the City of Charlotte, North Carolina. Amy lives in North Carolina with her husband, two sons, and four spoiled rotten cats.

* * *

Visit her website: amyclipston.com
Facebook: Amy Clipston
Twitter: @AmyClipston

Enjoy Amy Clipston's Hearts of the Lancaster Grand Hotel series!

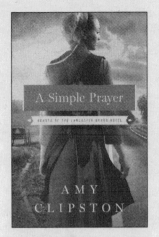

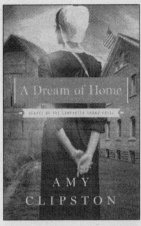

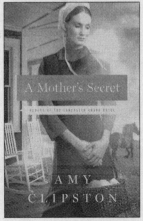

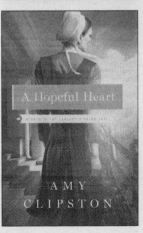

Available in print and e-book

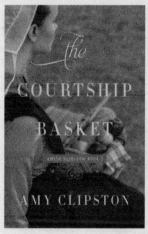
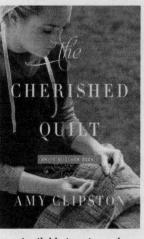

The *Kauffman*
Amish Bakery Series

A GIFT of GRACE — AMY CLIPSTON

A SEASON of LOVE — AMY CLIPSTON

A PLACE of PEACE — AMY CLIPSTON

A PROMISE of HOPE — AMY CLIPSTON

A LIFE of JOY — AMY CLIPSTON

Kauffman AMISH CHRISTMAS COLLECTION — Amy Clipston

ENJOY NOVELLAS FROM FOUR OF YOUR
FAVORITE AUTHORS IN THE AMISH
COLLECTION *An Amish Harvest*

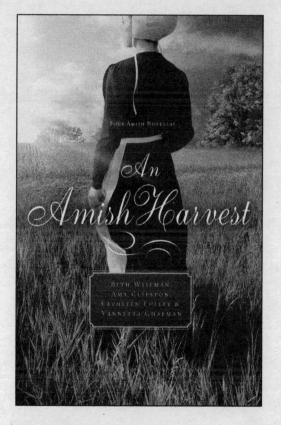

9781401686942-B